Traces of Greed

T D Bessler

To Marshall & Stella
Wonderful Friends
Thank you for Being
here
Enjoy

ISBN: 978-1-60910-404-7

Library of Congress Control Number: 2010910801

Printed in the United States of America.

BookLocker.com, Inc.
2010

“Be not thou afraid when one is made rich,
when the glory of his house is increased;
for when he dieth he shall carry nothing
away: his glory shall not descend after
him.”

Psalm 49:16-17

Acknowledgements

Publishing this work was a dream come true. Eighteen years ago Traces of Greed was born. Most of this work was written on a yellow note pad in an automobile that was parked in a local shopping center during my lunch break. Once completed I lost interest when I received a few rejection letters and decided to put it away for another time. Greed became the headlines in most national newspapers recently, so I began to hone my work and finished this manuscript for publication.

I would like to acknowledge some important people in my life that made this novel possible, and I am forever grateful for their work efforts and consultation that made this all a reality for me.

Thank you to Lisa Karen, my former executive secretary, for her hundreds of hours transcribing my notes to legible writing for all to read including myself. To Cookie Dispoto who, without question, devoted her efforts towards this work in formatting and correcting my page structure. Thank you to my wife, Jeanne, who gave me unwavering advice and was a wonderful critic who got me back on track when I wandered in the story. This novel would not be complete if it were not for my editor Harvey Stanbrough, who took me on his busy schedule and made me so appreciative of his craft. Thank God for the internet and finding such a dedicated professional.

Thank you all for your wisdom and fine work.

T D Bessler

Prologue

Stu whispered, “Becca, wake up.” Even in sleep, his wife’s face didn’t look very different from the face he’d first made up his mind to get a closer look at in the bookkeeping department of the Morris National Bank. She hadn’t smiled at him then, and she didn’t now. His breath tickled her. She swatted her ear.

“C’mon, Honey, wake up. Please?” He nudged her shoulder. No response. He nudged her again.

“What time is it?” she said without opening her eyes.

“Two o’clock. I can’t sleep. We have to talk.”

“Go downstairs and have some warm milk. You’ll be asleep in no time. If you still want to talk in the morning, that’s fine by me, but not now. You know how lousy I feel when I don’t get my sleep.”

“I didn’t just get an urge to chat and wake you, Becca. I’ve been lying here since midnight, thinking, trying not to wake you. But I really need you to listen to me. Not in the morning. Now, Becca!”

She pushed her pillows up against the headboard and turned her half-closed eyes in his direction. “Okay, okay.” She grumbled. “What has you in such a *state* at two a.m.?’

“Same thing that has me in a state, as you so nicely put it, all day long: working with my father. I have to get out from under him. I can never do a damn thing right in his eyes. Then he complains I don’t do enough. Today was the clincher.”

“What happened?” she asked without real interest. “And if it was so awful, why didn’t you bring it up last night?”

“Because you don’t like me to talk business over dinner, that’s why!”

“Whoa, fella! Don’t go getting mad at me.”

“Sorry. It’s just that I’ve been bustin’ my ass for this guy since I got out of school, and all it’s brought me is misery, every single goddamn day. Last week, there was a rise in interest rates and he told me to adjust the prime rate up one-percent on all the commercial loans. Well, the damn phones started ringing off the hook because customers were pissed-off at that big adjustment all at once."

"So let him handle them. I mean, you did do it because he told you to, right?"

"Yeah, he told me, all right. Only now he says he told me to adjust the rate by only one-half percent. I know damn well what he said, but he's just tired of taking all the heat. Well I'm tired, too. Sick and tired of taking heat he's responsible for. And I'm sick and tired of taking all the other shit he tosses at me on a daily basis. I need to be my own person, Becca, and he'll never let me. So I've decided we're leaving here."

Becca's eyes were open all the way now. "And where are we supposed to be going?" she asked in her extra-quiet voice, the dangerous one.

"Florida. We're moving to Florida. I called Des at the bank before I left work yesterday, and he wants me with him. No strings attached. He's looking for someone and he told me I'm his top candidate."

"Are you planning to do this on your own?"

"What do you mean?"

"I'm not about to leave here in order to trot off to hot, sticky Florida!" she snapped. "Especially not to live near my asshole brother!"

"This isn't about your not liking to live near your brother, it's about my hating to work for my father. It's a way for me to get out from under him. Besides, it's a good opportunity for us, for our family. Des was really encouraging. He may not be the sweetest brother-in-law in the world, but he knows what I can do and he says he wants me with him."

"Good opportunity for you? I doubt it. But it's definitely not my idea of a good opportunity for me. First of all, I hate Florida. Second, I hate my brother. Des is nothing but a slick conniver who's never given a crap about anybody. I know you find it hard to see that your father's right about anything, but he was right about Des when he was here to dinner last week and said he was a loose cannon bound to do a lot of damage sooner rather than later. You've told me yourself that his reputation in your business stinks. From what your father says that's not a state secret in Florida, either. Maybe you ought to think a little more about why he's offering you a job."

She took a deep breath and squeezed his hand. "I know you're good at what you do, hon. But Des is only going to use you. He'll get you into trouble. Mark my words, if you accept his offer, you'll be sorry, I promise you that," she said, her voice beginning to elevate to another octave.

"Now you're taking my father's side?"

"Stu, you know damn well I'm not taking his side. I hate the way your father puts you down nearly as much as you do, maybe more. I know how capable you are and how much he depends on you even though he'd rather die than admit it. But he's right about my brother. Believe me, I know better than you what Des is like, and I'm telling you, if you do this, you'll regret it."

She sat up straighter against the headboard. "Besides, I don't have to go down there to know I'd regret it. Stu, this is my home. I can't just get up and move and upset the kids because your father has treated you like a kid for the hundredth time. Speak up for yourself, goddamnit! Tell him he's wrong, that you did exactly what he told you to do. Christ, Stu, isn't it about time you stood up to him?"

"Don't you think I have? Many times! He always comes back with some answer—even if he's making it up right on the spot—that sounds like it's true. If he can't think of anything, he falls back on telling me to show him the proper respect. I'm tired, Becca. I'm tired of fighting him all the time and losing, over and over. I want to live my own life and to stop being the tail wagging behind him. I know your brother isn't the nicest guy, but he's not my father, literally or figuratively. I can handle him. You must have some faith left in me. I think this is a real opportunity for me. Please, let's not argue about it anymore. Let's just go."

Becca's face reddened. She gripped the end of the sheet, squeezing it in her fist until her knuckles stretched the skin of her forehand smooth. "Maybe you didn't hear me," she said quietly. "I'm not leaving here on the basis of what you've told me. So you make any plans you want to, but if they involve moving to Florida, you're doing it alone. Now I need some sleep!"

Flattening her pillows, she slid down between the sheets, turned on her side away from him, obviously hopeful she'd managed to bring the argument to an end.

"That's just like you," Stu said. "Turning your back on me when I need you. You know, Becca, maybe you've had it too easy. Maybe you should have worked; maybe then you'd see things more clearly. You have no idea what hell I have to go through every day."

Becca glared at him. "I know damn well what you go through each day! God knows you tell me often enough! What beats me is why you do nothing about it. When we hit Florida it won't be long before you're bitchin' about Des—but there, you'll *really* have something to bitch about! You think he's going to give you a nice cushy job so you can strut your stuff, but you'd better think again! He'll nail your ass to the cross every day, because that's the kind of Chairman he is. If you can't stand up to your dad, Stu, forget about being able to hold your own against my dear brother."

"Why can't you understand?" he yelled. "If my father were *just* my boss, it'd be different! Look, I've made my decision. I'm not going to be kissing ass the rest of my life. I'm going and that's it. If you want to stay here, fine. But you're my wife, Becca."

"Stu, grow up, damn it! You're in a difficult situation with your dad, but running away isn't the answer. If you feel you have to run, I guess I can't stop you. When you stop running, I'll be here." She put her head between her pillows, determined to shut him out.

He spoke loudly and clearly so she would hear every word. "Fine, bury your head. I'm leaving next Friday. I hope you change your mind."

Stu shut his eyes, even though he knew sleep would be beyond his reach for whatever was left of the night. He lay there, listening to the irregular beating of his heart, each beat a shard of hope that she'd change her mind and come with him.

But he knew she wouldn't budge. By morning, he had convinced himself that maybe some time apart wasn't such a bad idea. Maybe being on her own for awhile would remind her that being able to count on the person you'd taken marriage vows with was a two-way street.

That had been five long years ago.

To Queenie

Me & You!

Chapter One

As Halsey Stuart waited for George Thompson to finish placating an indignant woman in a pinstriped suit, he looked around City National bank. Being in someone else's bank was like a chef dining out. He viewed the place with a critical eye.

The ambience at City National was definitely a step down from the way Stu's Fortune Beach Bank presented itself. But you couldn't always judge a bank by the quality of the marble on the floor, a hard lesson he'd learned in recent weeks. He was glad his line of credit was safely in place at City National.

But right now he was in a hurry to make use of it, and George, the branch manager of City National, was taking longer than he should with the irate woman. That was the underside of George's unfailing politeness, and one reason, at thirty-five, George was at the pinnacle of his career. Any aspirations beyond bank manager he might secretly be harboring were just not in the cards. Stu glanced at his watch in a way George Thompson was sure to grasp, and within seconds the branch manager hastened to end his business with the woman.

George always walked as if someone were holding a stopwatch on him, but as he approached Stu his bounce was subdued. *Hope it's because he kept me waiting,* Stu thought. *Not because maybe he's heard rumors about Fortune Beach Bank.* Even if word had reached George, there was still no reason he'd have automatically frozen Stu's line of credit. Surely, he'd wait to find out what happened and whether he was leaving the area. As George stood in front of him, he just seemed nervous about having kept Stu waiting.

"Hey, Mr. Stuart, sorry for holding you up. Ms. Oakes, the one leaning against the deposit counter, is one adamant, sly old fox. She can't understand the early withdrawal penalty on her CD after she beat me out of one penalty already. I tried explaining again even though I know she understands the rules. You know how it is, someone always trying to beat the system. Anyway, how are things up your way?"

"Fine, George. Everything's just fine. I just stopped in to draw some money on my line of credit. Do you know how much I have left?"

"Give me a few seconds to pull your file up on the screen." George race-walked back toward his desk and pressed the computer keys with precision. "You've used exactly half the line. How much of the $50,000 remaining would you like?"

"I'm going out of town for awhile so I may need it all."

"Shall I have it transferred to your account, then?"

Stu pretended to consider that. "Better wire the funds less five thousand dollars to my father's bank in New Jersey." He took a card from the morocco holder he'd seen George admire before and jotted quickly. "Here's my account number and routing information. I'll take the five thousand with me today."

"That'll be fine, Mr. Stuart."

George rapidly prepared the note for Stu's signature and slid it across the desk.

Stu took out his Mont Blanc pen—a going away gift from his father when Stu had accepted the job in Fortune Beach five years earlier—and bent to sign off on the money. A loud bang yanked his head around. The glass door leading into the lobby slammed against the wall, glass shattering in every direction.

Two men strode in, nylon stockings shielding their faces, guns drawn.

"Anybody does anything but breathe, it'll be your last goddamn breath," the taller man ordered. "Do I make myself clear?"

I'll say, Stu thought. He had no intention of playing hero, and suddenly he didn't give a damn about the money, but keeping calm was something else. All he wanted was to get out alive.

He commanded himself to stop shaking. There were only a handful of people in the lobby. Slowly, he scanned their faces for who might do or say the wrong thing. Fortunately, Ms. Oakes had gone. Among the current customers no one looked stupid enough to argue with the gunmen, but one never knew how terror could change a person. There was one elderly man, second in line at a teller's window, whose fear was visibly clear across the lobby as a wet spot formed on the front of the his pants and spread down his leg. *Poor bastard! Hope he doesn't have a heart attack.*

"Hey, you! Yeah, you!" The second gunman pointed his gun at George. "Get your skinny ass over here! *Now!"*

George, of course, did exactly as he was told, approaching the two gunmen as quickly as his rubbery legs would carry him. He kept his eyes lowered, an unnecessary caution given the stockings pulled over their faces. They also wore matching dark blue windbreakers, absent any identifying insignia, with the collars turned up.

Just then, a woman came through the front door of the bank. She spotted one of the robbers and tried to tiptoe back out, but one of the gunmen noticed her too. He pointed his gun. "You're in now, bitch. Just keep on walking in."

Panicking, the woman made a run for the door. Three shots thundered and the woman lurched forward, crashing through the glass panel door. Half of her body was hanging out the front door, a thick piece of jagged glass protruding through her abdomen.

Stu's entire body clenched as he waited for more shots to be fired, but the gunmen had made their point. Everyone was rooted in place. For a few seconds, there was a deafening silence.

The taller gunman grabbed George by the hair, put his .357 Magnum to the quivering man's throat, and cocked the hammer ever so slowly with his thumb. "I'd be very careful if I were you and do exactly like you're told." George nodded quickly and repeatedly.

"Atta boy," the gunman said.

"Everybody else, on the floor!" the other ordered. "Let's go! Face down, everybody, heads facing away from the teller counter! Quick! Unless someone here is dying to be next." He chuckled, then growled, "Don't take my little joke seriously. We don't give a shit if all of youse want to die now—we're in this to the end."

Stu was already on the marble floor, which felt very cold against his cheek. The gunmen were loudly opening zippered bags, slamming drawers open and shut. The thought of the money flying into the bags. *The faster the better*, he thought. *Just let there be enough to satisfy them.*

There must have been, because one of the robbers laughed again. Footsteps echoed as they left, and something clunked to the floor. Then there was only a hissing noise, smoke, choking, eyes burning. *Tear gas!*

Outside, cycles fired up and roared away. In the stillness following the sounds of departure, people got up off the floor and scrambled for the double doors, passing the lifeless body and gasping for fresh air. Stu looked around, his reflexive sense of responsibility kicking in. Everyone seemed to be out except the dead woman and George. He wiped his stinging eyes with his shirt and, with the head teller, went back into the bank to find him. It didn't take long.

George lay on the floor under a deposit counter, out cold, blood running down the side of his head. An ugly blow had landed above his right ear, not lethal from the look of it.

Stu and one of the male customers dragged him outside. Within minutes George came to.

By then a crowd had started to form. Sirens were approaching, although they sounded a few blocks off. Stu looked at George. "George, are you okay?"

The manager looked up at Stu, the blood caking on the side of his face. "Okay? I don't know.... I don't know how any of us got the hell out of there alive."

"The thing to concentrate on, George, is that you're out of there. It's over. Look, I have to get going. I can't explain, but this isn't a morning I can get hung up giving a statement to the police. I have a plane to catch. Are you following me, George? Can you remember something?"

"I'll never be able to forget this." George replied.

"You'll be fine. Listen, George. Take the five thousand and put it in my account. I'll use my ATM card to access any money that I need the next couple of days. I'm sorry to leave, but I know you'll be able to handle things from here on in."

George nodded. "Thanks for saying that. I'll have to, won't I? I can't thank you enough for getting me out of there. God knows how much worse off I'd be if you hadn't gotten me out into the air. I'll make sure you're kept out of this. Just tell me what to do about that poor woman in the doorway?"

"Nothing," Stu said. "The police will take care of it. They'll be here any second." Stu rose, rushed to his car and drove off, his hands clenched white as paper on the steering wheel.

He tried to concentrate on being glad to be alive. He'd be more glad when he was actually out of Florida, but he had promised to see Des first, and he was a man of his word. Today, he was hoping Des would be a man of few words, because he couldn't stay long. He'd given Des five years. Fifteen minutes more wouldn't hurt, and then it was Stu's time. He suspected he'd need every bit of it to pick up the pieces and try to put his life back together. Again.

Chapter Two

Driving north up the Dixie Highway, once he'd put some distance between himself and the bank, Stu relaxed. He didn't like leaving the scene of a crime—it didn't fit in with the conscientiousness on which he prided himself—but he couldn't afford to spend the day with detectives or the FBI. He glanced at his watch. *Nine thirty-five... still time to see Des and stop by to hug Marie goodbye before the plane takes off.*

At twenty-six, Marie wasn't only a beautiful young woman but a vivacious daughter with a fast-track career path. She had earned her undergraduate degree at Lehigh, Stu's alma mater. It didn't surprise him when she got a job right out of law school with the prestigious law firm that was counsel to his bank. She did it without his knowledge. A courtesy phone call from the firm had informed him that they'd made her an offer. She'd made no mention of the interview because she wanted to get the job on her own. To avoid the appearance of a conflict of interest, he made sure she was never asked to do any work that involved the bank.

As he approached the Emerald Bridge separating the mainland from the island, he noticed that many of the boat slips were empty. A few yachts remained berthed, but the snowbirds had escaped the tropical heat, heading north for the Hamptons and Newport. He tapped his fingers on the steering wheel. *No matter where they are, chances are they aren't sweating life.*

Kids on bicycles were lined up along the bridge, fishing. Dangling a line from the Emerald Bridge was a native ritual observed by young and old alike, and would most likely be part of Stu's life when the time came to retire. It was a long way off yet, but recently when thinking of it, he salivated. He and Becca could travel then—he hadn't taken more than nine consecutive days off during the last five years. They'd go to Europe, a place they'd both talked about for years. Stu smiled. *Can't be too soon,* he thought. *But first I have to clean up the mess I'm in.*

Coming off the bridge Stu slowed for a moment. It was like crossing a border. The end of the bridge was where one world ended and... where Fortune Beach began.

As he came to the end of Fortune Boulevard, and stopped at the light, it occurred to Stu that no one but a Fortune Beacher could imagine what it was truly like to live a Fortune Beacher's life. Fortune Beacher's were born into a family of the privileged few. No other life would seem quite so worth living.

He made a left turn onto Atlantic Avenue, and proceeded along the ocean road, past the tree-lined elegant pastel mansions that overlooked the always-beautiful, sometimes dangerous water.

Glancing in his rear view mirror, he saw a car he thought he'd noticed with him a few miles earlier. The black Jaguar was close. Both men in the front seat were wearing wraparound sunglasses. The car edged closer, its front fender so close to his rear bumper he couldn't see their headlights, then swerved into the oncoming lane and came alongside him.

He glared at them. "Hey, what the hell is wrong with you?"

The Jaguar swerved again, this time into the side of Stu's car. He gripped the wheel tightly, but a second jolt forced him off the road.

Frightened, he focused on steering the car back onto the road, only to be hit again. His car just missed hitting a concrete lamppost in Mayor Hank Stone's driveway, then slammed into the hedges and stopped.

Stu's head hit the steering wheel. He moved gingerly, to make sure he was all right, only to see in the rear view mirror the two men getting out of the Jaguar. They walked toward him, each carrying a baseball bat. He reached to lock his door—too late.

One of the men yanked the door open. The other grabbed him by the collar and pulled him out of the car. He shoved Stu up against the tall hedges where no one would see them, and that scared him as much as the bats, which he hoped were only for effect.

As if he'd read Stu's mind, the other thug shoved his bat it into Stu's solar plexus. "What kind'a sport you like, fella?"

Stu didn't answer.

He nudged the bat. “I said, what kind’a sport you like?”

Stu stuttered, “G-g-golf.”

“Fancy tastes. Well lemme tell ya, you better tell your boss to keep his goddamn mouth shut to the Feds or you and him are gonna get whacked, you hear me? You screw with us, *both* of you sons of bitches are gonna get it with a seven iron right across your numb skulls. Got it? He better clam up or we’ll be back for both of you.” He yanked the bat away from Stu’s abdomen, and the men got back into their car and drove off.

Stu was shaken. He leaned against the hedge, trying to catch his breath.

Stu inspected the dark blue Caprice he’d rented. “Damn!” Three dents marred the driver’s side doors. He got in, backed the car out of the driveway, and drove off slowly.

Telling Des what had happened wouldn’t make his departure any smoother. But before he even got into that, as soon as he got to Des’ house, he’d call Walter Dobbs, a man who clearly enjoyed being Chief of Police in a town where criminal activity seldom interfered with his serious avocation of eating. Walter pursued his hobby in some of the finest restaurants on Fortune Boulevard, at none of which he’d ever been presented with a bill for more than a cup of coffee. From his vantage point, Walter had managed to acquire the goods on everyone in Fortune Beach. That was how he’d been re-elected chief every two years for the past eighteen years. No one could afford to let him out of town. The possible up side to Walter’s off-beat surveillance of the town’s main thoroughfare was that he would notice a black Jag that didn’t belong to anyone he knew driving up Fortune Boulevard.

As Stu drove, he caressed his sore stomach. Tomorrow it would be bruised, at least he was alive. The second time in a single day he might have ended up dead instead.

Why didn’t he feel more grateful?

Chapter Three

It would be easier to feel gratitude if he were headed any place other than Des' house. Des wasn't actually responsible for the attack, but it wouldn't have happened if Des were not somehow tied in to whoever those guys worked for.

Stu's brother-in-law, Desmond Cain, CEO and Chairman of the Board of Fortune Beach Bank, had a lot of enemies. He saw the world as two camps, winners and losers, and he believed suckers and greed go together like milk and a cat. All of Des' so-called friends wanted a lap at the bowl. They didn't care what he invested in and, in most cases, they didn't care how profits were made as long as Des was deciding where to put their money. Some of his land investments paid off handsomely, but others wound up complete losses. How anyone could just throw money at him was beyond Stu's imagination.

The fact was Stu didn't give a damn one way or the other. What concerned him was that Des was always screwing somebody over, and sooner or later someone was going to get even. Inevitably the bank—and Stu's own reputation—would be hurt. That had given him enough reason to want to get out of Des' orbit for good. Until now, he hadn't considered that he might be the conduit for vengeance aimed at Des. As he drove, his shock and fear at the attack receded, only to be replaced by anger aimed right where it belonged: at Des.

Stu had come to know Fortune Beach well, but Des alone knew all the secret players, the behind-the-scenes characters with fists full of money, drooling to get in on the next big deal because it could be the real payoff. From the beginning, knowing that the real action was happening out of his sight made Stu uneasy. He had mixed feelings about being left out of the loop: he was afraid that what he didn't know might be worse than he imagined, but he was glad not to be involved. Maybe keeping Stu in the dark had been Des' way of looking after his sister's husband. Des had only brought Stu into the picture when he needed advice on lending procedures, making sure he could dance around banking regulations without causing any violations.

He made his way around the curve in the road to the six-foot high white stucco wall surrounding Des' property. Full, huge Banyan trees extended their limbs like a giant octopus over the wall made it impossible to see the mansion from the road. Two massive black iron gates protected the front entrance. The brass plate on the gate read *1400 Tierra Del Mar.*

The gate creaked open and Stu pulled the battered Caprice into the courtyard and parked. As Stu began walking toward the house, Des came to meet him. "Stu. I sure appreciate you coming over on such short notice." He extended his hand. Stu looked at it for a second, and then shook it briefly.

"What happened to your shirt?" Des said. "It's torn at the collar. Hey, the side of your face is black and blue. What the hell happened?"

Stu told him, watching Des' surprise for loopholes, then said, "I'd like to know what the hell's going on, Des." He held up one hand. "But before you start, I want to use your phone to see if Walt Dobbs can catch those bastards."

"First, I had nothing to do with whatever the hell happened. This is unbelievable! Did you see the paper today?"

"Just the market section."

Des took the Fortune Star from under his arm and unfolded it. "Look." The headline read *DESMOND CAIN: CHAIRMAN OF FORTUNE BEACH BANK UNDER INVESTIGATION.*

Stu glanced at Des. "What the hell happened?"

"Look, I have a lot of investors, and everybody I deal with isn't always happy with how things turn out. Somebody's always pissed off at me for one thing or another, so they make a few calls and in come the bank examiners. Not long after that, the newspaper finds out and this is the result. I just can't figure—"

The front door swung open and Polly, the plump Jamaican housemaid, called out, "Mr. Cain, telephone."

He called over his shoulder, "Be right there." Then he turned back to his brother-in-law. "Stu, hang on a few minutes; there's more I have to tell you. Go around to the patio; I'll get you another line for your call. I won't be long."

"Des, come on... I have a plane to catch."

"I'll be right back," Des said, moving toward the door.

Stu went around the back of the mansion to the raised patio that extended off the library. Shaded by a yellow and white awning, the patio boasted an outside bar, handsome white wrought-iron tables, and enough chairs to entertain the United States Senate. The grounds cascaded down three separate tiers. The first level, designed for lawn croquet, looked like a pristine green carpet. The second level was an Olympic-sized pool, with its own cabana and wet bar. The third level was a huge waterfall designed by Fortune Beach's own waterfall-designer, Marco DeMartini.

Stu sat on a lounge chair and thought about the man who owned all this. Des, at fifty-two, was one year his senior, to the day. They had developed a silly tradition over the years of complimenting each other on their birthdays each saying how great the other had weathered life's obstacles. It was true enough about Des. He was tall, tan and slim. It hardly mattered that his light brown hair was beginning to recede slightly. His dress was always impeccable, and he had a smile that would stop a woman's wristwatch. Even on this Sunday morning, he was wearing a blazer and tie. Camera ready, always.

He came through the French doors from the library. "Guess what? They caught the two characters who roughed you up."

"You're kidding," Stu said. "I was afraid I'd never get to press charges against those bastards."

"I just got a call from Walt Dobbs. They got 'em."

Stu stared at Des. "How? I never even reported it."

"You didn't have to. Evidently, the two idiots didn't figure on the video cameras at the mayor's house. They picked up everything clear as a bell. They want you down at the police station to identify them."

"My pleasure." Stu checked the time. "I'd better get going then. I have to be at the airport soon." He stood.

Des moved quickly to block his way. "Stu, the goddamn bank is a mess and I know you know that." Des spoke quickly. "It's coming down around me from all sides. I'm having a hard time keeping it all together. You're the only one I can say that to. I know I've made a few mistakes now and then, but hell, the regulators will try anything to close the place down. These guys are on a mission, and I think they're trying to put us both in jail."

"Just a second… what do you mean us?"

"Well, they know you're an executive officer, my brother-in-law, and Vice Chairman of the Board. My guess is they're going to try to nail you too."

Stu's face flushed. Quietly, he said, "Des, I left the bank, remember? I *resigned*. I'd have been out of here long ago, but I had to stay because I felt obligated to tie up some loose ends. As for that second-in-command crap, I never played a part in any of your stuff. I knew about some of it, but that is as far as it went. You always ran on your own show. I just did my job. I'm going back home."

Des shrugged. "I'd advise you to think it over. The FDIC will come looking for you. Most of our problems from what I can see are in the loan area, and if you think that by leaving you'll be washing your hands of everything, you're in for a big surprise. You could be held personally liable for whatever happens here. You stand to lose exactly what I do—everything—so I suggest you rethink your plans. Call your lawyer if you think I'm not telling you the skinny."

It took all Stu's will to manage a calm outer appearance. "Des, why do you think I'm leaving? In the five years I've been down here working for you, never once did you let me in on what the hell was really going on. All you did was use me to clean up your shitty messes. I was your go-between so no one could point a finger at you. You were—are—the chairman, and that means the ultimate responsibility is yours. Why do you think those two guys tried to rough me up today? I was the go-between again. I can almost bet Johnny Mack sent those guys. He doesn't mind the bullshit fees and all the other charges you sock him with, but if you drag him into this public mess you created, he's telling you that somebody's going to get hurt. I promise you, brother-in-law, it's not going to be me. I never received one illegal plug nickel from anyone in all the years I've been here."

How badly Des needed Stu not to leave was written all over his face. He couldn't get out of this mess by himself and he knew it. Besides, if there were going to be any loan negotiation with regulators, Stu was in a better position to deal with any problems. For one thing, Des didn't have the patience. Even more important, his mouth always started working before his brain had a chance to kick in. Examiners had to be handled with kid gloves. Government employees couldn't care less about the bank or the people who worked there. They had a job to do. They weren't about to be intimidated by some fast-talking chairman in a thousand-dollar suit who found it impossible to hide that he thought they were less than lowlifes.

"The federal examiners will be going through every loan over three hundred thousand dollars with a fine-toothed comb," Des said. "They're going to review every memo and financial statement. They will be looking at our board minutes. It's a good thing I doctored up a few of those minutes now and then or our asses would be in even hotter water. They're looking for apparent major violations, something to nail our asses."

Des took a sip of his tea and shook his head. "I just can't figure out how this happened. The FDIC has never come down on us like this. We've always had an understanding with them. Someone must have made a call, and it had to be from the inside. I don't know who I can trust... except you." He put one hand on Stu's shoulder. "Stu, I *need* you! You're family. Please, forget about your resignation until we're out of this mess. You still have a financial interest here. I know you made some bad investments over the past few years. It doesn't take much to catch the market the wrong way. If you stay with me now, I'll take care of you like always. One thing you can't say is that I ever underpaid you. Four hundred grand including goodies? It takes some people a lifetime to make what you made in just one year!"

Stu pulled away. "Please, Des, spare me. You got every red cent worth out of my hide. You don't give a shit about me or my bad investments, so save your song and dance routine for a believer."

"Okay, Stu. No music. Just true words. With your stock holdings in the tank, are you going to let your interest in the bank go down the drain, too? Don't glare at me like that. I'm talking plain truths here."

Stu answered tactfully. "I knew it would take some time to unload my interest in the bank. But your money was right with mine and that meant mine was safe. Someone in your position finds it hard to unload any interest in the bank as well unless you want to tell the world you violated securities rules, not to mention how pissed off your local millionaires friends would be. They might be afraid of you individually, but when they're all affected, that's another story. They'll have your ass."

"Listen to me. I'll give you a hundred thousand dollar bonus to sign on again. Just stay another six months until this blows over. Look, you're going to be involved anyway so you might as well get paid for it."

"I made promises back home. I take my word seriously. Besides, I don't think Becca could take coming back here for another six months and she sure as hell isn't going to stay with our friends much longer."

"I'll get her a damn maid!" Des said.

"That's not the issue. She hates it here. She doesn't like the heat, the humidity." Stu gestured around the yard. "Or all this artificial shit, Des. And back to the subject of stock, you knew I was trying to unload a hundred and seventy-five thousand shares and you were the one who pulled the plug on it. Telling the market maker not to produce any buyers was a rotten thing to do to me. You know how much I wanted out."

"Stu, listen, it was for your own good. We can turn this thing around even if I have to call Washington."

"Christ, Des, stop! How many times did you go over the line and they looked the other way? Didn't you know, if you kept pushing the envelope, sooner or later they'd nail you?"

"That's not what I pay good money for!" Des shouted.

Stu shook his head. "I'm going home." He took a serrated breath. "I'll be back, but Becca isn't going to be a happy camper. I need some time to break the news to her."

"Thanks. Please, just get back here as fast as you can."

As Stu pulled out of the courtyard, he rolled down the window and yelled, "Call Walt and tell him I'm not pressing charges—not this time—but you'd better get word to Johnny Mack. Tell him I said next time he wants to talk to you, he'd better not do it through me."

Chapter Four

Becca plopped herself down at the oak table in the kitchen. It was 7:30, a chance for a solitary cup of tea before any of the Collinses awoke. As she sipped the sweet tea, she thought about how much she relished being back home. Wakefield was her town. She'd grown up here, traded picnics in the park with her mother for sock hops and Friday night drive-in movies and Saturday football games. If her childhood hadn't been as perfect as it looked in hindsight, that was her memory of it. Her roots were here, and she was back to stay. Florida was fine for alligators, pickup trucks and pit bulls. It was definitely not the life for her.

Still, Becca worried about Stu being on his own. Marie was nearby, but even super-responsible Marie was as preoccupied with her own life as any twenty-six year old should be. Not long ago Stu was running on a fast track, spending large sums of money he didn't have, caught up in Des' lifestyle. Long since disillusioned about Des as a brother, she had grown to mistrust him as her husband's boss. He was a user and a manipulator. Stu couldn't bring himself to believe that her intuition was right, but she knew the flamboyant chairman would dump him in a nanosecond if it weren't for his knowledge and banking expertise. *Small wonder our marriage developed cracks,* Becca thought as she rose to empty the dishwasher and put away last night's supper dishes.

Fortunately, before the cracks developed into chasms, she'd thought to bring Reverend Van into the picture. Though a little younger than they, he was someone Stu respected. Becca especially liked his common sense sermons, and Stu liked the way he didn't talk "minister-ese" either in the pulpit or when you happened to bump into him at the garden supply store.

It turned out he was as commonsensical and direct during a counseling session. At their third session, he'd suggested, "Stu, you could really use a job with less stress. Maybe a move back north would give you the opportunity to find a position where can do what you're good at in a less-worrisome atmosphere." The minister had glanced at Becca, then back to Stu. "I think it would certainly help heal your marriage."

To Becca's surprise, Stu's response was positive. He actually seemed relieved. She'd felt especially grateful that he also understood that it was time to re-build their lives. Stu would be here soon, they'd find a house, and be together again as a family.

"Good Morning!" a voice called from what sounded far away. But when Becca turned toward it, she saw Suzanne standing right there in the doorway.

Staying with Ray and Suzanne for a short while as she house-hunted was fine, but every family needed their privacy. Becca smiled at her friend. "Hi. I hope my puttering around down here didn't wake you."

"Didn't even hear you. It's just time to get my blood circulating, take a shower and get to the flea market. It's Saturday. Remember? You and I are going to find some bargains today."

"Well, normally I'd be ready for that, but Stu's arriving today. Alice and I are going to the airport."

"That's right! You're man's coming home, I forgot. No wonder you're puttering around here so early. Bet you didn't sleep a wink." Suzanne hugged Becca tightly.

"I don't know what's come over me. It seems like it's been forever since I last saw him, but it's only been a few months."

"It's love, Honey. Don't try to figure it out." Suzanne smiled. Well, I guess it'll just be me and Ray."

Suzanne began her morning ritual of coffee, a bagel, and thirteen vitamins. Her long blonde hair was tied back with a rubber band. Bermuda shorts and a sweat shirt reading *Miami Dolphins* comprised her morning attire. Her thirty-nine year old body reflected a rigorous daily workout. Suzanne believed that a woman might survive in what was still, after all, a man's world thanks to intelligence and hard work. But to triumph in that world it really helped to be physically attractive and in terrific shape as well. Becca, the homemaker of the two, thought Suzanne's ideas were a little too ambitious. It was hard to argue with her success though as owner of Collins Realty in Wakefield. She was one of the most successful brokers in the area. Becca hoped that Suzanne would add to her victories by finding her as great a house as the one she'd sold for them years ago.

Ray walked in, dressed for his morning run. "Well, are we all going bargain hunting or what?"

"Morning, Hon," Suzanne said, and kissed him. "It's just you and me, Darlin'. Stu's coming home today."

"That's great! Bet I know who's a happy person today."

Ray leaned over and gave Becca a morning peck on the cheek. She felt very secure with him around. Ray was more like a brother than a friend. It was hard to remember that, at first, she hadn't liked him. He seemed to have a moat around him, to keep people at bay. He didn't talk much, and when he did, he kept his part of any exchange to monosyllables. But over the years, she'd learned that his manner was a kind of self-protection that his profession elicited. Her tall, strong friend with the receding red hair and wary blue eyes was Wakefield's Chief of Detectives.

It took two years before Becca and Stu saw his guard come down and witnessed a side of Ray that not many people got the opportunity to see. Behind his crusty manner lived a kind, gentle, thoughtful man, quick-witted and especially funny after a few Margueritas. He just never forgot the awesome responsibility of having sixty officers under his command. With crime on the rise practically everywhere, including their town, his department had its hands full dealing with everything from drug raids to murder, not to mention white-collar crimes like fraud and embezzlement. His department also handled suicides, accidental overdoses, robbery and rape. It never stopped. The only way he could lead anything resembling a normal family life was to encase himself in a shell when he was with anyone except Suzanne and a few very close friends.

"Well, I'm outta here," he said, zipping the jacket of his jogging suit. "Be back in a bit for some of that great-smelling coffee."

"Don't get sidetracked or we'll be late," Suzanne said, pointing an English muffin at him. "It pays to get there when it opens."

Becca stood. "Think I'll see if Alice is wakeable before noon today. Can you remember ever sleeping so much?"

"Nope," Suzanne said. "Must've been in another life."

Becca ran upstairs. Alice was sleeping in one of the guest rooms that Suzanne was hoping would one day be occupied by one of her own children. The room was unusually large, and had a high ceiling. Sculptured white molding wrapped around the room like twisted Turkish taffy. Not much had been done with the room over the years except to make it presentable. A few anonymous pictures hung on the walls. A pair of heavy blue drapes and white sheers surrounded the windows on the opposite side of the room. Alice would be leaving for college soon and the room would be empty again, waiting for another occupant.

Becca pulled back the drapes. No movement in the bed. She sat on the edge and tapped her daughter's shoulder gently. Alice stirred.

"Mom, what's wrong?"

"I'm sorry I woke you, but I thought we might keep each other company this morning. Suzanne and Ray are going to the flea market, and Dad's coming home today."

"That's right!" Alice said, sitting up against the pillows. "We could go over my clothes, decide what I ought to take to Villanova and what's too kiddish, and then we can go and pick up dad."

Becca smiled her gratitude. Alice knew her mom was under a strain and, half-asleep though she was, she had made up the busy work on the spot. She had decided weeks ago just what she was taking to Villanova. It had slipped her mind that she had shown her mother a shopping list for them to tackle when they got around to it.

Sweet kid, Becca thought. "Sounds like fun. How about some pancakes first?"

Ray hit the front door out of breath from his run. The aroma of perked coffee made him inhale with anticipation. He heard the water running upstairs. If Suzanne was taking a shower, he'd have time to get a quick cup of coffee and scan the front section of the paper before she came down to rush him to get ready to leave. He glanced through the first few pages. It was just like any other news day. A local politician got arrested for having sex with his aide and spending state funds so the two of them could go on a vacation together. He was shaking his head and laughing as he turned the page and began reading the National News section. He stopped laughing:

FLORIDA BANKER UNDER INVESTIGATION

The Banking Department of Florida has called in the Justice Department and the Federal Deposit Insurance Corporation for help in the case of Fortune Beach Bank. The Banking Department uncovered numerous improper loan transactions and the possibility that the bank had violated numerous safety and soundness violations.

The Bank, which has two billion dollars in assets with its main office located in Fortune Beach, Florida, will now be investigated by the appropriate regulatory authorities.

Holy Mother of God! He read the article again. *That's Stu's bank. What the heck's going on?* Becca had nothing but praise for the bank since Stu had been there.

He glanced to make sure no one had come into the room, then carefully removed the page from the paper. This was no time to get Becca upset. Stu would be home today. There would be time enough for Becca—and him—to find out what had happened later. He finished his coffee and went upstairs to shower.

Becca was in her bedroom laying out her clothes. She opened the dresser drawer to get out her underwear and caught sight of herself in the mirror angled over the dresser. The years had treated her well. Her face still looked young and smooth, her blond hair was still bright with a little help from her hairdresser, and her green eyes were bright with a little help from the prospect of having her husband home. *Not bad for forty five, she thought.* She opened her robe and let it fall around her feet. Her gaze went to the full-length mirror on the open closet door. Her body was pretty firm, despite the fact that she didn't exercise as rigorously as Suzanne. And her legs were as shapely as the first time Stu had admired them. They could still draw a casual glance. But it was Stu's admiration she coveted, only his. They would be alone together, tonight. Goose bumps rose on her arms in anticipation, and she laughed to imagine what her seventeen year old daughter in the next room would say if she could read her very proper mother's thoughts.

Chapter Five

Marie couldn't have felt any better. Knowing how her father cared about neatness, she was making the bed in her tenth-floor condo and daydreaming about the events of yesterday, the day she won her first case! She'd also won first-time praise from her boss and, even more important perhaps, other members of the firm were bound to take notice.

Her client, Dan Styles, had been beaten unmercifully by three Layton police officers in a holding cell at police headquarters two years ago. He'd had two operations on his collar bone, had worn a cast for two months on his broken arm, and had undergone extensive surgery to his face, including reconstruction of a half torn-off right ear. After two years only a slight scar was visible around his ear, but the loss of hearing was permanent.

Both Styles and Marie thought it was a big price to pay for being three-tenths over the Breathalyzer limit one dark night on Highway 441. There was no denying Styles had had few drinks, but the police claimed he was uncontrollable and had punched them while they were trying to get him into the holding cell. Styles swore to her he hadn't attacked them, and Marie believed him. Layton cops were known for handing down sentences before going to court. *This time they got what was coming to them,* she thought. Marie and her client were both happy with the judgment of one million three hundred thousand dollars.

Buoyed by the victory, she was ready for her next case. Raring to go, in fact. But in the mean-time, after her Dad left, she'd settle for spending this Saturday in exorbitant leisure at the pool. She glanced out her living room window at the ocean, which looked placid and inviting. Maybe she'd go so far as to get a sand chair from the garage downstairs along with a good book and walk down to the beach.

Seawatch is a great place to live, she thought. *Everything's here: security, shopping, and recreation. Just park the car for the weekend and shut out the world.*

She searched the shelf for something easy to read. As she grabbed for a book, the phone rang.

"Hello."

"Hi, Hon. It's Dad."

"You on your way? Do you have time for lunch? I can have something ready when you get here."

"Marie, I'm real sorry, but I can't come by. I got hung up with your Uncle Des longer than I wanted to, and I can't miss my plane."

"Oh."

"I know. Believe me, I wanted to have a chance to say goodbye to you in person."

“Well, I guess I'll just have to tell you my news over the phone: I won my case! The judgment for my client was for one million three. My boss managed to smile twice at me."

"I'll bet he smiled more than that inside. Congratulations, Counselor! God am I proud of you! How in the hell did you get so much money?"

"It's all in the jury, Dad. We had a good case, but the truth is I never expected such a big award. Hey, I’m glad I perused this firm or I’d probably be stuck in some two-bit operation somewhere.”

"Well, I’m sure they’re very happy with you and your brilliant court work."

"Thanks Dad."

"Listen, Marie, I only have another couple of minutes, and I have to speak to you in confidence, okay?"

"Sure. You all right? Is something wrong?"

"I'm not sure. I'm returning to my old position at the bank... temporarily. Some problems have come up that your uncle needs me to keep a lid on."

"Dad, I'm not as surprised as I might be. There were rumors going around about some goings-on at the bank. Twice when I came into the conference room at the office there was a sudden hush, like a few of the partners were surprised to see me. I knew something was up with the bank, but I couldn’t catch it all. I tried to fish around, but I couldn't find out anything. What did Mom say about this?"

"Haven't told her yet. Thought I'd better do it in person. That's one reason I can't miss this plane."

"Good luck. You know how much she loves it here, and Uncle Des."

"I have to come back, Marie. The bank's got problems."

"But you haven't done anything."

"You're right, I haven't, but I could still be in some trouble, as your Uncle Des just took some glee in reminding me."

"I think I overheard there were examiners and a lot of other people there. Is that true?"

"So I'm told. If your uncle ends up with some serious personal problems, I may be standing right beside him."

"What do you mean by serious personal problems?"

"Well, if anything was going on illegally that caused the bank to suffer a loss in some way, even though I had nothing to do with it, I can be held personally responsible... and not just me, the whole damn Board of Directors."

"You're kidding? You *personally*?"

"The rules of the game when it comes to this kind of stuff are pretty clear. That's why I have to come back. I want to make sure no one decides to push the blame for whatever did take place, on me. Having to bear some of the responsibility is bad enough, but to stand accused—to have anyone say I myself committed illegal behavior—well, that's not going to happen. My whole professional life I've been scrupulous about avoiding even the appearance of anything improper. Keep your ears open at the firm. I've kept mine shut for too long. Since they're counsel for the bank, maybe you'll hear something that I should be aware of."

"I do know people in the banking division. Trouble is they know who I am. It's not going to be easy, but I'll do what I can."

"If your mother calls before I reach home, don't tell her anything."

"When are you coming back?"

"In a few weeks or so. Gotta go, Darling. I'll call you from New Jersey, let you know when to expect us."

"Okay, Dad. Have a good flight back. Love you."

Marie grabbed a sand chair from the garage and made her way to the beach. The ocean breeze smelled fresh. She slathered on suntan lotion. *Definitely a good beach day.* Later, she'd have an early dinner, and then head out to Worthington.

She played back her conversation with her father. She hated to hear him so worried. It made her feel a little guilty because, although she hated what might be in store for him, she was glad her parents were coming back. She had no one else close down here.

There was Pete, of course, the assistant golf pro at the club. He was good looking enough so that a number of women had signed up for lessons with him. Marie liked his upbeat personality, a trait she hadn't encountered much among her fellow lawyers. She'd been dating him awhile, but not exactly regularly. Her long work hours had a lot to do with that. She'd have to find more time for him, get to know him better. If her Dad got his way, he wouldn't be back for long.

The airport page announced, "Last call for Continental flight 1011 to Newark International Airport. Now boarding at Gate 27."

Stu picked up his pace and headed down the terminal runway for Gate 27.

The alert stewardess smiled. "Just made it, Mr. Stuart. You're in seat Five-A. Go right aboard and enjoy your flight, Sir." She pointed to the doorway.

"Thank you." He smiled at the attendant and entered the cabin.

Lowering his large frame into the roomy grey leather seat, Stu buckled himself in, grabbed a newspaper, and put on his reading glasses.

As the plane inched down the runway, he watched the incoming planes landing. The next few weeks were going to be difficult. The banking business wasn't fun anymore. It had become a bureaucracy of paper shufflers, he among them. How much of every day at Fortune Beach Bank had he spent writing policies and reading memos from some department head covering his ass? Everybody was afraid to risk a conflict with the bank's policies, and that fear was recorded in endless pages of small print.

Stu emitted a deep sigh. He'd try to clean up the mess at the bank and then move on. Maybe it was time to start thinking about doing something else for the rest of his working life. Becca and he could open a bed and breakfast in Cape May. They'd talked about it several times, but he had never wanted to leave banking. Now he looked at it—at everything—differently. Just the thought of living without another interoffice memo or FDIC regulation made him feel freer inside.

Stu bent closer to his reflection in the window. The small wrinkles on his forehead were not there a few years ago. The crow's feet around his eyes were more prominent, and grey was overtaking the brown in his hair. Then, before he could give another thought to getting older, the huge 747 was gliding among the clouds. It felt wonderful to escape the world below, even if only for a couple of hours.

"Care for something to drink, Mr. Stuart?"

"A bloody mary, please."

The attendant was soon back, pouring a shot glass of Absolut into the bloody mary mix and stirring. "Here you are, Sir. Enjoy."

Stu sat back to taste the spicy tingle of his drink, but thoughts about how his plans had been changed intruded. Never in his wildest dreams had he imagined he would go back to Fortune Beach Bank.

Luckily, the house in Worthington hadn't sold. Everyone was bottom fishing on price and Stu wasn't ready to give the place away. Having the house would make moving back to Florida easy, if Becca was willing to come.

The alternative was too painful, and he shut his eyes to avoid looking at it. Tired from the strain of the day, he drifted off.

When he awoke, there was someone in the seat next to his. Stu straightened in his seat and squinted at the stranger, a man about his own age, maybe a little younger, in an olive-green poplin suit with more wrinkles in it than a day old newspaper. The dark stains—coffee?—on his right lapel didn't enhance the man's appearance.

"Mr. Stuart, we have to talk."

Chapter Six

Stu was stunned to hear the stranger address him by name. "Excuse me?"

"I realize you don't know me, Mr. Stuart, but I know you. My name is Jack Hendricks. I'm with the Justice Department."

He pulled out a wallet with cracked corners, opened it to his photo identification, and handed it to Stu. The I.D. picture matched the thin, sallow face of the man who had turned up beside him out of nowhere. The printing said he was John Hendricks, and that John Hendricks was a Chief Field Investigator for the Justice Department.

Stu closed the wallet and handed it back. "And where are you headed, Mr. Hendricks? This flight doesn't stop in Washington."

"I'm assigned to the Fortune Beach Bank investigation. And I'm on this flight to tell you privately where you're headed."

"Look, Hendricks. I know there's a lot of nosing around the bank right now, but I can assure you, if there was anything going on to warrant the Justice Department being involved, I certainly would have known about it."

"That's what we thought at first. Now we're not so sure how much you know. Now, just in case you're not aware of everything, I'm here to give you an outline of your problems."

Stu turned and looked out the window with a blue blank stare.

Hendricks continued.

"Mr. Stuart, I'm here on the chance that you need to be told that this isn't just some trivial investigation. The Justice Department didn't get into this case to slap your hand because you failed to keep up with Community Reinvestment Policies. We're not the FDIC, who are, I understand, at the bank for that and some other reasons for which your asses at Fortune may end up in a sling. The Justice Department wouldn't be involved and I wouldn't be here if this were not a Federal banking matter."

Stu swiveled in his seat and stared at Hendricks.

Hendricks said calmly, "Mr. Stuart, your problems are far above and beyond any regulatory enforcement concerns. I'm here to advise you to cooperate in this investigation. Right now, we only want your brother-in-law, Desmond Cain, but if you don't cooperate with us... well, we'll seek an indictment on you as well. Before you decide, it's only fair to tell you that, as of right now, we believe Cain has been using you in a number of his dealings without your knowledge. Even if that proves out, you're still in trouble. From the profile we've built up of him, it's pretty clear that if he thinks you're going to blow the whistle on him when this thing heats up, you're going to need some protection. That's where I come in."

"Protection? From my brother-in-law?"

"From someone who might want to make sure you don't strengthen the government's case."

"You've been watching too much TV."

"What do you know about Main Street Investment?"

Quickly, Stu combed his mind for anything at all that he might know about it. Coming up empty-handed, he shrugged.

"Well, whether or not you know it, you're a general partner in the limited partnership. You own a portion of six commercial office buildings. You're not a poker player, are you, Mr. Stuart? I'm not going to ask you who's been accepting the lease payments or how you guys got the money to finance the project, because your face says you probably have no idea. But what I've just told you is true. Check around."

Stu thought, *how could something like this get by me? It can't be true.* Despite the comfortably cool temperature in the cabin, a trail of sweat started down his back.

"To be honest, we don't give a damn about this money or the payments. But someone at FDIC is sure to want a feather in their cap on this one."

A passenger turned his head slightly and Stu lowered his voice. "I don't have the slightest idea what the hell you're talking about."

"Mr. Stuart, we need to get on with this. We'll be landing soon."

Hendricks was right about that, at least. Stu heard the change in the huge turbines driving the aircraft as the plane seemed to slow down.

"Just for the record, we know who your limited partners are. They haven't disguised themselves quite as well as they think."

"Well, who are they? You say they're my partners. Seems to me I have the right to know who they are."

Hendricks shook his head. "Sorry."

"What the hell do you mean, 'sorry'?"

"I'm not going to remove any incentive for you to investigate on your own. But I'll tell you this much: one of the partners is a congressman."

"What?"

"There are more things for which you're likely to be held accountable. Better start finding out what they are—consider that a helpful hint. I'm not at liberty to tell you any more than that."

Stu wanted to grab the supercilious bastard and put some extra wrinkles in his suit. "Let me tell you something, Hendricks. My mother taught me never to trust anyone who says he's from the government and is here to help you. I admit I don't have all the answers, but I will soon."

"We won't wait around for you, Mr. Stuart, so you'd better hurry. I wish I could have convinced you how serious this is." He took something from his pocket and jotted a note on it. "Look. Here's my card. That's my beeper number. It'll reach me twenty-four hours a day." Hendricks let out a deep breath. "Might as well tell you, someone from our department will be watching you from now on. Don't do anything stupid, Mr. Stuart. You don't want to make your position any worse."

Without waiting for a response, Hendricks got up and went through the curtain separating the main passenger section from first class.

Stu stared at the card in his hand, feeling his ears beginning to close due to the change in cabin pressure. *Des is slick, but he's also smart. He wouldn't involve himself in a shady scheme with a congressman... would he?*

Becca ran toward Stu and put her arms around him. "I'm so glad you're home," she said against his ear. "Don't get a swelled head, but I've missed you, Mister."

"Me, too. You sure smell good."

Boucheron was his favorite perfume. He knew she'd worn it to please him. He wondered how pleased *she'd* be when she found out that her big brother might have involved him in some smelly business ventures. Well, he didn't have to tell her right now. After all, he didn't know anything. Maybe there was a whole lot less to know than that bastard Hendricks hinted. Holding Becca always made him feel things would work out. He kissed her.

"Hey, you guys," Alice said. "My turn." She gave Stu a big hug and kissed him on both cheeks. "Hi, Dad. Missed you, too."

"I missed you, Honey. Let's pick up my bags and get out of here."

They walked together to the claim area, one to each side of him. When they located the right carousel, Stu took a step back and looked at his younger daughter. "You get more beautiful month by month." He glanced around. No sign of Hendricks. "You're the best-looking female here—next to your mother, of course!"

"Oh stop," Alice and her mother said simultaneously. They all smiled.

Stu's luggage came tumbling out all at once. His golf bags, four pieces of Samsonite, and a black wooden trunk. Tailing everything was a bushel of Indian River red grapefruit, Becca's favorite.

“It’s a good thing I brought Suzanne’s van.” Becca said. “Or you’d be riding on the roof.”

Stu had a feeling someone was following them. He looked out the back window. No way to tell.

"Since you girls look like you both just came out of Glamour magazine how about stopping for an early dinner?”

"I always said you were a born idea man," Becca said. "Alice and I were hoping you’d suggest eating out—Suzanne and Ray are away until late tonight."

"Dad, let's go to Jimmy's Cabin. The food's so good there."

"Wherever you two want to go is fine with me. Just let's get there because I'm starved."

Jimmy's Cabin was the most popular restaurant within twenty miles. There was nothing fancy about Jimmy's, but the relaxed atmosphere of the place was contagious, which accounted for its popularity with the high-powered residents of Short Hills. Soft hurricane lamps on dark green tablecloths. The high-vaulted dark wood ceilings with knotty wood pine paneling that gave the restaurant its cabin look. Flickering light from an open flame pit danced against the cabin walls. Charcoal broiled steaks were the house specialty and none of the Stuarts hesitated when the waiter came to take their order.

Dinner, including their conversation, was uninterrupted and pleasant.

During the second cup of decaf Stu allowed himself to remember that soon Becca would find out he had to go back to Florida. Would the woman he loved so much and just had dinner with make him go back alone?

Chapter Seven

Marie had promised her dad to take a run over to Worthington to check on things that very evening, but Palmetto Hills Boulevard wasn't a road to be traveling at night, alone. Still, a promise was a promise. She kept her gaze glued to the road for the twelve miles between her condo and Worthington. At Old Cypress Trail, she turned left and drove until the house at the end of the cul-de-sac was in view, barely, sitting as it did back from the road where the darkness was nearly complete. She put on her high beams to light up the front door so she wouldn't have to fumble for the house keys in the dark.

When she put the key in the lock, the door swung open by itself. Startled, she stopped in her tracks, but after a moment she realized that her father, in his hurry to leave, simply hadn't done a very thorough job of locking the door. *Good thing I decided to come over tonight.* She felt around the foyer wall for the light switch, flipped it on and gasped.

All the sheets from the furniture were ripped off and lying on the floor. Pillow cushions were thrown everywhere. Suddenly it occurred to her that someone might still be in the house. She stood very still and listened. No sound. *That doesn't prove no one's here, girl. Call the police—if the phone line hasn't been cut.* She moved to the phone on the table near the sofa and picked it up. The trembling in her hands lessened when she heard a dial tone. She hesitated. If the intruders were still there, she'd have sensed it. She put down the phone and hefted a table lamp. *Too bulky... not heavy enough.* She tiptoed over to the desk and picked up a square crystal paperweight with sharp corners, an award her father had won several years ago. Moving very cautiously, Marie made her way down the hallway until she reached her parents' room. In the doorway, she stopped, listened hard and flipped on the bedroom light.

"Holy Christ!" She swiveled quickly to make sure no one had come up behind her. She was alone.

The mattress had been pulled off the bed, and there were several deep slits in it. The sheets were thrown into a ball in the corner of the room. The dresser drawers were open. Some clothes were hanging out, and others were scattered on top and on the floor. Marie walked to the door of the master bath. Affixed to the wall by a large hunting knife was a folded piece of paper. She pulled the paper free, and unfolded it. In letters cut out of a magazine, she read,

THIS WAS EASY.
WE CAN DO IT AGAIN.
THE BANK ISN'T YOUR PROBLEM—WE ARE!
GO BACK HOME AND STAY THERE.
AND KEEP QUIET!

Her face grew pale and she began to tremble. The tears she'd been successfully holding back came free. She had to call the police. But she wanted to get out of there as soon as she could. The police couldn't undo the terrible destruction, and the note was a sure sign the intruders had finished their work and left before she arrived, so calling them could wait. Moving slowly, as though walking through water, she went into the kitchen and turned on the outside flood lights. They would stay on until her parents came back.

She looked through the sliding glass door that opened onto the enclosed patio. She tried the sliding door. Locked. Thank God for small blessings. The area around the kidney-shaped pool seemed all right as well, but when she looked past the pool to the other sliding door, which opened from the master bedroom onto the patio, her eyes narrowed.

To make sure she wasn't imagining things, she reluctantly returned to the bedroom. She'd been so thrown at the condition of the room, she hadn't even gone near the door. Now she verified what she'd spotted from across the pool: the screen door was torn and the door itself had been pried open. She closed it the best she could and quickly left the violated house.

As soon as she got into her car, she locked all four doors. *Should I call the police first?* She opted to call her father once she got home because the police would want her to wait at the house and she was not about to stay there any longer.

Driving back home on the quiet dark road she could see nothing but the center line and the flicker of headlights behind her as she looked in the rear view mirror. It began to rain lightly, then more heavily. From time to time, a bolt of lightning knifed through the sky, momentarily lighting the road in front of her, but the rest of the time the wipers didn't improve things much. She checked the rear view mirror again. The headlights behind her were closer. A moment later, she made the turn in the road, and looked again, waiting for the car to pass her.

But the driver didn't pass. It followed her through the turn and a moment later Marie jerked against her seat belt as it jabbed her bumper. She peered hard into the mirror again, but the rain made it impossible to see the driver's face, or even gender. *Who the hell's doing this? Did someone follow me from the house? I have to get away from this maniac.* She tightened her hands on the wheel.

Fury and fear vied for the upper hand. She thought of stomping her foot on the brake, throwing the sonofabitch through his front windshield. But what if it didn't work? If whoever it was survived, she might wind up getting herself killed.

In the distance, she saw lights, bright lights. Wonderful lights. Beautiful lights. Her courage got a bounce from them, and she accelerated. The car behind her kept up. *Damn.* They were doing seventy-five miles an hour. She was trying to decide whether speeding up even more would help when she noticed in the distance a combination gas station and convenience store whose lights indicated it was open. As she approached the station, she turned the wheel quickly to the right. The car careened through the lot, almost taking down the gas pumps, and screeched to a stop a mere five feet from the front entrance of the store. Her whole body was trembling.

She rolled down the window, and looked back. She could just make out the other car, stopped in the middle of the road. She stuck her head farther out, and raindrops pelted against her face.

Suddenly, outrage overcame every other emotion, and she burst from her car screaming, "You bastards!"

Repeated horn blasts drowned out her voice as the car raced off down the road. As the tail lights disappeared in the distance, a voice behind her yelled, "You crazy, Lady?"

She turned. In the doorway of the convenience store stood a thin woman apparently the night clerk. "You could've taken down my pumps. What were you doing, drag racing in the rain? You rich people are all alike, only interested in having your weird fun."

Marie opened her mouth to apologize, but the woman backed into the store and slammed the door, then locked it and turned out the lights. The woman was right about one thing. It was a crazy world.

You just had to keep fighting the craziness, or it would win. The lawyer in her, avid always for specifics, got to work. *See the car, Marie. Dark color, could be deep green or navy. Low-slung, definitely. Graceful lines. A Jag.*

Chapter Eight

The white sports van pulled into the long, dimly lit driveway. Stu was removing the luggage when the dogs started barking. He couldn't help grinning as he headed for the back door; he wanted to see them, too. As Becca put her key in the lock, two canine faces appeared in the glass door panels, barking and scratching to get out. They pushed past Becca, who had been gone, only a matter of hours. They were waiting for Stu. Surrendering to the inevitable, he dropped his suitcases and braced himself. Both dogs hit him at once. He took the full force of their weight, ending up on the ground, his face assaulted by two very wet tongues to the accompaniment of Becca's laughter. After a long moment, he staved them off long enough to get up. They stood still then, waiting for Stu to return the affection of their greeting. He petted each of them lavishly, rewarded by canine cries of happiness.

He was finally home.

Alice had gone on inside. The house was dark and she was going for the light on the end table when the phone rang. She stopped short, not knowing what to do first—turn on the light or answer the phone, which was ringing again. She fumbled for it, knocked over an ashtray, and picked up the receiver.

"Hello!"

Marie said, "No need to shout. Hi, Alice. What's the matter?"

"Oh, it's you."

"Thanks."

"I didn't mean it that way. Look you'd have to be here. The dogs are all over Dad, and Mom is laughing the way she does when she watches those old comedies she loves on video, plus its pitch dark in here."

"You're having a blackout there?"

Alice finally located the lamp switch and turned it on. "Not any more."

"Hey, does this conversation sound as weird on your end as it does on mine?"

"I told you, you'd have to be here."

"I'm kind of glad I'm not, given the evidence I've heard so far."

"Evidence, huh? You talk lawyer talk all the time now?"

"Alice, I need to talk to Dad. Is he there?"

"Hold on, he's coming." She glanced over her shoulder. "Dad, it's Marie."

But as Stu walked toward the phone, Becca beat him to it. She tossed him an apologetic look. "Marie? It's Mom. Is everything all right? Is there anything wrong?"

"Hi, Mom. Yes. No. In that order."

"I just get nervous when you call, especially in the evening. Sorry for jumping in. Can we send you something?"

"Not a thing, Mom, just your love. But talk to Dad later. I won a big case the other day. He'll tell you all about it."

"Honey, that's terrific! Any chance you'll be coming up here for a visit soon?"

Silence.

"Marie? Stu, I think we were cut off."

"I'm right here, Mom."

"Oh, good. Listen, your father's glaring at me for grabbing the phone. I'll call you about a visit. Here he is."

"Marie? Something come up?"

"Look, Dad, just be cool and listen without showing any emotion. Okay?"

"Sure... the dinner was great... I wish you'd been with us, too."

"Good, now listen. I went out to the house and it's a mess."

"I don't understand. I left it spotless!" By an enormous effort of will, Stu kept his tone conversational.

"I'm going to tell you everything. Just don't react."

"Details about your work never bore me. Go on."

"When I got there it was dark and the lights were out. When I went to unlock the front door, it was already unlocked. It just swung open. I went through the rooms—"

"By yourself?" He caught Becca's glance, formulated his next question carefully. "Nobody else in it with you?"

"Whoever had been there was gone by then. The way things were thrown around, I knew it wasn't a regular burglary, that somebody was looking for something. Dad, I found a note stuck in the bathroom wall with a knife! I could hardly believe it."

"I can," Stu said, managing by a thread to keep his temper in check. "No, I'm not in any hurry, Darling. I'd love to hear it."

As Marie read the note, tension built in his neck and his jaw clenched. "Anything else?" he said evenly.

"Yes, Dad, I'm afraid there's more. I got scared—"

"About time, I'd say."

"Dad, remember, I'm fine now. Got that?"

"Yes."

"Okay. Well, I admit I got the willies and had to get out of there. On my way back to the condo, a car came up behind me and hit my bumper a couple times. I have to assume it had something to do with what happened at the house. Do you think whoever it was could have been following me?"

Stu said, "Hold on a minute, Hon." He put his hand over the mouthpiece. "Becca I can't very well tell Marie how beat I am—she's just bursting with her good news—so would you mind starting my unpacking? As soon as she's done, I really want to get to bed. Do you mind, Darling?"

"Of course not. Just don't be too long. You do look kind of beat." She grabbed Stu's smaller bag and headed upstairs.

"Okay, she's gone," Stu said, keeping his voice quiet. "Now, are you really all right?"

"Word of honor. I pulled into a gas station and the car went on by blowing the horn. Imagine that. I couldn't see clearly because of the rain, but I think it may have been a dark Jaguar."

Stu felt like smashing the receiver into the wall. "Is there anything you're holding back? I don't have to pretend any more, so make sure you're telling me everything, Marie. If anything happened to you—"

"Everything's under control, really. I called Pete Langworth. You know him, the pro at the golf course? We're getting to be really good friends, and he's going over to the house to help me clean up.

He's also going to be staying with me for a few days until I feel safe again. Dad, I'm not sure what's going on here, and at this point, you can't be either—especially not long distance. By the way, I called Uncle Des and told him what happened."

"Oh? What'd he say?"

"He's having the bank's security patrol go out every few hours around the clock to check on the place for us. Anyway, that's everything. I didn't want to spoil your homecoming but I felt you had to know. Sorry, Dad."

"Honey, don't you be sorry. You're great. Stay just as you are—only try being a little more prudent. You shouldn't have gone into the house alone. Why didn't you call the police?"

"Because I wanted to call you first, no need to worry about that any more, Pete'll be with me. Dad, call me tomorrow at the office when you can talk. I'm afraid you're not going to have an easy time when you get back here."

Or while I'm here. "Don't worry about me. Concentrate on taking care of yourself. I'll get back to you soon. And congratulations again on your case!"

"Love you, Dad."

"Love you too."

After he hung up, Stu continued to sit on the sofa, absorbing the consequences of Marie's call. Any idea of taking a short vacation was gone. He and Becca hadn't been away together for a long time, but that was going to have to wait. There were more important things to do. Who were these people violating their home? What did they want from him? All this was more than he'd bargained for. *Damn Des and his grandiose schemes!*

He would have to give Becca the news here, and sooner than he'd have liked. But not tonight.

He turned out the light and was headed for the stairs with his large suitcase when the phone rang. He couldn't move real fast, but was about to pick it up in the kitchen when it stopped.

Upstairs, Becca was sitting on the edge of the bed in her nightgown. She had a book in her hand and was hanging up the telephone as Stu entered the room.

"Who was that?"

"Ray. They won't be home. They got talked into staying the night, won't be back until sometime tomorrow morning."

"Thanks for putting my stuff away." *If you only knew how fast I'll be repacking it....*

Becca shrugged. "I'm just glad to have you home."

Stu changed into his pajamas, put on a robe, and walked down the hall to Alice's room to say goodnight. She was already asleep.

Becca was still reading when he got into bed. He hadn't realized how utterly bushed he was. Small wonder. He couldn't remember a longer day. He kissed Becca and turned on his side, hoping everything that had happened wouldn't keep him awake. But nothing could have. In no time at all, he gave in to sleep.

Half an hour later, Becca had enough of her book, put it on the night stand, and turned out the light. For a few minutes, she listened to Stu's light snore, content to have him back where he belonged. But what with Alice at dinner and his long phone call with Marie, they'd barely said hello to one another. She looked over at Stu. *He can't be that tired.*

She moved closer to him and, spooning his body, pressed tightly against his back and began to kiss his neck while running her hand over his smooth chest. She caressed his nipple, gently, then pinched it lightly the way he liked. Stu didn't awaken all at once. Slowly, he turned on his back, his eyes still shut. Becca continued her exploration of all the familiar places. A moment later, Stu quite awake now, was kissing her as though they hadn't been together for a year. His hands came alive, meeting her touch for touch. The sheets got tangled up and were pushed aside altogether as their bodies joined.

Afterward, Becca's head resting against his chest, she said, "Welcome home."

Stu felt his stomach clench, but he was determined to ignore its hint. There was no way he was going to spoil her gift with his news. "Thank you. A guy couldn't feel more welcome than that. You're really something, Becca. When's the last time I told you I love you?"

"Just now, for about twenty solid minutes." She laughed. "That was up to the gold standard."

She kissed him and turned on her side. He did likewise, but this time sleep eluded him. He did love Becca, more than he sometimes let himself think about when it might keep him from making the most practical—or in this case, only—decision. He owed her the truth. It was a debt he'd have to pay soon. But even as the lavender-gray of first light crept around the edge of the drapes, he still hadn't figured out how.

Chapter Nine

Sunday was a long, slow day. Alice went to the mall with a friend. Suzanne and Ray stayed away to give them time alone. Becca and Stu went out to brunch and sat together over the Sunday papers. Stu was too preoccupied with his own problems to concentrate on the world's, but if Becca noticed that he was on the same page for a very long time, she didn't say anything.

Nor did Stu. Not a word about what had happened to him, or to Marie, or to the bank.

When they went to bed, early, he knew time was running out. Monday morning came quickly. The sun cast a beam of light on the flowered green and white wallpaper. Stu decided to take the dogs for a walk. This was the time of day he most enjoyed. He liked to think and plan while he walked in the morning. Of course, this morning he didn't really expect to enjoy it quite as much as usual.

Sure enough, as soon as he set out, his mind went immediately to Florida. The problems at the bank were serious, and he could put himself in jeopardy by not being there to defend himself.

As he walked along the dirt path with the dogs, he realized that in a few days he had to leave which left him little time to talk to Becca and, potentially just as difficult, see his father at the bank. At the very least he had to find out whether his money had arrived from City National.

Maybe he'd also tell his father what was happening in Florida. Then again, maybe not. He'd have to wait and see what mood the old man was in before he decided. On reflection, borrowing fifty thousand dollars had been a bad decision. When he got back to Florida, he would write a check and reduce his credit line; he wouldn't need that money. House hunting, as far as he was concerned, was over. Des would give him that one hundred grand bonus for returning. That would be enough to live on for awhile, even if it hardly solved his potential financial troubles.

As he hit the front steps, he could smell the coffee. Becca, in a running outfit, was on her way out the door as he went in. Running was part of Becca's morning ritual now. She didn't enjoy it, complained it was boring, and claimed it abused her body, but it's how she stayed in shape.

After a quick shower and what felt like a life-and-death search, Stu found the keys to Becca's car under a magazine. He started up the Saab. It felt good to be behind the wheel of an old friend. The car had forty four thousand miles on it and wasn't even broken in yet. The morning air was cool, but the car radio informed him it would heat up to ninety by noon. Stu hoped that the weatherman was right. He wanted to play golf with Becca before he went back to Florida. He had decided to tell her of the change in their plans on the club course.

He reached the Morristown square within minutes. Being back in familiar surroundings it felt better than he liked to admit. The two oldest buildings in town were the church and the bank. Both were historic landmarks that had been used by George Washington and his troops. The Presbyterian Church was where Stu had spent most Sunday mornings with his parents. Rich in history, it was the visual focal point of the town. Its grand bell tower stood tall against the huge oak trees facing the square. He had always enjoyed walking through the park, admiring from different vantage points the magnificent church with its stained glass windows and arched dome.

Across the street stood the Morris National Bank. The huge granite building now two hundred twenty five years old was rumored to have been used as a hospital. It provided shelter not only for the injured, but also for those who were sick with smallpox, fever, and frostbite during the horrendously severe winters.

The four granite pillars supporting the structure were worn smooth. Each of the brass doors leading into the bank weighed about four tons, but was so precisely balanced and sensitive that a child could open it with just one hand.

Every time Stu entered the bank he felt as though he were walking back in time. White and black marble made up the floors, walls and teller counters. Each teller counter still had the original brass security bars. Two, forty foot murals decorated the north and south walls. The paintings memorialized the American Revolution. They portrayed the local residents and troops as they strove to survive those grueling winters.

Stu's father, Harrison Stuart, was Chairman, President, and Chief Executive Officer of the bank. He had held the position for the past forty years through lean and prosperous times. He was now seventy four years old, with one year left until mandatory retirement. He didn't want to leave, but he was a man who believed fervently in the importance of rules and he would abide by this one. Stu sighed. When his father retired, the bank would change, and not necessarily for the better.

Harrison Stuart had started his career as a messenger boy and worked his way up. There wasn't a department of the bank in which he hadn't done a stint. He was polite and a quick learner, and he moved through the corporate ranks rather quickly.

The bank had always been a serious place—banking, after all, was a serious business—but when Harrison took over the presidency of the bank, that was the end of even occasional harmless jocularity. Bankers were entrusted with other people's money, and that was a trust beyond the normal course of doing business. Life savings, including his own, had been invested prudently, to insure that the principal was never at undue risk. If depositors wanted more return than he could provide in this manner, he himself phoned his competitor down the street and initiated the transfer of the client's deposit balances.

Stu admired his father's commitment to his ideals, especially that a bank officer held a position of trust. But admiring the man and liking him were not the same. Harrison had never considered the milestone events in his son's life to be of sufficient weight to merit his presence. He was never there when Stu needed someone older to confide in. He never offered encouragement when his son, like any youngster, needed that more than anything. Stu's mother, Janice, had always seemed genuinely in love with her husband. Doubtless, she had initially been attracted by his rugged complexion, deep set blue green eyes, and squared off chin, but the fact was Harrison was *different* with her: she saw the side of him that was tender and loving, a faithful husband who worked as hard as he did because it wasn't easy staying on top. Maintaining your place on the narrow apex required a tremendous amount of devotion and energy, and Janice knew that. It sometimes made him moody, but in fifty two years she'd learned how to maneuver through those rocky times.

Becca and Janice had a lot in common. Both had that extra sense, that unique touch that was so important in keeping a marriage together. Their love for their husbands added a leavening of understanding. Each also shared a willingness not to pry into the business matters of her man.

Stu glanced at his watch. This wasn't a day he could afford to let get away from him. Crossing the lobby quickly, he headed for the elevator to the third floor. There, passing through a set of glass doors, he spotted Doris Wells, his father's secretary for the past thirty two years. Doris oversaw all the daily activities of the executive offices, and was the inflexible barrier between the public and Harrison Stuart. No one got to see the president without her approval.

"Well, good morning, Mr. Stuart," she said. "I haven't seen you in a dog's age."

"Hello, Doris. It's good to see you again. You look as beautiful as the day I left here."

"Don't you always know the right thing to say? We all miss you around here."

"I must say it feels good just being back up north."

"I hear you're up for good now. I hope you decide to come back to work with your father."

"How's he doing? Is he all right?"

"He's fine. A little grumpy now and then." She smiled. "But he still keeps us hopping around here."

"Is he busy?"

"Not this moment." She glanced at her phone console. "He's on the phone. No, wait, he's off."

She punched a button. "Mr. Stuart, your son is here to see you. Yes sir." She hung up. "You can go right in."

"Thanks, Doris."

Stu took a breath and opened the door to his father's private domain. His father was seated behind his huge leather-topped desk, phone in hand, apparently on a brand new call. And scowling.

Chapter Ten

He glanced up, but the scowl didn't fade. He gave a perfunctory nod, Stu's signal to enter the inner sanctum.

"Listen," Harrison said. His low voice held more command presence than any shout. "I'm not going out that long on those bonds. Find me something that matures within five years or less. I am not going to strain my liquidity position in this see-sawing economy."

That apparently didn't end the matter. Stu tuned-out the conversation and looked around the office to see whether anything had changed.

He should have known better. Usually, behind the desk of the biggest office in any corporation, there would be a large window. But in Harrison Stuart's office, the window looking out on Morristown Square was behind a conference table. Behind the president's desk stood what he considered a window on the world: two large bookcases filled with fine editions of his favorite "great books." Alongside his prized ten-volume collection of the works of William Shakespeare was a well-thumbed copy of Machiavelli's *Prince.* Between the two bookcases hung a lithograph by Jimmy Dwyer—his famous painting of "The Closing"—so appropriate for this room. The other walls were adorned with so many citations, plaques, proclamations and pictures that it was hard to discern the subtle herringbone pattern of the wallpaper behind them. Harrison Stuart had been State Campaign Chairman for the Republican Party during two elections, and there were numerous pictures to certify the gratitude of politicians in and out of the state.

A glass plate shielded the leather top of his nineteenth-century desk from being scratched by a careless visitor. The glass also protected from curious fingers a sheet of thirty two uncut one hundred dollar bills issued by the Treasury Department at the Bureau of Engraving and Printing. Harrison enjoyed looking at the bills himself, but they also served a purpose: they intrigued many who came to see him and provided a topic of conversation during which Harrison used a person's response to gauge his character. President Eisenhower had given him the sheet along with a personal note that was displayed beside it:

Dear Harrison:
To my old friend and loyal supporter,
But best of all a lover of horses.
Ike

The story of Harrison Stuart's relationship with President Eisenhower had thrilled Stu as a boy. As Harrison told it, he had met the great man when he was in school at Gettysburg. When Eisenhower took sick in 1956, the presidency was largely run from the Gettysburg farm. To earn extra money, Harrison volunteered to do odd jobs around the farm. One job was taking care of some of the general's prize horses, and another was cleaning Ike's office. Eisenhower was a great doodler when he was on the phone with important dignitaries. One day, Harrison got up the nerve to ask whether he might keep some of the doodles he'd rescued from the waste basket.

Ike laughed and said, "Why not?" From then on, he would occasionally actually save a particularly good doodle to give Harrison. Harrison's collection included a few ingenious caricatures of world figures. They were priceless memories of his longtime friend.

The friendship had begun casually. One morning while Harrison was cleaning out the stable stalls, Eisenhower stopped to chat. That brief chat led to many others on subjects as diverse as world economics and which brush would give the shiniest coat to a favored horse. In time, a friendship grew that would last a lifetime.

Stu glanced at his father, still focused on his phone conversation.

"One more thing," he said. "I got notice of a call option on two Hanover Township Education Bonds. I'm going to need some type of replacement with comparable yields. Yes, about two million. Okay, then. Get back to me tomorrow." He hung up, shaking his head, and finally looked up. "Nobody gives 100% effort any more. Sorry about the call, but you have to stay right on top of the bastards. Good to see you, Son." He stood and offered his hand.

"No problem," Stu said, taking a seat in front of the desk. "You're looking well. Everything good with you and Mom?"

"Well, there isn't a doctor within twenty five miles who likes either of us." He knocked the side of the desk. "So that's good. But we don't get to see you kids much and we miss those grandkids of ours a lot. They're all so grown up. Where's the time gone these last ten years? Here I am, still trying to make a living." He smiled his most ingratiating smile at his little joke.

"Dad, you haven't changed a bit."

"I trust that's a compliment. When do you think you'll be coming back to work here?"

"Well, that's one reason I came by. But before we talk about that, would you have Doris check my account here for a wire transfer that was to come in from my personal account in Florida?"

Harrison nodded, pressed the intercom, and passed on the request.

"Thanks. Dad, I'm not going to be coming back right away."

"What's that mean?"

"It means I'm not sure exactly when I'll be coming back. Des' bank is in a financial mess—problems not only with the FDIC, but also with the Justice Department. The fact is, I've received threatening notes, and my home has been broken into and ransacked. I've been run off the road and I had a confrontation with a couple of thugs. Even Marie has experienced a couple of problems."

"If someone's harassing Marie, I'll personally—"

"I'm taking care of it, Dad." *Why don't you know that without my saying?*

"Christ, I don't like what I'm hearing. I told you years ago that brother-in-law of yours was a slick operator. How the hell he became part of this family is beyond my comprehension. I know a few people at the Florida Department of Banking, remember? They confirmed he wasn't a straight shooter, told me the only reason he was still operating the bank was that they hadn't been able to pin anything on him. I wish I'd known all this shit before he moved his way into the family. He always had someone else do his dirty work." The blue-green of Harrison's eyes became a laser. "Does that include you?"

"Of course not! Look, at the time the opportunity looked attractive. When I look back on it I should have listened to you, but things weren't exactly good between us at the time." *You forget that was the real reason I left?*

"You really want to go into all that again?"

"No, Dad." *Of course I want to. I want you to know, once and for all, how I feel about the way you've always treated me. But you'd fight me inch for inch on that, too. You don't want to know. Not then, not now, not ever.* He sighed. Forcing his father to rehash their problems wouldn't help Stu solve any of the big ones loading down his plate right now. "Besides, I don't have the time. I have to talk to Becca, tell her that I'm going back."

"She doesn't know? Goddamn, boy, you got no balls! What are you going to do when you get back there? What are your plans?"

"I'm not—" The intercom buzzed and Harrison picked it up. Stu walked over to the window so it would not seem that he was listening in on his father's conversation. He glanced idly down at the street, all those people in cars knowing where they were going. He only noticed the maroon Dodge parked across the street from the bank because two men were leaning against it, looking up. Right at him! One of them said something. The other nodded and started around to the passenger side of the car. They must have spotted Stu staring down at them. The first guy got behind the wheel, and when he reached the passenger side, the second man glanced up once more, giving Stu a chance to recognize Jack Hendricks, his unwanted plane companion. *Jesus, Hendricks wanted me to see it was him. Show me that when he told me the Justice Department was going to be watching me, he meant it literally.*

As the car speed off toward the intersection, he could just imagine what the old man would have to say if he told him, which he suddenly understood he didn't have to do. Finally, he understood what he *did* have to do.

His father hung up. "Here's the information on your wire. Your money got here."

"Thanks. Dad, I need a favor."

Harrison Stuart glanced at the note he'd just made and smiled thinly at Stu. "Don't let me hear about any hard times."

"Don't believe everything you see. I borrowed that money for a down payment in the event Becca saw a house up here. Those plans are now in abeyance, so I'm going to pay back most of the money right away. Besides, the favor I need has nothing to do with that."

"I'm listening."

Stu recounted the part of the Florida situation he thought his father would take most seriously.

Instead, Harrison Stuart laughed.

"What's so funny?" Stu said, trying to keep his voice in check.

"Looks to me as though they're ready to get that sonofabitch Cain. But a *congressman?* You have got to be kidding me!"

"I'd hardly kid about that. Look, at first I couldn't believe it either, but now I'm sure it's real."

"What makes you so sure?"

"Dad, for once just take my word for something. Can you do that?"

Those cool blue-green eyes bore into Stu again. After what seemed an endless moment, his father shrugged. "Sure," he said. "What's the favor?"

"I need to know what's going on. With all your connections, maybe you can find out for me how serious this really is."

"All right. I'll try to check out this guy Kendrick—"

"Hendricks, Dad."

"Right." He jotted the name down. "I'll see if I can find out why he went to all the trouble of being on the same plane as you just to talk. Meanwhile, you find out more about this congressman."

"Dad, if he wanted me to know the congressman's—"

"Look, nobody likes sticking their neck out. You asked me to give you some help and I will, but the more information you can get me, the easier it's going to be to find out what's going on."

"I'll do my best."

"I remember walking the halls of the Rayburn Building, grabbing this congressman and that one to get support for one banking bill or another. I had powerful access to those people back then. I still have a little, but not like before. The new congressmen have their heads up their asses. They're trying to do right for everybody, and in the end, the damn country is being flushed right down the toilet." His indignation lifted him right out of his chair. He began to stalk the carpet. "This banking crisis we're in is a disaster that Congress created. The politicians didn't take the time to understand what this business was all about before passing ridiculous regulations that we have to live with. None of them admits that, of course, because they won't get reelected, so the goddamn cowards blame it on us." He stopped short, looked at Stu. "I'm telling you this because I have some enemies of my own on the Hill—and they're the survivors—so I'm not sure what help I can be to you. But if we *both* try our damndest—"

"I understand, Dad. I didn't know you were still so involved."

"Only when I get pissed off. The wrong people are paying the price for what happened in this business. I only hope I live long enough to see those guys get kicked out of office for what they've done to us bankers and to this country!"

Usually when his father got irritated enough, the discussion would end up being about Stu's failures. To forestall that possibility, he changed the subject. "Dad, I planned to go back tomorrow, but the way things look I may not make it. I'll definitely be leaving though. I don't like Marie being down there alone."

"Damn right! I don't like it one damn bit." He snapped his fingers. "I know. Tell her to stay at my place in Boca. Hell, I haven't used the place the whole winter. I hate going down there. I only bought it because you guys were down there and I could see Marie once in a while, but that never panned out because I got too busy."

"You ever going to believe that life isn't all business, Dad? I'll pass your invitation on to Marie, and I'll call you before I leave. Maybe I'll have some more information."

"Listen, when you go down there don't take any crap from Cain. You do what you think is right, Son, no matter how much heat you get from him. You have to stay strong, that's the main thing. Stay strong." Harrison squeezed Stu's shoulder. It was as close to an affectionate gesture as Stu could remember, and it touched him.

"This time I'm going to take your advice, Dad. Some of this stuff is over my head, especially the political part. I'm lucky to have an expert teacher I can call on."

The two men shook hands. At the last moment, Harrison Stuart placed his other hand over Stu's. Stu blinked. *Why in hell did it take all this to put the old man in my corner?*

Stu got into his car, tense not only with what awaited him in Florida, but with the things he had to get done before he left.

To his surprise, it helped that his father knew most of what was going on. If something happened to Stu, his father wouldn't let up until he found out who was responsible.

As he cruised down the highway, Stu turned his thoughts to telling Becca.

Chapter Eleven

Three Wakefield police cars were angled in front of the Collins' house. Stu thought, *something terrible must have happened to Ray!* He parked the car and got out. His anxiety fueled by a dispatcher's voice blurting coded jargon from one of the police cars, he was halfway up the driveway before he registered that it was Ray to whom the uniforms were talking. Suzanne and Becca stood by, listening intently.

"What's wrong?" Stu said. "Where's Alice? Where is she?"

"Stu, calm down," Becca said. "Everybody's fine. It's the van that's the problem."

"Check out the front windshield," Ray said.

Stu peered through the huge hole on the passenger side window. A golf club lay on the front seat. *Fortune Beach again! Are the boys in town to finish what they started?*

Ray walked over to the van and took a closer look at the club, which was still partly covered by the large white handkerchief they'd used to remove it from the car. "This is a very small town. Everyone knows my car and no one would screw with it. Someone from outside the area did this. I'd sure like to catch the little prick myself."

Two of the officers nodded agreement. "We'll have someone come over and do a light dusting of the handles and windows, but I don't think they're going to find anything. We'll be keeping an eye on the place during patrols."

"Thanks for getting here so fast," Ray said. "I'll look at the report later this afternoon."

As the officers headed for their cars, Ray grabbed Stu's shoulders. "Forget the car for a minute, how the hell are you? What a homecoming! We sure missed you."

"That goes both ways, Buddy." Ray and Stu went way back. Being a cop had made Ray nosey, and wary. They became friends slowly, and best friends very slowly. Now, there wasn't a man Stu trusted more. Apparently that went two ways also. One evening Ray had happened into a local sports bar where he and Monica were having a drink. A few days later, Stu had attempted an explanation. Ray had stopped him. "You don't owe me any explanation, Stu. Not about anything." And he'd never mentioned it again.

Now they walked together down to the pool. "Ray, what happened to your van today was no accident. I didn't want to say anything in front of the girls."

"What do you know about this?"

"What I know is that it's connected to why I have to go back to Florida. I was supposed to be home for good. Becca doesn't even know yet."

"Hey, I'm not sure what you're trying to say, but I've been hanging onto this article I pulled out of the paper," Ray said, tugging at his pants pocket. "So I'm not quite as surprised as I would have been."

Stu glanced over the article, then filled Ray in on events at the bank, the run-in he'd had with the two goons on the road, the unexpected visitor in the wrinkled suit, and what Marie had found at the house.

"Goddamn, Stu. They're coming for your ass on all fronts. When the feds get involved—" He shook his head. "Sounds to me like the shit is gonna hit the fan down there very soon. I hope you can handle it. Is there anything I can do? There must be people down there you can trust."

"I'm not sure. One way or another, everyone's connected to my brother-in-law. I guess I'll just have to watch my back."

"Stu, you aren't asking my advice, but I've got some. When you fill Becca in, be careful what you tell her, remember it's her brother and things can get very sensitive. You don't have to tell her everything. If Suzanne knew half the shit I'm into she wouldn't sleep at night."

"I'll keep it in mind, but honestly, she can't stand the bastard either."

"And don't forget that I know my way around Washington also if you need help."

Stu hadn't forgotten. When Ray graduated from high school he did what many restless kids did: he joined the Marines. In early 1963, Ray was in the presidential honor guard. He was on duty at the White House the week the entire country watched the on-camera coverage of the murdered president. Ray, angry as hell and wanting to avenge President Kennedy's murder, called on every hour of his training to get through his duties during the funeral. He had told Stu once how he'd clutched the handle of Kennedy's casket like a vise, because he felt that more than a life had ended that day. Ray finished his tour under Lyndon Johnson's presidency as a secret service agent then came back home. But he'd kept in touch with many of his honor guard buddies, many of whom ended up in government.

"What I'm saying is, if you ever need help, Stu, I know people who will help find the right people to talk to."

"I won't forget, Ray. And thanks. You know, I wouldn't be so concerned if someone hadn't gone to all the trouble of being on the same plane I was on coming up here, just to scare me. Believe me, he did."

"Who was this guy? What'd he say?"

"His I.D. said his name was Hendricks and he works for the Justice Department. But he seemed to know a lot more about me and I might feel a little better if I knew more about him."

"His first name didn't happen to be John?"

"The I.D. said John, yeah. Why? You know this guy?"

"I doubt it. The Jack Hendricks I used to know wasn't in Justice. He was Secret Service—stationed at the White House when I was. A switch to Justice doesn't fit the Hendricks I remember, but you never know."

"Could you check it out? It'd mean a lot to me."

"Bet your sweet ass. I'll have an answer—"

The back door slammed and Becca strolled toward them. "Stu, I'm ready to knock five strokes off my game."

Becca seldom hit the ball long, but every shot was straight down the fairway. Stu, on the other hand, had a natural slice that meant he never knew where the ball would finally come to rest on each shot. After they played the fifth hole, they decided to stop at the halfway house for a sandwich and a cool drink. Stu ordered, and they sat at one of the picnic tables nearby. He knew no more delay was possible, but it was hard to start the conversation.

"I'm definitely not getting talked into giving you any strokes the next time we play," he said. "The way it's going, it looks like you're going to have the pick of the rack at the pro shop again!"

"Stu, if you'd only relax instead of trying to hit the cover off the ball...Your game seems even more tense than usual today. Can't you just relax while we're here and swing easy?"

"Maybe some other day, but definitely not today. Listen, I'm afraid our plans have to be put on hold for awhile."

Becca only looked at him.

"I have problems in Florida. The bank's in a real mess. Stuff's been going on and the federal regulators have come in... and there's a chance I could be involved."

Becca's face turned ashen. "You? Involved? In what?"

"I'm not sure yet, but it could be some things that were under my jurisdiction and responsibility when I was there."

"Still, if you can prove you had nothing to do with whatever it was, what are you worried about?"

"Becca, the bank's federally insured, so if anything happens to it I, along with a number of others including your brother, will be held responsible."

"Responsible how?"

"Well, if the bank goes down the tube and losses are incurred, the board and executive officers may have to share in some of those losses. They could possibly attack our personal assets."

"Good! They can have them all, so long as they take the bills that go along with them."

"Becca, I think Des is involved in some crap that he can't get out of. I don't know the whole story yet."

"You don't have to. I'm not surprised the sonofabitch has his grimy hands in something. And I wouldn't put it past him to point the finger at you. I'd get out of there right now, brother or no brother, before he can screw you."

"What I have to do is go back there to make sure that doesn't happen. If I'm up here, I can't tell where the finger is being pointed. I haven't stopped looking for another way out since I got here, but there just isn't any. I'm so sorry, Becca.

"What about the job with your father? How's he going to take this change of plans?" Becca asked.

"The job will still be there if I want it. I'd rather do something else."

"What's this all coming down to, Stu?"

"Becca... I have to leave soon, and I hope you'll go back with me. The day this is over, we'll be on a plane back up here. I promise. But I've got to protect my name. I haven't done anything wrong, Becca. I swear."

"No need for that with me. I know you haven't done anything wrong. And you know I'll be with you, and I mean that in both senses." She smiled thinly. "I'll enjoy going back. I can't wait to get my hands on that greedy bastard brother of mine if he even tries to involve you in any of his shenanigans. Now, let's play these last four holes. I feel like knocking the cover off the ball before I help you pack."

Chapter Twelve

A burst of black smoke and the stench of burning rubber lingered like bad perfume throughout the air as the wheels of the 747 touched down at Fortune Beach International.

Stu was exhausted from the flight. He'd delayed his departure for two weeks to help coordinate the move back to Florida so that it would not all be left to Becca.

Arriving at the baggage claim area, he spotted his carousel and then his luggage. Marie was waiting by the ramp with her hand on the strap of one of his cases. She wasn't alone.

"Hi, Sweetpea. Hope you weren't waiting too long."

"No, not long. How was your flight Dad?" She stopped and indicated her friend. "By the way this is Pete Langworth from the club. He helped me out at the house the other night." she said excitedly.

"Of course." Stu offered his hand, and liked Langworth's firm handshake. "Glad you were around. I can't thank you enough for helping Marie."

Langworth glanced at Marie with his long sculptured grin, then back at Stu. "Delighted to help any way I can, Mr. Stuart. Even though you've never taken a golf lesson from me."

Stu grinned. "I was hoping you hadn't noticed."

"Just kidding, Mr. Stuart."

"If you saw how poorly I played in New Jersey you might not be." He glanced at the carousel. "There's the rest of my luggage. Let's get it and get out of here."

"Dad, the bank sent a car over to the house, so you don't have to rent one. I drove it over here... thought we might need two cars. But you didn't bring that much."

Within a few minutes they were on their way to Worthington. Driving down Palmetto Hills Boulevard, he was reminded of how different he had felt about arriving in Florida five years earlier, buoyant over having beaten out a hundred and forty-seven other candidates across the country who had applied for the same position. Even though his brother-in-law was Chairman of the Board he didn't want any favors. Stu wanted him to know that he was the cream of the crop. When the plane had landed that balmy August evening, there in the parking lot sat a new Lincoln with keys under the floor mat, and a welcoming note from Des stuck to the visor telling him that dinner arrangements had been made for him at the Worthington Golf Club

How elated he had felt that August evening. Finally on his own now, away from his father's critical eye. If only things had turned out differently. If only Des hadn't turned out to be everything Becca had warned him about and worse.

Pulling up to the house, Stu was caught by surprise. Everything seemed to be in its place. There was no sign of an intruder being there.

"Well, Dad, what do you think?" Said Marie.

"Everything looks just great! What a good job you've done."

"I didn't do it alone. Pete helped a lot. He rounded up all the maintenance people at the club and orchestrated what you see here."

"Pete, I can't thank you enough for your help on this," Stu said. "My wife and I appreciate what you've done."

"Like I said before, glad to be of help, Mr. Stuart."

The two of them stayed and ate with Stu. Tired as he was, he was happy to have the company and for a chance to observe Marie and Pete together. Langworth was as attentive as he was helpful. Stu liked his manners and the modesty he displayed when the discussion turned to his joining the mini-tour telling Marie that he has decided to stay at the golf club rather than travel every week living out of a suitcase.

Stu was standing in the bedroom, trying to decide whether unpacking could wait until tomorrow night, when the phone rang. It was Becca.

"Hey, Hi Sweetie."

"Sounds like you got down there all right. Is everything okay at the house?"

"Everything's fine. Marie and Pete, her new friend, met me and stayed for Chinese take-out. They just left."

"Who's Pete?"

"I *think* he's her boyfriend. He's one of the assistant golf pros over at the club. He's been watching out for her. Nice young man. Tall, lanky, with black hair. A good looking kid though. How are you doing?"

"Just a few loose ends to tie up and I'll be on my way down. Miss you already. Ray wants to talk to you a few minutes. Here he is."

"Stu, I've got more for you than I expected on Jack Hendricks. After a couple calls that got me nowhere, it finally occurred to me that one person who knows practically everyone in Washington is Ralph Daley."

"Should I have heard of him?"

"The point is, *he* hears about practically everyone. He's an old pal of mine from back in my Secret Service days. Now he's Chief of Operations for the Government Accounting Office. They keep tabs on everyone in government. Anyway, Ralph didn't ask me a whole lot of questions. Took my word for it this was important. He put someone on the project right away. When he reviewed what this guy came up with, a bell went off. When he told me the story, my bell went off too. I can't believe I'd forgotten."

"Ray! Forgotten what, for Christ's sake?"

"Hendricks was in the Secret Service when I was assigned to the White House. The story was he botched up a route they were taking toward the government center in Boston when President Kennedy was visiting his home state. He sent the pace car in the motorcade off to the left down Walnut Street, which was a one way street, with the presidential limousine following. It wasn't the authorized route and they had a hell of a time getting out of there. Hendricks received a reprimand and was given sixty days' leave of absence to find another agency that would take him under an authorized transfer. The botched incident was the talk of White House personnel for weeks. Daley had a vague memory of trying to help Hendricks with his transfer. Ralph believed the guy was entitled to one mistake especially when dealing with the pressures, and stress of the job he had. But it was such a long time ago, he couldn't even remember whether, in the end, he *had* been able to help."

"I guess if it's the same Hendricks who's tailing me, someone did. Thanks for trying, Ray."

"Not so fast. While Daley was talking, I remembered Hendricks too. You know, so many people go in and out of your life... still, I can't believe I'd forgotten this one."

"You knew him?"

"Let's just say, when I managed to get hold of him today, he remembered me."

"This is unbelievable. So what's this, a million-to-one shot?"

"He was glad I'd called too. Someone must have slipped up because he didn't know that you were back in Florida. Someone's ass is going to be in a sling for that one."

"Yeah. Mine."

"Stu, shut up and listen. I told you I forgot all about him? Well, he had more reason to be memorable. He told me there were not many people who stood up for him back then. I happened to be one of those who did, and he thanked me for taking a chance on him."

"What did he say when you brought me up?"

"No doubt about it, he was surprised. Listen, Hendricks knows what it feels like to be in trouble for something you didn't do."

"I don't get it. He did mess up that motorcade you mentioned."

"Turned out he was set up. Through his earpiece, he was instructed to turn left. He knew it wasn't the right route, but he was told there were problems ahead and to make the turn. Turned out, the Secret Service quota was filled, and Senator Berry's nephew wanted in really bad. They staged a screw-up to open the position. Could you imagine putting the President of the United States in danger because someone wanted a Secret Service job?"

"That's scary as hell. Ray, I can tell you, I'm no big shot, but right now my own situation feels scary as hell to me. Did you and Hendricks talk about it?"

"He obviously couldn't tell me a whole lot, but he said to tell you that being tough right up front, the way he was with you is how Justice usually gets cooperation. I got the distinct impression he knows you're not involved."

"What does he want from me, then?"

"Your help. He needs to understand the politics of how things were done at the bank. Stu, if your brother-in-law and the congressman are up to their eyeballs in illegal shit, who knows who else may be involved? That makes this case very sensitive, and that's why Hendricks was assigned to it. Apparently, over the past several years, he's built himself an excellent reputation for *not* messing up a job."

"You really trust this guy?"

"I do. And I trust you to do the right thing."

"Which is?"

"Right now, nothing. When Hendricks gets back down there, he'll be in touch. He'll want a meeting. Meet him."

"I'm going to have to trust you on this. I don't know what I can tell him, but I'll do my best. I owe you, Buddy. How you doin'?"

"You don't want to know. Besides trying to nail down the bastards who broke my windshield, we have a couple of murders on our hands. Can you imagine Wakefield with a double murder? There's going to be a lot of front porch lights on for the next few nights. A bunch of kids found six heavy duty leaf bags alongside of Route 10. When they opened them up, they found the torsos of two males. Heads in one bag, legs and arms in the other. Can you imagine? I really feel sorry for those kids. We haven't been able to identify the bodies, but everyone is frightened because like they say, things like this don't happen in our town. Well, until now they were right."

"I know how they feel."

"Concentrate on knowing that Jack Hendricks knows how you feel. Call me if you need me. 'Bye, Buddy."

Stu hung up slowly, then lowered himself onto the bed to rest a few minutes.

His own scream woke him. The bedside clock said 2:50 a.m. Stu wiped the sweat from his forehead, undressed, and slipped back into bed, thankful the nightmare that had awoken him was only a dream.

Chapter Thirteen

Stu's silver Lincoln headed over the crest of the Emerald Bridge that connects the mainland to Fortune Beach. The smell of diesel fuel permeated the salt air as squawking seagulls hovered, scouting for their morning meal. The early sun ricocheted off the Atlantic waters like silver ribbons glittering in the sunlight, rippling slowly with the tide.

His own little world was going to be different from now on. His fantasy of accumulating great wealth was now gone. He'd been given a second chance with Becca, and he wasn't going to risk his marriage again. He was back here only to accomplish three things: protect his back, protect his professional reputation, and salvage his family's financial security.

His single largest investment, Fortune Beach Bank stock options, was now in jeopardy. Given the mess the bank was in, regaining shareholder confidence was going to be a stretch. Stu had no doubt that the lion's share of correcting the problems would fall on him.

Maybe he deserved to be slapped with that. It appalled him how easily he had been drawn into the life of junkets to Vegas, weekends in the Bahamas, tarpon fishing in Costa Rica. He'd been a fool, and eventually his tab for bank-related entertainment exceeded even Des' high tolerance. Des had weaned him off the lifestyle quickly, and his social welcome quickly cooled.

Becca had never said much, but one late night as Stu tried to slip in through the kitchen after a night of too many Sambucas, she flicked on the light switch. "This bullshit has to stop, and I mean now!" she said. "Do you really think I'm going to sit back and watch you destroy yourself and our marriage?"

"I was only—"

"Stop! Don't say a word because you don't know what the hell you're saying, and this conversation is going to get a lot worse. Just think about how I feel with everyone around town talking about your screwing around. Tomorrow is a new beginning for you, or else you're on your own. You got a reprieve here tonight. Don't screw it up or I won't be here when you get back!" She stormed off toward the stairs heading for bed.

Stu had heard every word and rather than start an argument that would only make things worse he decided to sleep in the spare room the rest of the night.

Still, he'd managed to hang onto the reputation he'd developed with the Fortune Beacher's as someone whose financial advice they could trust, especially when it came to negotiations over foreclosed real estate. Stu could smell just how hungry a seller was for a short sale, and he used that knowledge to help numerous clients acquire property at bargain basement prices.

The car phone beeped. Des, of course. "Thought I'd catch you in the car. How do you like those wheels?"

"Fine. I'm nearly there."

"Settle yourself, then come and see me. I want to introduce you to some of our guests."

"As soon as I can find my office."

"No rush, our visitors aren't going anywhere. See ya."

Stu turned the corner where Main Street and Fortune Beach Boulevard intersected, which was believed to be the very spot of the wealthiest intersection in the world. Two blocks ahead on the right, Stu pulled the car into the parking lot of Fortune Beach Bank. The handsome Spanish architecture matched the façade throughout the downtown area. His old parking space hadn't been painted over with another name. Des was one cocky bastard.

The bank entrance, with its arched portico and dark blue Spanish tile driveway, was as impressive as it was intended to be. The double glass entrance doors were etched, and twenty-four carat gold leaf braised the corporate monogram.

Two armed guards were busy offering assistance at the bank's entrance with a municipal cash deposit from the weekend parking meters, while customer service representatives were busy helping FBB clients, some of whom were personalities known throughout the world. They wintered in Fortune Beach and banked where they got the most attention. Des always made sure he provided whatever they wanted. "The best service never costs as much as losing a client" was one of his favorite axioms.

Harry Hibbs nodded at Stu. "Good Morning Mr. Stuart. Good to have you back, Sir." Harry had been warmly greeting customers at the bank's main entrance for more than thirty-five years. He never complained about his salary or the aching feet that supported his 375 pound body all day.

"Why thank you, Harry. How are things?"

Harry raised his bushy grey eyebrows. "All these people runnin' round here—"

"We'll get everything back to normal pretty soon, Harry boy."

When Stu reached the executive area of the bank, he wasn't surprised to find Charlotte Webster waiting for him. Charlotte was a stout woman with thinning gray hair, a hundred dollar smile and a very close resemblance to Barbara Bush, not only in appearance but in spine. On the cusp of sixty five, Charlotte had given notice that she was retiring after thirty-four years of service.

"The news that you were coming back was the first good news we've had here in awhile," she said. "We'll be all right now."

Stu smiled. "I thought you were getting out of here?"

"If you think for one minute I'd stay home and miss all this action now that you're back, you're crazy, Mr. Stuart."

Stu's office faced the eastern end of the building. He could see the Atlantic Ocean over the roof tops of the oceanside mansions a block away. Charlotte edged into the doorway. "I have Mr. Cain on the phone. He wants to know when to expect you in his office. He kind'a sounds impatient."

"Tell him a few minutes; I'm on the phone."

Stu wrote up a list of what he wanted to accomplish when he came back from his meeting with Des. He buzzed Charlotte, who came to the door again.

He handed her the list. "I'll need this stuff when I get back. The comptroller will have it."

"Sure, Mr. Stuart. Let me make sure I've got everything straight. You want copies of today's statement of condition, the last quarter's call report, the yearly budget, and information on the bank's loan portfolio? Will the comptroller have that last one?"

"You're right. Just have someone in the lending division get me a trial balance on the commercial loan portfolio. I'll take it from there."

"Lately, Sir, the examiners have been spending all their time in the commercial loan department. I get the feeling by the way they're asking questions and rifling through the loan files, there's nothing routine about this examination and I've been through plenty of exams in my time." She shook her head. "We've never had people from the Justice Department here either. The scuttlebutt around the bank is that the employees think we're going under, and fast!"

"If that's what people think, well, that's just one more thing we'll have to take care of, won't we, Char?"

The entrance to the Chairman's office was through two smoked green glass doors. Another set, at the far end of the office, led to the conference room. Des rose to greet him. "Stu! It feels like you never left. Welcome back."

Stu looked past Des into the conference room, where four sets of eyes looked intently back at him. *It sure as hell feels like I never left, only worse,* he thought.

Chapter Fourteen

Extending his right hand, Des walked around the desk and put his hand on Stu's shoulder, saying, "Hey did you get settled?"

"Not really, but I have the rest of the day to get caught up."

"Well, before you do that, I want you to meet some of our country's worst and dumbest." His glance indicated the people seated around the conference table next door.

"Are you making any progress on our problems with them?"

"Those bastards won't give an inch. I'm not sure what their agenda is, and you can bet your sweet ass they're not going to tell us either. We have to be as helpful as we can with information, even if they're turning the whole goddamn place upside down. Can you believe those sonsofbitches are checking my gas credit card down in accounting? I own thirty percent of this fuckin' place, and those assholes are checking where I had my last meal!"

"I detect they're beginning to get under your skin, Des."

"Shit! I know, I know... I have to be cool."

"That's the drill, exactly," Stu said. "These people are trained to piss you off and wear you down until you stop watching what you say, because then you never know what might come poppin' out. You have to understand the mentality here. These are government honchos you're dealing with, not your blue-blood buddies from Fortune Beach. If they can nail your ass for something—anything, no matter what it is—that's points for them. They have nothing to lose and if you think you have deep pockets wait until you see what they can spend to prove their point. Understand?"

"Christ, no, I don't understand! What'd I ever do to deserve this slow torture? Let's just get it over with!"

Stu decided to let that pass. "Look, Des, they're probably going to be here for months, so get used it."

"Why the hell are you so calm all of a sudden? Give it a few days and we'll see how calm you are then!"

"The point is we have to stay alert through this so that when they leave, we're still standing. Now, why don't you give me the short version of what's happening here?"

"From what I see, everything around here is a big goddamn secret. They will talk to you when they're good and ready. Meantime, they're sniffing around all my records like dogs in heat. Reading board minutes until the print comes off the damn page, trying to tie loan minutes to the actual loan documents to see if things happened exactly the way they were approved, and shit like that." Des threw up his hands in disgust and started to pace the office.

"Des, I told you to watch yourself. Those doors are glass."

He swung around and looked into the conference room, then glared at Stu. "Why not just put a leash on me and maybe a muzzle too?"

That may be the best idea you've had in weeks, Stu thought. "Think for a minute—is it in your best interest to show them you're nervous?"

"I *am* nervous, and if you had blood in your veins instead of ice water, you'd be just as antsy as I am. I have a lot to lose here." He turned toward his desk to take a seat.

"Des, what's wrong with you? You can kick the shit out of your investment friends you hang around with, but when it comes to this you're in another character. I really don't know how you're going to take this, but I'm only going to say it once, so try to hear me: You asked me to come back here, and I'm here. While I'm here, I'm going to do everything I can to make this mess go away. We're going to lose some battles here. There's no winning here at the end of the day and it's going to cost us. I'm not doing this for your sake, but for my wife and my kids. Got it?"

Des' eyes darkened, but he nodded.

"Good. Now that we've got that straight, why don't you take me into the conference room and introduce me?"

No one stood as Des entered with a stranger in tow. *Not a good sign,* Stu noted. *But then, they aren't here to display good manners.*

"Gentlemen, ladies, we'll be joined this morning by Mr. Halsey Stuart. Mr. Stuart has just returned from a brief trip north. As you know, he's the executive vice-president and head of our commercial loan department besides being my right hand on many matters we deal with."

Stu nodded around the table. A large black man stood. His hair was graying and half-glasses rested on the end of his nose. He walked slowly around the table, leaning heavily on a wooden cane with a brass duck handle. Stu was about to change his mind about the lack of manners when the big man passed right by them and headed for a side table set up with coffee. He poured himself a cup, added two sugars, and took a sip. Then, still ignoring Stu, he turned toward Des. "Good morning Mr. Cain. I brought my assistant with me today. I trust you won't mind?" His voice was rich and deep and as confident as if he held a gun.

"Not at all. Stu, this is the FDIC lead examiner, Lionel DuPree out of Atlanta," Des said, smiling.

And you, brother-in-law ought to be nominated for an Academy Award, you sound so at ease right now. "Nice to meet you, Mr. Stuart," DuPree said, offering his hand. "And this is my assistant, Cecile Fontane, whom I am sure you will get to know during our stay here."

"Ms. Fontane," Stu said, and shook her hand, noticing that she wore a little too much scent. He figured her to be about thirty-five, a very attractive black woman. Her soft smile made him wonder how tough an examiner she really was.

Des spoke again. "Stu, this gentleman is Roger Jacobson from the Florida Department of Banking. This is a dual exam, and Roger is representing the State's interest."

"Good morning, Mr. Jacobson."

The examiner acknowledged Stu with a nod. Jacobson couldn't be anything else but an examiner. He wore a black suit that was one size too small, with a thin maroon tie that made Stu want to yawn.

Des looked at a man seated at the far end of the table. "I'm afraid we haven't met."

"Dave Docker, Justice," the man said without standing. "I'm representing Mr. Jack Hendricks, who was unable to be here today." Docker, who was very thin, had a twitchy way of moving his neck when he talked.

"Anyone else like a cup of coffee before we start?" Des said, ever the gracious host. "If not..." He took a seat at the head of the table.

Everyone found his place, and Stu took the chair with the best remaining view of everyone.

Lionel DuPree ran his hand over the desk. The black acrylic rectangular table was inlaid with gold and silver Spanish Escudo coins. "Nice. Real nice," he said.

"Thank you. Our clients are used to fine things. They like to do business where their taste isn't offended."

"The coins are real, I imagine."

Watch it, Des.

Des shrugged, leaving it wide open. "Lionel, as I assured you, Stu is back," he said. "And we of Fortune Beach Bank are glad to have him back. I thought you ought to meet right off, get acquainted. If there's anything he or I can do to make life easier while you're here, all you have to do is ask." He glanced at his brother-in-law. "Right, Stu?"

Stu smiled. "Most assuredly."

"Thank you both," DuPree said. "We're glad to see Mr. Stuart here. We've been reading a lot of his memos and we do want to ask him some questions when he gets settled. I know it's his first day back. Mr. Cain, we did want to mention that we noticed you have very little senior management for a bank of this size. It's very thin in my view, and that's one more reason we're glad to see Mr. Stuart back."

"Well, we run an efficient ship," Des said. "Why be top-heavy?"

"Because that way there are more controls. Executives with duel responsibilities don't work, and besides, a few intelligent heads are better than one—or even two."

Mr. Jacobsen looked at Stu. "Mr. Stuart, Roger Jacobson, Banking Department. Once you're settled, I'd like to be filled in on one of your larger borrowers, a Mr. Johnny Mack, and the Ocean Beach Development Corporation?"

Stu didn't dare check out Des. He looked directly at Jacobson. "I can tell you right now, Mr. Jacobson, Johnny Mack is a successful developer in this part of the state. He's been a customer of this bank for the past twenty years. His accounts have balances in the high six figures on average, and the overall risk to the bank with his personal signature is fairly minimal."

"We're not questioning his ability to build homes or his personal net worth, Mr. Stuart. We just don't understand some of the transactions, that's all."

"Like what?"

Cecile Fontane raised her right eyebrow just a bit. "May I?"

"By all means," Jacobson said.

"Thank you. Mr. Stuart, Mr. Johnny Mack signed a bank commitment for 5.5 million dollars, and from what we can see, you lent him six million. I don't understand how that's done. I also see where he's supposed to pay two points for the loan. That comes to one hundred ten thousand dollars, just as the commitment states. But when I traced the entries back, all I could find that he paid was twenty five thousand dollars. Can you tell us where the remaining eighty-five thousand dollars is entered? Perhaps we missed it?"

"Ms. Fontane, I can only assure you that all the transactions I have seen with this borrower have been fine. I'll of course check into what you're saying and get back to you."

"Please do. I'm just a little confused, that's all."

"As I said, I'll give you an answer as soon as I can."

"There's no rush, Sir. We'll be here for quite a while." She returned a slight smile.

In that instant Stu knew she wasn't to be underestimated. Charlotte was right; this wasn't a normal examination. They were going back through documents and general ledger tickets reviewing entries. He had better get moving and find out what was going on before they thought they had a fool as well as a thief in their net.

"I'm sure we can give you all the answers you need on this matter," Des said. "All we ask in turn is a little patience. Now, is there anything else we can do to help?"

"We're working up a list, Mr. Cain," DuPree said. "There's a lot more we just don't understand about the operation of the bank and the involvement of its directors. What we'd like to do is leave this subject for another meeting in a few days. Say I give you a call when we're ready?"

"That's fine." Des rose from his chair.

Everyone stood and shook hands all around. The four examiners left the room.

Stu waited until they were down the hall before he turned to Des. "What the hell? Do you know anything about this?"

Chapter Fifteen

For a moment, Des only stared. Then, tautly, he said, "Since when do you talk like that to your boss?" A thin smile broke across Des' stony face. "Or to your favorite brother-in-law? Hey, we're going to beat those nerdy bureaucrats, you know? You and me."

"Is it possible that you still don't get it, Des? If you don't get your act together, and I mean right now, those nerdy bureaucrats are going to *hang* your ass. Let's start with the loan to Mack. What's the story? I need facts, and I need them fast."

"Keep your voice down. The fact is, I am, or was, a silent partner in the Ocean Beach project."

"What do you mean, am or was? It's one or the other."

"Well, the project is almost complete. Look, Johnny needed capital to get it started. He was up to his neck in the Riverview deal. No other bank was going to lend him the money to get this new project off the ground. If I were going to lend the money with the risk on my end, I wanted a piece of the project." He grinned ingratiatingly. "I knew it'd be a home run right from the beginning."

"How'd you get something like this through? This would need board approval."

"What difference does that make now? You asked for facts. Okay, what else do you want to know?"

"Where's the commitment fee money? And how'd he get to borrow five hundred thousand more than was approved?"

"He never paid more than twenty-five thousand dollars for the commitment in the first place. I waived the rest of the fees. The project was stalling because homes were not closing fast enough even though they were sold. To keep the subcontractors on the job until the units closed, they needed more funding. So, I had Mack sign a note to me and I agreed to advance him the five hundred thousand to keep the project going. We didn't need this construction loan going belly up, so I waived the fees. I called down to the note department and had the fees reduced on my authority."

"Are you that crazy? Self-dealing is a clear conflict of interest! You're involved in the project, Des! You share personally in its profits! And you're telling me that when the project ran short you used the bank's money to continue to fund it? Brilliant! And you never told me a damn thing! You bypassed telling me anything and put me in jeopardy! Des, you violated every regulation in the book. If they uncover all this, you're out of here in a minute! How about a fine for the bank of about a million dollars a day if they want to stick it to you?"

"Okay, okay, look. I know I stuck my neck out a mile on this one, but how are they going to know about my involvement unless someone tells them?" He was staring directly at Stu now.

"You said you're a secret partner... just how secret?"

"Only Johnny Mack and now you—no one else knows about this."

Stu studied the view and his conscience. Then he turned and looked into the hopeful eyes of his wife's only brother. "Des, I don't know what I'm going to do about this. By telling me, you've involved me up to my ass." He shook his head, then sighed. "I'll deny that you spoke to me about this."

Des said, "Just do what I brought you back here to do: keep a lid on things... a tight one. Don't pretend my management style is news to you. You knew right along some of what I've been involved in. You were well paid. Still are. And remember the bonus I promised you. I've always looked after those who look after me. Don't forget that, and we'll be rid of those nosy bastards in no time."

Stu couldn't believe his ears. "Just like that? That's what you think? Well, let me straighten you out on one little matter. The hundred grand? I wouldn't take one red cent of that money now. All I need is for those guys looking around in my account and finding a hundred-thousand dollar bonus when the bank's having financial problems. I'll never get them off my ass. Besides, the stockholders are going to take it on the chin again this year. That bonus would stick out a mile on the proxy. I could use the money, but I'm not about to dig my grave any deeper. I told you right off, I'm here to protect my own ass, not yours."

"Our asses are rubbing right up against each other, brother-in-law."

"Yes and no. First of all, you're in no position to show me that cocky attitude. We both bear responsibility for the condition of this place, but if I'm going to hang around and try to clean up this mess, you'd damned well better be square with me. Lie to me once, and I'll drop you like a sack of dirty fifties."

"Why would I lie to you at this stage?"

Because by now, lying is second nature to you. "I don't have all the questions I'll want to ask you yet, but I'll be back. We—I—need to be *prepared.* There are too many of them to fight off any other way. I still don't know whether you realize it, but you've brought the wrath of the whole regulatory process down on us. With the heat that's on in Congress, you're just their kind of flesh. They've already spent five billion dollars trying to clean up the banking mess, and the taxpayers are still pissed at how it's been handled. We're talking about big money here, Des. If I didn't know better, I'd think I was working in a goddamn savings and loan."

"It's all a bunch of bullshit, Stuie boy! As soon as another problem crops up, they'll be off on that. One thing for sure about Congress, these guys get elected on the basis of who they know and how much they need to spend—or steal—to get themselves elected. Take away their knack for bullshitting, and there's not one of them could find the zipper to their pants without a schematic."

"You may be right about them, but it's your weaknesses that got us in this spot. You always wanted a little more, and a little more. Someday you're going to want once too often, and that someday just might be now."

"That's what I have you around for," Des said, laughing. "To protect me from myself. Besides, what's life all about? I walk this earth like everyone else. In order to get anywhere you have to take chances. That's what makes this country great. People like me, who go across the grain of society's rules. If there were no risk takers, who the hell do you think would be working around here? The little guy only works because he's given the opportunity by someone else who created a job. People like me are the ones who provide those opportunities. Keep that in mind, Buddy, when you're feeling self-righteous. Sitting on the shoreline keeps you dry, but how about getting in the white water with me and finding out whether you have what it takes to stay afloat? That's what life is all about, Stu, getting in the water."

"If this weren't so serious, I'd tell you to go screw yourself. Count yourself lucky we're not made of the same stuff, because the goddamn bank would end up six feet under, and we'd both be making license plates."

"Hey, how about a quick lunch later?"

"I don't think you've heard a word I've said. Look, I have to try to put out some fires around here today. I'll see you later."

On and off during the next few hours, Stu's concentration was interrupted by a nagging sense that he might not have made the right decision in coming back. Who knew where the hell the trail might lead? As he began to read what Charlotte had waiting on his desk, he became certain there was something going on here bigger than what Des was telling him.

It was mid-afternoon before he remembered to phone George at City National to tell him he was returning the money he had borrowed from his credit line. George sounded bouncier than usual, and on impulse Stu asked him why. Turned out he was leaving the bank to go into partnership with his cousin who owned an insurance business. No wonder he sounded happy. These days, even being a branch manager held hazards.

Being an executive vice-president certainly ought to carry battle pay, he thought. He had to find out just how bad things were from his vantage point. He was sure the regulators already knew, and that they would not tolerate any further weakness in the bank's capital position. If things didn't change soon, they would be running the bank in a few months. He'd seen it in their eyes this morning. Even now, they were closing in.

He had to get to the bottom of these problems and fast. Then he had to come up with a plan to re-kindle investor confidence in the bank. *Damn, my mind's a blank. Now think... what would my father do?*

Chapter Sixteen

Dusk arrived at the same time Stu's Maker's Mark bourbon was slid in front of him. Tiger's was his favorite watering hole and within walking distance of the bank, and he was ready to refresh himself from a long day of disasters. He needed to think how to go about this project. He still wasn't sure how bad things were, but what he did know was alarming. The bank had a vault full of non-performing delinquent loans that were increasing quickly in his billion dollar bank. So far this year, the bank had charged off thirty million dollars. If the bank continued to deteriorate with loan customers not paying the bank back, it would be heading for a Cease and Desist Order from bank regulators. *I should have paid more attention to what was going on around me and my department,* he thought. *I'm almost as guilty as Des.*

He'd signaled the bartender for another bourbon when he felt a tap on his shoulder. He turned and was greeted with the soft, ruby red smile of Margaret Neff, owner of the *Fortune Star.*

"Hi Stu. I heard you were back, and from what I hear they need you badly over at your place right now."

Peg was an expert reporter and journalist. She had been molded by her father, the original owner of the fifty-six year old *Fortune Star.* He had delivered the news to those who wallowed in opulence looking for their daily fix of being seen or quoted in media of their peers. Now it was her turn to produce a quality newspaper and keep the headlines powerful for her aristocratic readers. She was smart, well dressed and could read a face or detect a trembling voice better than a priest at confession. Stu knew her attributes and knew he had to be careful or he might wind up on the front page in Fortune Beach driveways the next morning.

"Care to join me?" Stu said.

"Sure. I'd much rather have a drink with you than Des. I can't stand that sonofabitch."

Stu laughed. "Didn't your daddy ever tell you, ladies don't use such language?”

She sat down. "I need to talk to you. I hear you're about to be taken over. True?"

"That's what you want to talk about? Really? Come on, Peg."

"Stu, you're better off letting people know what's going on than having these rumors continue. Locals in town are getting nervous. They don’t want to pull their deposits, but they’re scared. What’s Des doing about it?"

"Hey, it’s my first day back, Peg. Even if I wanted to tell you, I'm in no position to talk to the papers. Des is your man for that story"

"Well, I can tell you something. Even if only half the rumors are true, it's not good for the town or the bank. If you go down for the count on this here in Fortune Beach, that's national news. You know anytime a fish farts around here, the world seems to smell it. Stu, fair warning. We're ready to go with a story that we believe is accurate. It's in your interest to make a comment before we go to print with it."

Stu forced a smile. "You’d better get your facts straight before you go to print, Dear. I'll get back to you."

"I'll hold you to that. I see my friends have arrived so I have to go, but one more thing because you're such a nice guy. Stu, people in this town talk, especially folks who have too much time on their hands, and I know you know that. If you think you have things under control, you're mistaken. Watch yourself, be careful."

She walked away, shuffling through the tables and greeting admirers as Stu gulped down the last of his drink. He pushed the glass away indicating he was leaving, but decided to pick up a pepperoni pizza to go. Just then Tom Wallace walked in and sat at the bar. Tom had a small partially bald head atop of his large frame, on its way to becoming huge. He’d started at the bank right out of high school, working his way from teller to head note teller, a position that carried responsibility for booking all loans onto the bank’s computer system. If there was one person who could clue-in

Stu about any unusual internal loan situations at the bank, Tom was the guy. Stu signaled the bartender to send him over.

Tom approached. "Hi, Mr. Stuart. I saw you earlier today and looked like you were really busy. I don't think you saw me."

"Sorry. Impossible day. One thing after another. Buy you a drink?"

"Thanks, great. It's good to have you back, Sir. Chances are I'm going to have to give one of the kids a bath tonight. So I guess I can fortify myself for the event before I go home."

"Hey, I'm about to have a bite to eat. Would you like to join me? I'd kind of like some company. My wife isn't back in town yet. Your wife mind if you pass on that bath?"

"Let me call and see what's what." He moved away to make his phone call.

While waiting, Stu spotted Peg, who was settled in with two friends for dinner: Walter Dobbs and Hank Stone, the chief of police and the mayor. *What an odd trio having dinner together. Between the three of them there's nothing in this town they don't know about.* He wondered what they could be talking about. *I'm sure the bank's in there someplace.*

Tom returned. "Wife gave me the green light."

"Glad you could stay."

They ordered, then made small talk until the food arrived. Finally, Stu decided it was time. "Tom, I know you personally book every loan in the Commercial Loan Department, and I'll bet nothing escapes your eagle eyes. Tell me, what's going on in there?"

Tom wiped his upper lip, which was suddenly producing beads of sweat. The man was no fool. "Mr. Stuart, how am I supposed to answer that? We have an extremely busy department, and at times I feel we don't get the credit we deserve for the responsibility we have there. We see a lot of stuff there, but we have to keep our silence because of the people we deal with. I know you know that."

"I know it isn't easy down there, but tell me, are there any issues that have you concerned? Things I should know about?"

"We have many issues that bother me with partnerships and stuff like that, but I'm not so sure why you're asking. How do I know you weren't sent here by Mr. Cain to test my loyalty? I don't want to lose my job. If I talk to you, who am I really talking to?"

The man was way off base, but no fool. Stu leaned toward him and spoke softly. "You know why I came back. I came back to try to fix the mess we're in, which I'm sure you're aware of by now. The truth is I have a lot at stake here, but so do you and everyone else who's given their all to the bank. Look, Tom, I can't fix things alone. Will you help me?"

Tom didn't answer right away. He seemed to be thinking through his options. Finally, he nodded. "Okay, but I hope you know what you're getting into." He took a deep breath and plunged ahead. "I think the shit's going to hit the fan pretty soon. Not only do we have delinquent loans that you're familiar with, but many of them were questionable right from the start and nobody's asking what happened. I'm no analyst, but I don't think it takes one to know the way people have been getting these loans, and even the transactions taking place at the closings are questionable. Now bank examiners are crawling all over the department. We have some people from the Justice Department asking questions about certain congressmen and, quite frankly, I don't know what I'm going to do. They haven't gotten to me yet. I don't know what they're waiting for, but I'm nervous as shit. Maybe they think I'm in on some of the stuff."

"I don't think that's the reason at all. They just have a lot to do. So what's your take on what is going on with some of the loans?"

"Let's just say Mr. Cain has exercised a great deal of authority in the department. I know your responsibilities in the lending area, Mr. Stuart, but Mr. Cain has said more than once that he's the ultimate boss and he wants things done his way with no ifs, ands, or buts about it... that's his pet phrase when he talks to me. You know, he doesn't even go through channels when he wants to tell me something. He picks up the phone himself. He's even come to the department a couple times. The bottom line is, he's approved loans, under his own authority, without any personal guarantees and contrary to policy. He never gets the wife's signature on the note when it warrants. He changes some loans approved by other officers, usually to aid a borrower that he knows. He put new accounting procedures in place, and no one said a thing about it. It's getting to the point that—look, it's just a job. I make thirty-two thousand a year. I have a little bank stock put away for the future. I really don't want to get in the middle or question the authority of the chairman."

"I understand," Stu replied. "But in order to make things right, I have to be able to evaluate your assumptions, and how can I do that if I don't have the facts as you see them?"

The waiter interrupted to prepare the Caesar salad, and Stu could see Tom was using that time to decide. The waiter left for another table and it was obvious Tom would rather be giving his kid a bath. "Well," he said, spanning the room while he spoke. "There's Mr. Cranston."

"Alex Cranston, our board member?"

Tom nodded. "And your daughter's employer. I'm not trying to be a smart ass, Sir, but people talk and I needed you to know that I know."

"No problem. Go on, please."

"Mr. Cranston is involved in so many deals at the bank that I don't know which end is up. Not only does he have a financial interest in many of the loans, but he represents the bank as our counsel at loan closing. At times he also represents the borrower, if it's one of his clients. You okay, Mr. Stuart? You look flushed."

"I'm fine. Please, don't stop." The vein in Stu's neck was protruding noticeably. "He's been doing it for some time; I don't understand why the auditor hasn't picked this stuff up."

"Is there more than one loan that you know about with Cranston?"

"Well, I'm sure you know the Bartley Towers project on Atlantic Avenue, right?"

"The high rise? About two hundred units?"

"That's the one. Mr. Cranston has a twenty percent interest in the project even though you don't see it on paper."

"How do you know that?"

"I was at the closing with the documents from the bank. The attorney fees were being taken out of the loan proceeds, and Mr. Joe Servin, one of the other partners, was upset at what he was being charged, especially the funds being taken out of his loan proceeds. He said to Mr. Cranston that he should have charged him much less because he would only be hurting himself since he was a twenty-percent partner. He was making money on both ends of the deal. It's like the bank is his piggy bank. I heard it all."

"How come this attorney thing wasn't picked up before? Who the hell prepares the commitments around here?"

"Mr. Cain himself changed the attorney that was to represent the bank at closing to Mr. Cranston. Mr. Cain told me to issue an addendum to the original commitment."

"And board action isn't required for attorney selections."

Tom nodded. He wiped his sweaty forehead with his napkin. "That enough, Mr. Stuart?"

"God knows it ought to be. But no, I know you've got more."

"Do you want another about Mr. Cranston or someone else?"

"There are others?"

"Are you kidding? There are dozens!"

Chapter Seventeen

Dozens? How could so many questionable transactions slip by me? Was Tom being over dramatic in his explanation or was he trying to throw Des under the bus? If Tom wasn't bullshitting him, his stories might be just the break Stu needed. It was hard to believe what the guy knew, and what he didn't know.

Stu pressed. "Let's hear more."

"How about Mr. Penza?"

"Rocco Penza, the architect and former board member? What's his claim to fame?"

"Well, remember he borrowed five million dollars on the Clairmont Hotel project? The one that's now in bankruptcy? I overheard the examiners talking about it in our area. From what I get of it, the appraisal used to approve that loan was over-inflated, and someone upstairs wasn't reviewing the work of the appraisers. He was given double what the project was actually worth."

"Who did the appraisal?" Stu asked. His neck muscles began to tighten again.

"Donaldson Associates."

"They're thieves! I told the loan committee six months ago to stop using them! They appraise high just like their bills."

"Here's something you might not know. Not only are Penza and Donaldson located in the same office complex, I hear they both live on the same street."

"So I guess you're saying this was a neighborly favor. Unbelievable! It can't be!" Stu brushed back a strand of hair that had fallen over his face.

"From what I'm told the project is fully advanced, but the building is only half-completed, if that," Tom said softly, looking around to be sure no one was overhearing the conversation.

Stu lowered his voice too. "I heard through the grapevine that Penza has personal problems, and I was told he had money tied up in the project, but I never knew any of these other details. How does this stuff take so long to surface?"

"Mr. Cain knew. He's in on this one also."

"Are you sure? Be careful... this is very serious stuff. I know he has his faults, but this is criminal."

"I'm no fool, Mr. Stuart. I know your connection, but if I'm going to stick my neck out, I'm not going to tell half a story. It's the truth."

Stu nodded. "Okay. Go on."

"Well, when I sifted through the file after I heard the loan was being reviewed, I found that on the first construction advance, we gave out all the money without one cinder block being put into the ground. In other words, the whole project was worth $2,500,000 according to the appraisal and we gave him $5,000,000 in one shot." Tom snapped his fingers. "Just like that."

"I know there has to be more to this story," Stu grumbled. "I can feel it. Did anyone bother to file a mortgage on the property?"

"A man like you has to have keen instincts about a situation like this. When we closed the loan, the proceeds, all $5,000,000 went into Mr. Cranston's personal checking account."

Stu's eyes grew wide. "Wait a minute; what does he have to do with all this?"

"That I don't know. It's out of my area, but I assume Mr. Cranston is running the project to some degree!"

"Well, I know one thing: Cranston's smart. He's not going to take a chance on being picked up on a bank audit putting funds into his account. I don't even see how he could have done it."

"Easy. Just think about it. Who checks the mica-encoded numbers on credit slips to accounts? No one. Well, someone uses the correct corporate name on the slip to show it went to the right account—in this case, the Clairmont Corporation—but the mica numbers used were for Mr. Cranston's account."

Stu wanted to slap the table. "Goddamnit! Who's been paying the interest on the loan? I've never seen it delinquent until we got the damn bankruptcy notice last month."

Tom shrugged. "Our loan is fairly current, but we have no equity. I'm told by the branch administrator that we get a slip from a teller who takes the principal and interest payments at the window. Not only is there no trace of who's making the payments because they're paying in cash, but there's more to the story of their dealings. They reduce the principal balance significantly with the cash payments and then borrow the money again later against the construction line without even an inspection on the property being completed. Nowhere in the file does it show someone went out there to see what was going on with the project. When they did it enough times—and not one of them was a reportable transaction from what I can see so far—they decided not to push their luck and they bankrupted the company before the IRS and whoever else began snooping around." He paused for a moment. "So Rocco goes off the board, and we get stuck working this shitty loan out. Seven months before he declared bankruptcy, he made a large principal payment and then withdrew a construction advance for the same amount of the loan. That was his last laundering job and no one was the wiser because he'd done it so many times before." Tom sat back in his chair.

As the food was delivered to the table sizzling on metal trays, Stu poured himself another glass of red wine. Tom began devouring his entree, but Stu interrupted him. "Tom, what's up with the rumors about loans to a congressman? What's the real deal? Is it true?"

"I'm not sure about that. There's just so much funny stuff going on, Mr. Stuart." He took a large bite of his steak and chewed it thoughtfully, smacking his lips. "I do remember... quite some time ago... being asked by Mr. Cain to mail copies of closing documents to an address in Washington, but I don't remember any more about it."

"How about the address?"

"Sorry. All I can remember now is that I had to write the address on the back of a loan file. When Mr. Cain called I was busy with some other project, and he wanted me to mail out this stuff immediately, so I wrote the address and the name down on the back of the loan file I was working. I got it out at the end of the day."

"Tom, that file's really important. I'm relying on you to find it."

"I'll do my best, Mr. Stuart."

"I know you will. Tell me, do you know anything about Main Street Investors?"

"That's another large loan to a partnership with some condo projects, I think. Never saw any problems with it, but I have to admit, I haven't spent any real time on the file. "

"I need to know the details. Gather all the information you can on the loan. Bring it to me tomorrow. Okay?"

"Sure thing. Is that one I missed?"

Stu shrugged. "I need to do some work with it. Let's get outta here. I lost my appetite."

It felt good to get out into the open, even though it was still warm and muggy. There was no moon, and the stars were bright against the dark sky. Tom had left his car parked in the bank lot as well, so they headed back together. The streets were quiet except for a few cars parked in front of Romano's, which was noted for the best Northern Italian food on the beach.

Stu said, "It's amazing to me how much information you carry in that head of yours. How do you do it?"

"I've been in this department a long time, and the players don't change. Just the loans do."

"Listen, Tom, I need one more thing: get me all the commercial files on Johnny Mack, his partnerships, corporations—any deals that involve him in any way, no matter where they might be."

"It's going to take me a—"

It felt as though a razor blade cut across the back of Stu's neck and he heard a light *whoosh.* He turned to ask Tom whether he'd felt anything and—

Tom was clutching at his throat. His eyes were bulging and his mouth gaped open as he strained for oxygen. Blood poured between his fingers. He reeled violently backward, his huge body crashing through the front window of Gucci's. He lay writhing in the shards of broken glass, clawing at something protruding from his throat.

Stu leapt through the opening to see what Tom was grabbing. Protruding from his neck was a small wooden arrow about a foot in length, feathers soaked with blood. Stu rolled him halfway over, looking for the other end. It was hard to see in the dim light, but he felt the steel tip of the arrow and knew it had to stay in place until help arrived. "Tom, hold on! Do you hear me?"

His hands wide open and visibly shaking, Tom reached out for help. Stu grasped his hands and felt the warmth of blood on his hands.

"Breathe, Tom! Please breathe! I'll get help!"

Why hadn't the sound of the alarm brought help yet? Suddenly people appeared out of Romano's, looking puzzled at the commotion across the street. Stu yelled, "This man needs help! Please, someone call an ambulance!"

As people scattered in all directions, Stu turned back to Tom. His flow of blood was now worse. Stu knew he would not last long if the blood wasn't staunched quickly.

A waiter was still standing nearby. Stu looked at him. "Go get me Saran Wrap and towels from the restaurant. Hurry, hurry up!" He said to a waiter standing like a frozen ice cube. It seemed like five minutes, but seconds only ticked away when the chef showed up with the wrap.

"Wrap that towel around his neck and I'll pull off a sheet and wrap his neck. Hurry! We have to contain his blood. He's losing way too much. Wrap it over the arrow when I pick up his head. I'll break off these feathers to make it easier." Stu grabbed the bloody feathers and twisted ever so carefully until he heard a snap.

The pressure of the Saran Wrap over the towel seemed to slow the flow of blood. In the distance Stu could hear sirens getting louder.

Stu turned back to Tom to tell him help was on the way, but his face had turned blue and his eyes were closed. His breathing was shallow. "Tom, stay alive! Think of your wife, your kids. Please stay alive! You can do it!"

The Fortune Beach Ambulance arrived. Two attendants moved quickly through the crowd.

"There's an arrow in his neck. Be careful."

"I can't believe the blood this guy lost. And he's still alive?"

"I can hardly get a pulse on him," said the other attendant.

They moved quickly inserting an IV into his arm and placing a brace around his head to keep him steady. Another minute ran down as they drove off in the direction of Good Samaritan Hospital.

Stu waded his way through the crowd to the bathroom at Romano's. Someone said to someone else, "Did you see that guy? They must have got him, too."

What? Stu thought. *What are they talking about?* He had to be alone for now. He locked the bathroom door, leaned up against it, and closed his eyes. When he regained his composure, he viewed his reflection in the mirror over the sink. His face, shirt, and hands were covered in blood. He looked as though he was the one who'd been shot.

He cleaned up as well as he could. As he wiped the nape of his neck with a damp paper towel, he felt a stinging sensation. He felt around the area, and discovered a slight burn on his skin. *That's right... something grazed the back of my neck. The feathers on the arrow! A half inch over and—That arrow was meant for me!*

Chapter Eighteen

The brass door handle jiggled. Stu glanced quickly toward the door. Someone wanted to use the bathroom. A knock. Another knock.

Then a mumbled voice. "Stu, are you in there? Hey, let me in."

What in hell is Des doing here? Stu barely breathed as the door handle jiggled once again. *Does he know one of his employees might not make it through the night?*

"Stu, are you all right? Open the door."

"Not until you tell me what you're doing here, Des."

"Jesus! I can't believe what you're saying. I heard about the incident on the Plectron at the house, so I drove over here to see what was going on. I saw your car in our parking lot, the bank was dark. I came on over here where the crowd was. I ran into Hank Stone outside, and he told me you were involved. What the hell happened?"

Stu opened the door, his eyes focused on Des' every move as he stepped outside the room.

"Christ, Stu, what the hell happened? I mean, I heard what happened, but what really happened? Look at you! You look like you've been in a train wreck. No way are you going home alone tonight. I'm taking you back to my place. I think you need someone to talk to."

"No!" Stu said. Then he assumed a quieter voice. "Thanks. I mean, I appreciate the thought, but I really want to be alone. Everything is still so real for me on what just happened here."

"Well, at least let me drive you. In the morning I'll send someone to pick you up."

Stu didn't feel up to driving, and he figured if Des had other ideas he could defend himself. "I'll take you up on that ride, and thanks. Let's get the hell outta here. I'll tell you what happened on the way."

Des' red Austin Healey was parked outside the restaurant. Stu squeezed into the passenger seat and off they drove. The car set low to the ground, it felt as though they were part of the road. Stu wasn't in any mood for a speed test and he let it be known.

"Whatever you say." Des slowed to seventy.

"We could have a dead employee on our hands."

"I heard two people were shot; that's all I know."

"No, they got it wrong. Only Tom Wallace was hit... in the neck. I think he's probably dead."

"The guy in the note department? I know him. Who would want to harm that guy?"

Stu knew that Des was basically just a good salesman, so maybe he really didn't know what happened. He told Des the details.

"He was barely breathing when they took him away. I have to call the hospital—maybe someone in the emergency room has a few miracles up their sleeve for this guy."

"Find out if they moonlight at banks." Des said sarcastically. "Sorry. I couldn't help it. Look, take a couple days off. This was a hell of a day for you. Relax the best you can, get yourself together, and come in when you're ready. Whatever you need let me know."

Stu shook his head. "I have too much to do right now. I don't want to look like a fool when those examiners question me. Right now, they seem to know more about what's been going on than I do and that's embarrassing. Which reminds me, you and I have to sit down and clear the air about some of the things I heard today. I can't avoid the land mines if I don't know where they are. If they've got the goods on you, the faster we face up to that, the better chance we have of repairing the damage before we both end up in the slammer. I'm convinced that you have a lot to tell me."

"Not really. There's not all that much to know. Are you asking me if I cut a few corners now and then, went against the rules a little bit? Sure, that's the only way you can do business down here. That's my role, Stu; I'm a rainmaker for the bank. In case you haven't noticed lately, that's a job. None of those examiners you met can do a real job, you understand? Their specialty is second-guessing the people who do the real work. They're government people; always remember that."

"Des, they have a job to do here and apparently they're going to do it, because they're busting our ass right now. Seems to me our job is to get with it and get the bastards the hell out of here. I'll be in some time tomorrow." He wiped his face with a tissue as the beads of sweat formed again on his forehead.

They pulled up in front of Stu's house. "I'm sending over one of the guards. No argument. You won't even know he's around. He'll be parked just down the street for the next few days."

Stu figured he'd be sleeping with one eye open anyway, so what could it hurt. "That's not a bad idea for a few days."

"Sure you want to come in tomorrow?"

"Yes, but I might be a little late. Thanks for the concern and the ride. Send your driver over around 10:30 in the morning."

Stu undressed, throwing his blood soaked Brooks Brothers suit in the garbage. He didn't want to see any of it again.

He took a shower and had headed for bed when he noticed there were two messages on the answering machine. Becca wanting to say hello and that she was starting the long drive down with Alice early in the morning.

The second message was from Marie, and something in her voice didn't sound right.

Her phone rang ten times. *Why isn't her machine on?* Stu told himself not to panic and dialed Becca.

Ray answered.

"Stu! Glad you called."

"Boy am I glad you answered. Got a minute to talk before Becca gets on?"

"Sounds serious. What's up, Buddy?"

"I believe someone tried to kill me tonight. Chances are the guy I was having dinner with is now dead. Someone shot an arrow into his neck. I think that arrow was meant for me."

"You're shitting me. Tell me what happened, nice and slow," Ray instructed.

Stu began to re-tell the events.

"Sounds to me you're in deeper than it's safe to be."

"After tonight, my guard's up, believe me."

"You must be getting under somebody's skin or at least someone thinks you are. I have some days coming to me. I can hop a plane and be there before morning."

"I really appreciate it, but please stay there. Ray, I don't want Becca or Alice down here right now. Can you keep them awhile?"

"Are you kidding? We were sorry to see them leave."

"Thanks. I'll call you when I have some more details for you to chew on."

"Did you happen to get a look at the arrow by chance?"

"No... I was afraid to pull it out of his neck."

"Well, check it out with the detective on the case if you can. Find out if it was on the short side but kind'a fat. If it was, it sounds like a crossbow. Had a case like that once. Maybe there's some ego involved here, too.

"You lost me."

"We asked the guy why he didn't use a gun; he said any asshole can pull a trigger on a gun, but shooting a crossbow takes real skill."

"Proud bastard, huh."

"Stu, be careful. Hey, *here's* Becca now."

Hearing the laundered version of what happened, Becca urged him to come back. "Look, I'm concerned for you. Anytime you get involved with my brother, somehow he's always in the middle. I'm not saying he had anything to do with what I just heard, but something caused this, and he's got to be involved somehow. If you let me come down there I can really ratchet things up for him and he knows it."

"Please don't put extra pressure on me. Let it go. I have to finish what I came down here to do."

"I'll call you every day. And you come up in a few weeks."

When he hung up, he was glad he'd promised. Even a couple days away from here seemed wonderful.

Stu tried reaching Marie again, but still no answer. *Where is she? Is she all right?* After five more tries, he called Pete's house, but his phone had been disconnected. He couldn't even drive over to Marie's. His car was back at the bank.

He lay back, but exhausted as he was, sleep was out of the question. When the phone finally did ring at a quarter past one, he grabbed for the receiver. "Hello?"

"Dad?"

"Marie, where have you been? I've been calling you all night. Are you all right?"

"I'm fine, but I had a little scare tonight. My car was stolen."

Relieved, Stu said, "It's just a car. Besides, it'll probably turn up."

"Already did. It was found parked on the Dixie Highway with its flashers on and the engine still running."

"Sounds like someone wanted the car to be found."

"The police called me, so Pete and I went over to get the car."

"Was anything missing?"

"My glove compartment was rifled, but whoever it was didn't take anything. Something was weird though...."

"What's that?"

"On the floor on the driver's side was this leather thing that looked like a pocket and had a slit for a belt to go through. I asked the police officers if they knew what it was. One of them said it was a pocket quiver."

"A what?"

"A pocket quiver... it goes in your rear pocket and if you're into archery you put arrows in it."

"Marie, where is that thing?"

"The police took it."

Stu took a shallow breath. "I want you staying here tonight. Pete still there?"

"Dad, what is it? What's going on?"

"Tell you later. Put Pete on the phone."

Stu instructed Pete to follow Marie to his house. "Don't let her out of your sight. I expect you in half an hour."

"Yes Sir."

Stu hung up and stared at his trembling hand. Someone was trying to scare the hell out of him, and it was working.

Chapter Nineteen

When Detective Santora of the Fortune Beach Police Department finished quizzing Stu regarding the details of the shooting he also informed him that Tom had died in the hospital. Stu's shoulders slumped upon hearing the news and with a quivering voice asked him about the weapon used in the murder. The detective confirmed that the arrow was from a Swiss target crossbow. The shooter was definitely no amateur.

Marie moved back to her condo after a few days. She needed time to prepare for an up-coming trial. Stu reminded her to be careful, and to be cognizant of everything around her. They decided to meet for lunch Saturday at the condo where he would get the opportunity to ask some thorny questions about her boss, Alex Cranston. Charlotte had gathered the files as requested along with bits of information regarding Main Street Investors. Stu sifted through the voluminous material, noticing that the most troublesome seemed to be the loans to Alex Cranston and Johnny Mack. Still, he had to complete his review of the numerous files that towered unevenly on the table next to him.

He decided to detail the files on Johnny Mack. Perhaps as he listed the sequence of events on paper he would be able to assemble a profile of this character who seemed to play such a pivotal roll with so many Fortune Beach elite. He'd met Johnny several times in the bank during loan closings scheduled by Des, and at a few social events Des hosted at his mansion.

The Johnny Mack file was in complete disorder. Documents were hard to trace, because they didn't follow any selective date order. Stu spent much of the morning assembling the file to get a clearer picture of Mack's dealings with the bank.

In 1981 Johnny Mack built his first house with help from a small bank in Lantana, Florida which subsequently had been closed by the FDIC. He lost ten thousand dollars on his first venture because the home took longer to construct than he'd originally estimated. He didn't find a serious buyer until six months after construction was completed. Reduction in the sale price and interest expense wiped out any profits. He decided to give it another try. Johnny, on recommendation, went to see Des, who convinced him to build a home on Plantation Beach where there was money and opportunity. Des lent him $250,000 to purchase an ocean front lot where he constructed a home in less than six months. Des made sure Johnny's mother signed the note and took her house as collateral for the loan. Before the house was completed, he had five buyers. He sold the house to Chief of Police Walter Dobbs' son-in-law and realized a $120,000 profit. From that day forward, he vowed that waterfront property was where he would make his fortune. Over the years Johnny became a quality builder along the coastal waterways of Florida, never again being without a buyer before completing a home. He loved dealing with the rich. They knew exactly what they wanted and had the cash to back up their demands.

Thumbing through the files, Stu found an article from 1988 in the Sun Day Times naming Johnny Mack as the Florida Builder of the Year. Much of the credit went to Desmond Cain who gave him a second chance to make it. The money from the bank, along with some luck and hard work, had made him a success. His latest project was the construction of 275 homes sites, known as Flamingo Dunes, along the Intracoastal Waterway. The article pointed out that Ocean Beach Properties, the builder, obtained a partial commitment of thirty-five million dollars from the bank to begin the project. The town of Ocean Beach was a sleepy little residential community snuggled in along the Intracoastal approximately twenty miles north of Boca Raton. It was considered a great place to retire, a snowbirds' paradise that harbored glistening white beaches, fishing, and two eighteen-hole golf courses. The standard of living was inexpensive with most of its residents old enough to qualify for Social Security and early bird dinners. It was the perfect place to live until Morecom Data came to town.

Morecom Data was a California based conglomerate with offices in Washington, Dallas, Chicago, and now Ocean Beach, Florida. The company chose this sleepy retirement community because it was the only town that still had huge amounts of undeveloped land along its pristine waterway, along with hundreds of acres west of the Florida Turnpike for future development. When Morecom Data arrived, they came with strong credentials, power, and lots of money.

Morecom Data supplied the ammunition that the politicians needed to stay in office. They would provide six thousand jobs to the economy of southern Florida. They kept their word, and sent the small town reeling with change. Shopping centers, banks, gas stations, restaurants, movie theaters, night clubs, schools, new roads and higher taxes quickly followed. Ocean Beach was a town in the midst of transition. The standard of living changed dramatically from the days of waiting by the mail box for the monthly Social Security check to arrive. The elderly began to migrate to other nearby towns. Anything that would make a lifelong resident, and new retirees want to relocate, Morecom Data did their best to oblige. Their homes sold within days of being listed. Those who sold received a bonus of twenty percent over the market price of the house because the demand was so strong to move into this new, youthful exciting, vibrant community in Ocean Beach.

Stu asked Charlotte to get all the files on Morecom Data and their related accounts with the bank. He had to examine the total connection. Perhaps the files would give him a clue as to how far their tentacles really reached around town.

The phone rang. "Hello, Stuart here."

"Mr. Stuart? Hi. It's Jessica Warren. I don't expect you to know me, but I'm the new secretary to Chairman Cain. It's so good to hear your voice on the other end. How are you? I heard about your unfortunate ordeal. I'm glad you're all right. I'm sorry for that guy, Tom; he was a really nice person from what I'm told."

"You're right. He was a nice guy. Is there something I can do for you?"

"Oh, I just never thought those little arrows would be able to do any serious harm. There so small. I thought they were more for like decoration. It seems so archaic to me. When was the last time you heard of someone getting killed by a crossbow?"

"Not in these times. How do you know so much about this stuff?"

"Well, Des mentioned it, and it reminded me of the little arrows on his wall."

His ears perked up. "What little arrows? I never saw them."

"The little ones in his den, over the stained glass window in the corner. You never saw them at his home?"

"This is the first I ever heard about it."

"He was some sort of a champion archer or something. I can't remember exactly what he told me, but I do remember the little arrows in the frame."

Stu couldn't believe what he was hearing. *Things like this just don't happen out of circumstance. What's going on?* Des' bimbo calls to say she's sorry for what happened, and then says that the murder weapon is similar to the one hanging over his brother-in-law's window at home? Did she make this call intentionally?

Thoughts raced through his mind: *If Des had anything to do with this, why didn't he try something last night? Why would he want me back if he just wanted to get rid of me? Doesn't make sense. It couldn't be that I know too much. I know very little about Des' clients. Then again, I do handle most of the divisions in the bank except for Des' friends. Am I going to be the next patsy at the bank like Becca warned? And just what was Tom's involvement in all this to warrant him getting killed?*

Jessica said, "Hey, you there?"

"Yes... yes, I'm here."

"Listen, the reason I called, I have a note from Des on my desk. He wanted me to see if you can attend a kickoff cocktail party at his house for our cancer drive. He thought you should be there."

"Where is he?" Stu asked.

"He had to go to some meeting with one of the examiners."

"When and what time?"

"Tomorrow night at seven."

"I'll be there. Are you going?"

"Do you think I'm going to miss a party at Des' house? Not a chance." She chuckled.

"See you tomorrow night," Stu said, hanging up the phone.

For an instant he found himself staring at the tall, lanky palm blowing in the breeze across the street. His reverie ended as a pile of loan files hit his desk with a thud, shocking him back to reality.

"Well this is all of them, at least what I could find. What golf hole were you dreaming of when I came into the room?"

He grinned. "Charlotte, you know me too well."

"Did you make the shot?"

"You bet. Sixteen inches from the hole."

"Good shot. Now get to work." She smiled and left the room.

As Stu opened the first file, another headline by the *Sun Day Times* caught his eye: *MORECOM DATA CORPORATION: FRIEND OR FOE?*

The story was about how the corporation had turned Ocean Beach inside-out in less than five years. It went on to say that the United States Government had owned approximately 250 acres of undeveloped land along the Intracoastal Waterway that was converted to a wildlife sanctuary in the late 1980s. Signs began to appear years later, indicating a residential community, Flamingo Dunes, was about to be born. Everyone was up in arms over the sale of property by the government and what the development of the land would do to the community, but the sale was completed, and the government washed its hands of the matter. What remained were many unanswered questions: Who bought the property? What was the purchase price? When was it sold? Why didn't anyone know about the auction?

The questions lingered for more than a year in the local press and were finally laid to rest as just another government screw up with no one taking the blame. The paper indicated that Morecom Data Corporation was the purchaser of the two parcels: the Flamingo Dunes Parcel and three hundred fifty acres of undeveloped land west of the Florida Turnpike. Construction of the company's office complex would bring thousands of new jobs, and an upscale residential community would be developed, providing additional housing for their employees.

Morecom Data entered into an agreement with Ocean Beach Properties to develop Flamingo Dunes with all the financing to be provided through Fortune Beach Bank. Johnny Mack became the builder/developer and was to realize millions from the completion of the project. *The whole transaction smells like limburger cheese on a hot exhaust muffler,* Stu surmised as he continued to read. Morecom Data was a major borrower and depositor of the bank. Des took primary care of the banking relationship, making sure the company was the bank's top priority.

Notes to the file indicated that the bank audit firm didn't like the cozy relationship established between the company and the bank's chairman. The audit revealed in its management report that other account managers should be involved in a credit this large in the event the chairman was out of town. More importantly, it was just good banking practice to have others involved. It was an unusual comment, but due to the ten million dollar unsecured line of credit and other borrowings, the auditor on the job was making sure his ass was covered. Stu thought the comment would have brought a response, but there was none, with the exception that Des was a silent partner in the deal.

Stu mumbled, "Just one more left. I might be able to get out of here for a round of golf." He keyed the intercom. "Charlotte, call Pete Langworth at the club and see if he's free. Maybe he'll play a few holes with me."

"Yes, Mr. Stuart."

All the recorded documents and collateral were kept in a separate file and locked in a fire proof vault each night. Any new documents that were placed in the file had to be filmed for security controls in the event of a disaster.

Stu was hoping to get through the last file quickly, but it was so thick that it was taking longer than expected. Turning the page to review the transfer of title documents between Morecom Data and Ocean Beach Properties, Stu stared at the bottom of the page. His face flushed to the color of Charlotte's lipstick. It was just like Tom had said! The firm of Cranston, Weatherby and Stone were the attorneys representing Morecom Data, Ocean Beach Properties and the bank. But the biggest surprise came when he read that the attorney signing the closing papers was none other than Marie Stuart. Stu was shaken. How can this be?

Not only was the attorney connection improper, but his daughter was signing documents for the firm knowing that he was Vice Chairman of the Board.

Charlotte came in. "Mr. Stuart, are you all right?"

"Sure, I'm fine."

"Pete Langworth can't make it. He's giving lessons all afternoon."

"That's all right. Tell him we'll do it some other time. I just lost my appetite for golf anyway."

"I'll tell him, Sir. Can you please pick up on line three? A Mr. Hendricks wants to speak to you. I couldn't hold him off."

"Jack Hendricks?"

"That's what he said his name was and that you'd know him."

"Yes, I know him." As Charlotte left, Stu picked up the phone. “Hello?”

"Hello Stu. I hope you don't mind me calling you that. I feel like I've known you longer."

"No problem."

"I wanted to wait awhile before I called, let you get your feet on the ground."

"Thanks."

"The grapevine tells me that you have pretty good connections around Washington. Not only is your father checking me out, but I also got a call from Ray Collins, your buddy, a guy I haven't seen in years. This whole thing is a real scary scene. If I didn't know better, I'd think I was the one being set up. Sure brings the definition of small world to the forefront doesn't it?" He laughed.

"Remember it's not always what you know," Stu said. "What can I do for you?"

"It's really about what you can do for yourself, Stu. My associates tell me that you had some excitement here yesterday. It's a shame that young fella had to die."

"It sure was a shame, but I believe I was the killer's real target."

"Not a chance. If someone wanted you dead, it would not be a difficult thing to accomplish, believe me."

"But Tom had nothing to do with *any* of this."

"Well, fact is, you're wrong. We think he was up to his ears in collusion at the bank. It was just a matter of time before he was going to be interrogated about the transactions going on in his department. I know you were with him before he died. I can only surmise that he was looking for an ally to support some of his activities. Maybe he knew time was running out for him, and he wanted to push some of what he knew off on someone else. Have you looked at the file on Main Street Investors yet?"

"Right now I'm overwhelmed by the files. You said I'm a partner in this project along with some congressman whose name I still don't know, yet I'm having a difficult time even understanding how all this stuff got by me."

"Why don't you meet me later and we can review it together?"

"Okay. That sounds reasonable, but you'll have to sign a confidentiality agreement. I'll see you at my home later this evening. How about seven? Do you know where I live?"

"Yes, I'll see you at seven."

Stu hung up, stunned by what he'd uncovered: the arrows at Des' house, the questionable transactions involving Ocean Beach Properties, and most disturbing, Marie's signature on documents from the firm. He decided to call her.

A woman with a soft English accent responded.

"Law office, Cranston, Weatherby and Stone, how can I assist you?"

"Yes. This is Halsey Stuart. Can you please connect me with Marie Stuart?" He waited a few seconds.

"Dad? What a surprise."

"I don't like bothering you at work, but dads have a right to, and I needed to speak with you."

"Sure. Is everything all right? Something wrong? I can hear it in you voice."

"Yes, something's wrong." He hesitated. "Why is Cranston allowing you to sign documents for the firm that involves bank transactions?"

"What are you talking about? Why do you sound so upset?"

"You should know better. You're a lawyer and you made a promise. You're supposed to know about conflicts of interest."

"I do. I never signed anything involving the bank. I watch it carefully. I know the program. I sign a lot of documents here, but I make sure they have nothing to do with the bank."

"Well your signature is on a firm document I just reviewed."

"That's impossible!"

"I'm going to photocopy the signature and bring the original with me. I'd like you to come to the house later tonight say six-thirty. I won't be able to sleep unless I get this matter settled."

"I'll ride over tonight and take a look at what you have, but I'm telling you now, I didn't sign anything."

"Well, that makes me feel better for the moment. What are you up to?"

"I am representing a guy who's being sued by City National Bank for fraud. They claim he filed false tax returns and financial statements."

"Let me guess. The loan's in default and the bank is taking the hit. Am I right?"

"You got it, to the tune of eight hundred thousand."

"What do you think?"

"It's not easy to convict on fraud unless the bank has some good substantial evidence and can prove it to a jury."

"Who made the loan over there?"

"George something. Thompson, I think."

"Wonderful. I know the guy. He's not there anymore."

"I know, and I can't find him. Can you help me?"

"I'm not sure. I'll get back to you on that."

"See you tonight."

"'Bye Honey."

If Stu really had to get to George he could do it easily. Probably within a few minutes. He did him a huge favor back at the hold-up, and besides Stu liked him. Banking wasn't for George, so why bring all these bad experiences back to him? Stu decided it was wise to forget just where George said he was moving to. Perhaps he would remember another day... maybe.

Stu placed a call to his father. His secretary, Doris, answered the phone in her deep, raspy voice. "Good morning, Chairman's office."

"Hello Doris. How are things? It's Stu."

"Mr. Stuart. How are you? It's so good to hear your voice. Sorry you're back in Florida."

"Me too. Is my father around?"

"No, I'm sorry. He called a few days ago and said he was under the weather. It sounded like the flu. I haven't heard from him since. It's a little unusual not to hear from him, but I didn't want to call the house. Every once in awhile you just need to be left alone. We all have another life, you know, so I decided I'd wait a few days before I bugged him."

"That's funny. It's the first I'm hearing about this. I'll call the house and see how he's doing. It's up to you to keep the fortress together, Doris."

"Mr. Stuart, this place runs like a well-oiled machine whether he's here or not, but please don't tell him. Everyone knows exactly what they're supposed to do or else."

"Take care, Doris."

Stu called the house. It was unusual that his mother didn't call.

"Hello?"

"Mom?"

"Stu, thank heavens! I'm glad you called. Your father isn't feeling well." Her voice was noticeably trembling.

"Why didn't you call me, Mom?"

"Your father forbade me to call. He said you had enough on your mind, and besides it was only the flu."

"I understand. Can I speak to him?"

"Sure. He's right here, sitting up in bed reading the *Journal."*

"Thanks, love you."

"Hey Son, you have a handle on things down there?" Harrison's voice wasn't the same. The energy he usually portrayed through his speech was missing.

"Yeah I do. How about you up there?"

"Oh, it's nothing. I'll get over this bug in a few days. I'm not used to sitting in bed. What I need is a few sets of tennis instead of all this shitty medicine I'm taking. Sorry I didn't call you. It's not like me you know, but let me tell you, I got a call from Ray Collins. I guess you gave him my number. He asked me for some advice and told me his connections in Washington. I was impressed. He was checking this guy Hendricks out so I didn't bother."

"That's okay, Dad; I can handle it from here."

"Hold on a minute! I might be under the weather, but I'm not dead yet. I did a little checking on my own about this congressman who's on the take."

"You did?"

"Damn right I did! My sources are confidential and I talked in general terms, so it's going to be hard for someone to put two and two together... unless, of course, they're the ones on the take, and if they are, they should know that we know."

"Just how general were you?"

"Very, believe me. Anyway, there are rumors flying around Washington that something's about to blow."

"What does that have to do with what we're talking about?"

"It could mean plenty. The comments are centering on a congressman who's being investigated in some land deals. Do I have to draw you a picture?"

"Jesus. Why didn't you let me in on this?"

"Because I don't have all the pieces to the puzzle yet, Son. Remember, it's only rumors right now. I'll be told before any action takes place. The press isn't even aware of this yet."

"You must know who it is." Stu said.

"Let's just say I'm getting close."

"I want you to be careful, Dad. Strange things have been happening down here."

Stu told him about his brush with death. His father gasped. “You’d better get out of there. I don't like the smell of what's going on. That Des is an evil bastard. I don’t trust him."

"Dad, how about you and mom come down here for a few weeks? It will do you both good, and besides all the money you’re paying for this condo is going right down the drain. What's the sense of owning it if you don't use it?"

"I can't. The bank comes first. I already missed more time than I should have."

"That's just an excuse. Call Becca and you can all come down together for a few weeks. Don't worry about the bank. It’ll be there when you get back. And besides, the people you have working for you wouldn't dare make a move without calling you if it's important."

"That's true."

"Well, what do you say?"

"It's a good idea. I haven't seen the place in over a year, and it would be great seeing Marie again. It's been so long... I think I'll do it."

"I’ll be talking with Becca later. I'm sure all she needs is the news that you guys are coming down and she’ll be right behind you. I’m sure Doris can work out the travel details."

"I'll see to that, but what I don’t want to miss is more information about our friend in Congress. I’m sure the name will be circling the Rayburn Building soon enough, if it isn’t already."

"Well, let me know when you’re coming down. I'll meet you at the airport. Thanks for all the effort on my problem down here."

"’Bye Son."

Stu hung up and felt good about the call to his father. *He was actually decent. Maybe we can get along after all.* Stu decided when his father arrived he would devote more time trying to heal the wounds of years gone by, but his father had to meet him halfway.

Stu spent the entire afternoon reviewing budgets. It wasn’t exactly what he’d had in mind for the afternoon, but he had to get to the bottom of the expenses that were attributing to the bank's losses. He knew the bottom line before he started his review. He and Des would go at it line by line, arguing about how to lop off millions, and who would be affected by the cuts. The bank was losing millions every month and the capital was being eroded by the cost of maintaining so many bank properties. Bad loans were still bubbling up to the surface. The Florida economy was in the tank, and they had to take steps to stop the flow of red ink. He began by writing memos to Des, eliminating several expense items that were not important anymore as far as he was concerned.

The bank yacht had to go. Over the years it had brought in a lot of business, but now it was costing the bank sixty thousand dollars monthly.

He'd have to cut Magic Gardens Landscaping too: twenty-thousand a month to maintain the bank's landscaping. Des owned a seventy-five percent interest in the company. For the record he made sure that competitive bids were received on the banks outside maintenance each year when he submitted his bid. Somehow, he always remained the lowest bidder.

Des had a forty-percent interest in Caldwell Stationery of Fortune Beach. The bank's stationery budget was increased by six hundred thousand dollars last year. Stu lopped off four hundred and fifty thousand and sent him a memo about it.

Trying to find every company Des had a piece of wasn't easy. The partnerships and small businesses that he'd fronted with the bank's money for which he received an interest were difficult to get a handle on. He slashed any expense area that showed significant recent increases, assuming Des was involved somehow.

Stu had enough. His head was exploding from a sinus headache. He decided to go home, call Becca, get a drink, and take a swim in the pool, maybe unwind before Jack Hendricks appeared at his door. He hoped Marie would get there early so she wouldn't have to hang around and hear the discussion, but then he thought maybe she should.

The pressure from the water jets leading into the pool felt like thousands of little needles pulsing against his skin. He grabbed the phone and called Becca. When he'd filled her in as much as he could, he hung up the phone and swam a few laps before greeting his evening guests.

Chapter Twenty

Des and Jessica sat on the white couch in his office. The white Corinthian leather was soft and warm to the touch. The grandfather clock chimed six times, noting that everyone had left for the day, except the night crew and the security guards. The executive area within the bank was off limits after hours to everyone except those who had an encoded security card to enter the area. Des knew everyone who was coded into the system.

He poured a second round of dry martinis into the tall, frosted glasses on the coffee table. Jessica's face was flushed, but she picked up the glass slowly and sipped the clear liquid carefully so as not to spill any on the couch. Des caressed her chin, then delivered a soft, sensual kiss on her lips. She smiled and returned the kiss, then feathered her hands through his sandy hair as she thought back over the past few months of their courtship. It was like being on a roller coaster ride.

Jessica was no one's fool. Getting to the executive office hadn't been as easy as she thought, but persistence, good looks, and a little hanky-panky could open any door.

Each morning she spent two hours preparing herself for the work day. If she wanted to land a big fish, a weak hook would not do. Her twin sister Karen had married at eighteen, had three kids, a big mortgage, and couldn't afford dinner out but one night a month. Jessica wouldn't repeat her sister's way of life, but without a college degree, her body and looks had to make up for her lack of education. She decided to stay close to where the money accumulated, and do some investigation on her own with the help of Police Chief Walter Dobbs.

A few months ago she was pulled over for speeding on Atlantic Avenue at 1:00 a.m. She was stopped by none other than Chief Walter Dobbs who was coming home from a night out with a few of his new rookies. Jessica was on her way home as well, passing through Fortune Beach. She was driving on the revoked list. The chief seized the opportunity to help a girl in her circumstance and let her off the hook providing they meet casually for a late night cup of coffee. Upon arriving at the Star Dust Diner, the chief quickly got to the point of what he was really looking for. It was no surprise to Jessica, who knew exactly how to handle the situation, keeping in mind what she was really after in the long run.

Jessica brought life back into the fifty-eight year old police chief that he'd believed was lost forever. Here he was with a twenty-two year old beauty, screwing his brains out five days a week.

Jessica was cunning and knew all along that one has to give a little to get something meaningful in return. Many an evening as they lay naked together in the back seat of the chief's squad car, she would ask who the people of influence in town were. On several occasions Des' name came up. Chairman of the Board of the local bank, handsome, opinionated, rich and single.

She decided to set her plan in action to meet this bank chairman. She read in the Fortune Star that the bank was being honored by Fortune Beach as its Corporate Citizen of the Year at the world famous Grande Peninsula Hotel. She dressed to the nines, borrowed her girlfriend's white sable fur coat, and attended the affair. At 7:00 p.m. she stepped out of the rented white limousine that cost her one hundred seventy-five dollars. Perception was everything, and a grand entrance could get a person into the strangest of places.

She slowly exited the car, making sure everyone got a glance at her perfectly proportioned thighs and the curvature of her long, slender legs. Her long black strapless gown looked marvelous on her. The slit up the front was just enough to allow every muscle in her lower body to move with ease and grace, and tight enough that others couldn't take their eyes off her. The black velvet choker with diamond and ruby clusters added a special touch. Her flaming red hair was pulled back in a French braid and clasped with a black bow with a single faux ruby in the center. She looked absolutely gorgeous. She made her way to an empty seat and spent dinner telling everyone at the table that she was the athletic director at the Swanson Retarded School for Children in Miami Beach.

The annual presentation went quickly when Des finally reached the microphone to address the audience. She was impressed that he looked so young and handsome, considering he was in his fifties. He was tall, tan and very rich. Her opportunity came when she saw him on the dance floor with his back turned to her, talking to a short fat man. She moved up next to him, then slipped. Her right shoulder hit the back of his legs and he fell as well.

Des looked in awe at the long-legged beauty lying on the floor next to him. Her gown was split even further up the front from the fall, and she'd made no attempt to cross her legs. He couldn't believe he was on the floor looking up this beauty's dress after just being awarded Citizen of the Year. He got up slowly and pulled her up with him. She stood as close as she could possibly get, trying to look embarrassed.

"I am so sorry, Mr. Cain. Your speech was wonderful, and I'm so sorry I caused all this commotion. My heel must have hit a wet spot in the floor. I'm so embarrassed."

"Are you okay, Mrs. ...? Your dress... I'm sorry, can I get a pin or something?"

"No, that's okay. I think I have one in my purse." She smiled, still blushing, and offered her hand. "I'm sorry. I'm Jessica Warren."

He reached for her hand. "Nice to meet you, even under these difficult circumstances."

They talked the rest of the evening. What she said about her life was mostly untrue, but they seemed to hit it off. Des never talked much about his past and wasn't willing to discuss his weaknesses with anyone. He thought she was fascinating and would make a great trophy along with the others who had given him such great pleasure.

When the champagne and music ended and the night was over, Des offered to drive her home. She knew she could have him, but she had a long-term plan in mind: keep him on the hook and don't give in too fast; don't make the mistakes the others made; play it out and make him work for what he wanted; if he starts to lose interest, change plans, but keep cool. *He'll come around,* she thought. *They always do.*

She decided to take a cab home to avoid letting him think she was an easy mark. Letting him check out her body was one thing, but she wanted to appear proper and diffuse any wrong impressions that onlookers might have about them. She never forgot this was Fortune Beach.

Des felt comfortable with her and wanted to see her again, and they exchanged phone numbers. He put her in the cab, gave her a kiss on the cheek and sent her on her way. The hook was about to be set.

The affair with Walter Dobbs had to end. He had provided her with what she wanted to know and he'd been paid in spades. She thought it might not be easy to break it off so she wrote a soft, anonymous letter of awareness to Mrs. Dobbs at his home saying that her husband was on the prowl. Four days later Walt met her at the Publix Supermarket in Layton and told her he couldn't continue to meet. She wanted to make it look good, so she produced the biggest crocodile tears she could muster, then promised she would go her way on one condition.

"What's that?"

"I need a job, Walt. I'm an executive secretary and I just got laid off. Could you maybe use your influence to get me a job at the bank?"

"What bank?"

"Fortune Beach Bank. The main office at Fortune Beach."

"No problem. You'll be working in two weeks! I'll have someone call you."

They said their goodbyes and gave each other a final kiss.

The chief grinned. "Hey, it was good while it lasted. You added ten years to my life. I thought I was one of the walking dead. When we see each other again just wink, okay?"

"You've got it, Handsome."

Within a month's time, Jessica found herself in the executive secretary pool at the bank being rotated to different divisions within the organization. It didn't take long for Des to notice her. He was at the water cooler in the marketing department when he looked over and saw her at a desk in front of the manager's office.

What's this? He thought. As he approached her she looked up and smiled. Her luscious lips parted, and it was evident by her smile that she was glad to see him. His heart began to race. He couldn't believe this circumstance. "Jessica?"

"Good morning, Mr. Cain."

"What are you doing here? Aren't you a little out of your field?"

"You could say that. I got laid off a few weeks after we met. The funding never arrived for some reason or another and they had to let me go. I needed a job until something opened up for me."

"Well, I hope you like it here. I assume you're a secretary?"

"Yes. It's not so bad. I can type 120 words a minute; take steno and all that stuff. I took some courses a few years ago and became quite good at it."

"Well, you definitely add something to the organization. I just hope we get some work done around here."

She smiled. "Oh that's not a problem... we will."

Des wanted to ask her out but he had to be careful with so many people around. He couldn't afford loose talk around the bank though everyone knew he screwed just about everybody in the place under the age of thirty-five.

As the days passed he became even more frustrated because he couldn't get her off his mind. She crept into his every thought, making it difficult for him to concentrate on business. Finally the opportunity came one morning when his secretary buzzed his phone.

"Mr. Cain I have some preliminary budgets here for you to review from the accounting department. Would you care to see them?"

"Fine. Drop them off on my desk, please."

The door opened and someone placed the papers on his desk as instructed. He continued writing until he caught a familiar scent. He looked up and there she was. He smiled. "Well, this is a pleasant surprise."

"Good morning. They were a little short handed so I was asked to deliver these to you. I was told you don't bite."

"You should know better than that."

"I do."

He smiled and nodded slightly. "I can't remember having a better time than when we met at the hotel that evening. Would you care to join me for dinner at Musketeers tonight?"

"Are you sure it would be all right? I don't know about going to dinner with the chairman of the bank."

"Don't be silly. Who would you rather be with? I'm not as bad as they say I am."

"Actually, they all say you're really nice. Okay, why not?"

He got up from his desk and walked her to the door.

At the door she suddenly turned and Des found himself inches from her face.

"What time tonight?"

He could hardly think. "Uh.... How's seven sound?"

Her eyes were much bluer up close. He took in every detail of her fine facial features in the natural light. Her soft smile widened, her succulent lips encouraging him to kiss her right there at the door. Her perfume filled his nostrils and he couldn't wait any longer. He leaned closer, ever so gently, until they kissed. His breathing was becoming shallow. Soon she would set the hook, but not yet. Just a little more tease. Their lips touched once again and the kiss became more sensuous as he held her face in the palms of his hands. She moved her mouth with his, making sure that the impression she gave was that there was much more to come.

"That was from the night I saw you at the hotel," he said, almost out of breath. "When I put you in the cab, I forgot to kiss you. Perhaps I did, but not the way I wanted to."

"You have a good memory."

He kissed her again, gently, and then pulled away again, trying to catch his breath.

She touched his lips with her finger. "I'd better go now. See you tonight at seven."

Des was in deep water. Now all she had to do was set the hook. She decided to reel him in ever so slowly, just enough to keep his interest and desire. Her mother always said that the way to a man's heart was through his stomach. She knew better.

Musketeers restaurant was the current rage of Ft. Lauderdale, very chic and upbeat. It catered to the rich forty year olds. Candles flickered on the tables, and the mood was set for romance while a three piece combo played soft background music. Couples talked and held hands, looking into each other's eyes and exchanging whispered conversations.

Jessica was pleasantly surprised. She decided to relax, play her part and let him do the rest.

Des was looking for good conversation, a slow drive home and a turn in the sack. He was about to be outmaneuvered.

After dinner, some dancing and a few glasses of port wine, Jessica smiled up at him. "I'm sorry, Des, but I've had a long day and I'm completely exhausted."

Des dutifully drove her home, then gently kissed her good night while placing his hand on her thigh. She moved his hand away quickly and kissed him on the left ear, sighing, "Goodnight, Des."

She orchestrated several more dinners over the next few weeks, making Des even more determined to have her as his next trophy. She managed to elude his advances, but always left him with just enough kissing and body language to keep his interest without jeopardizing her plan. Shortly, she became executive secretary to the Chairman of the Board. Her salary went up and life became a series of adventures.

Celebrating her new job was appropriate so they decided to dine at his home. Des would have the private dinner catered using the gourmet chefs at Romano's. Everything was set to perfection, including a bottle of his favorite Bordeaux. *Now all I need is Jessica*, he thought.

She didn't show.

He was furious with her and he wasn't about to be made a fool of by anyone. He ran out of the house, jumped into his Austin Healey and drove in a rage to her home. He rang the bell several times, but no one answered. Her car was parked nearby under a huge Banyan tree. He rang the bell again. Suddenly a light went on and the door opened slowly.

He pushed it open completely with his hand. "Jessica, what the hell's going on? Where were you?"

"Oh Des, I'm sorry. I came home and decided to lie down for half an hour and didn't realize the time. I can't believe I slept so long."

"Do you know what I've been through? All the work at my home?"

"I'm sorry. I just—please, come in. You don't have to stand at the door."

He walked into the foyer of the small ranch-style house. It was neatly decorated and the rooms had a soft scent of spice. Her clothes were thrown over the arm of the couch. Her high heel shoes were lying next to the ottoman. She was dressed only in her terrycloth bathrobe and although she'd just awoken from a deep sleep she still looked ravishing. He couldn't stay mad at her.

"I thought something was wrong. That's why I came over. To tell you the truth, I was really upset. What made you so tired?"

"I don't know. I'm usually pretty spunky at this time of the day." *It's time*, she thought. The plan had worked. She'd wanted him on her turf where she knew her surroundings and felt more in control. She put her arms around his neck and pushed her frame tight against his. "I am sorry you're upset. I hope I can make it up to you." She pressed her lips to his and kissed him passionately.

Des adapted to her every move.

She moved her body up against him even more tightly, and he slipped his hands under her robe and cupped her bare buttocks. She drew him closer as they held onto each other, backing him into the bedroom down the hallway. They fell on the bed breathing heavily.

Jessica ran her fingers up and down his body. She was pleasantly surprised to find that he was in great physical shape, no bulges anywhere. By the time she was finished with him tonight, nothing else would matter anymore. He would be hers for as long as she wanted him.

Des was out of control. She was wonderful and everything he expected. They rolled off the bed onto the soft carpet without noticing. They were drenched in perspiration and totally spent, too exhausted to move, as they lay naked looking at the ceiling and touching each other gently.

She turned her head to face him and smiled softly. "So?"

"So what?"

"What do you think?"

"I think you're the most amazing woman I've ever met."

She smiled again. *He's in checkmate.* "I feel the same way about you. The minute you touched me, lights went on."

Still, she had to keep him off guard. *Too much of a good thing becomes old too fast, she thought. If I want this to work, I must outthink his desires..*

The martinis were beginning to affect her judgment. She became light headed and her face became flushed. She had to keep her senses about her as Des moved closer on the couch in his office.

He gently whispered, "You're mine" in her ear and kissed her on the neck.

She was hoping the night watchman would come up for a security check, but that didn't happen. She lay her head back with her eyes closed as he began to slide below her neck. The feeling of his hot breath against her breasts felt good and she wished she could stay on the couch for hours, but that would be a big mistake. It was time to end this.

She grabbed his head with her hands and pulled him up to kiss him. It was a long, smooth, soft kiss. "Des, not now. This isn't the place. I can't do this here... not in the office where we work."

"You're right... although I wish you were wrong."

"Let's talk about something else, okay? Let's see... I called Stu and he's coming to the house tomorrow night for the cancer benefit."

"Good. I'm glad he's coming. The list is getting bigger every day. I can't wait till this is all over."

"Talking about lists, did you know that just about all the examiners are going?"

"Good. I knew they wouldn't miss a free meal. Let them see that there are real people behind those loan files who breathe the same air as we do. Some of our customers can't breathe so well because they're squeezing the shit out of them. Maybe if they meet a few of these people they'll look at things differently around here."

"Do you know that a Congressman Zale is coming?"

"You're kidding! ...I only sent the invitation out of courtesy."

"Who is he?"

"He's a friend of mind. I helped him over the years and he hasn't forgotten the little guy. The rest of them seem to forget when they find fame in Washington."

Des liked Don Zale. He never sat on the sidelines, and he never forgot who helped him get where he was today. Zale was a powerful, persuasive congressman and Chairman of the House Banking Committee.

Chapter Twenty-One

Stu lapped the pool twenty times. When he thought he could go no farther, he squeezed out two more laps, then headed for the shower. He was getting dressed when he heard voices in the next room. He slipped on his shoes and briskly walked into the living room. Jack Hendricks and Marie were sitting at the kitchen table eating a pizza.

"I guess I don't have to introduce you two, do I?"

Marie shrugged. "I showed up with these two pizzas and Mr. Hendricks helped me to the door. I guess you invited more than me over tonight."

Jack said, "Sorry Stu. I'm a little early. I was waiting in my car when your daughter showed up. Very attractive young lady. I can only assume she takes after her mother."

Stu looked at Marie. "Honey, I forgot to tell you Mr. Hendricks would be coming over to see me. Frankly, I thought he was going to be here a little later."

"Dad, sit down and have a slice of pizza. Why isn't there anything else in this house to eat? When's Mom coming down?"

"I'm trying to work something out with your grandparents."

"Grandma and Pop are coming?"

"I think so."

"That's great! I haven't seen them in so long. I'll fix you a plate. Why don't you get me the documents you were talking about earlier?"

Stu walked into the bedroom, unlatched his leather attaché case, and brought the documents into the kitchen. "Here take a look at these and tell me what's going on. You should know your signature."

Marie looked at her father and then at the closing documents between Morecom Data Corporation and Ocean Beach Properties. Her signature was prominent as could be under the line reading *Cranston, Weatherby and Stone.*

"This isn't my signature! I didn't sign these! Those bastards! The dirty bastards!" She looked up at Stu. "This isn't my signature, Dad! I know how I write my name"

"I didn't think it looked quite right. Who do you think did this?"

Marie was furious at what she'd just seen. "I don't know, but I have to find out. How many other documents are around with my signature on them?"

Stu snapped his fingers. "I'll bet it was Cranston. I'll bet on it."

"Dad, how could he? I think you're wrong. He's involved in the bank, he's on your board, and the firm is counsel to the bank."

"That's why I think it's him. I don't trust him. He's involved up to his neck in everything that goes on with us and has made millions over the years. I am not saying he physically did it, but he knows about it and directed someone to sign your name to that paper."

Hendricks said, "I think you're wrong too, Stu."

"Wrong? Then who do you think signed her name to this?"

"Tom Wallace."

"You're joking! What the hell would Wallace get out of signing her name to this document?"

"Money. He did it for the money is my guess. Check the documents carefully. I think Cranston signed them by mistake and Wallace called him about it. Cranston after some thought wanted his name off the documents, so Wallace used White-Out and changed the signatures using Marie as the signer for the firm. Here, look for yourself. Can you see it? Do you see how it was changed? I can see an outline of the C in his name."

Marie held the paper up to the light and saw that what Hendricks was saying could be true, but she wasn't sure. "I see that the letters don't match up exactly right, but I'm not sure."

"Wallace wasn't smart enough to do this on his own. He got his instructions from the firm and was paid for making the change. We always believed there was a tie between Wallace and the firm. All this couldn't go on unless there was someone inside the bank giving aid to these jerks, so we were looking for anything we could get our hands on and we happened to come upon this. I can tell you Lionel DuPree knows about it also."

"He hasn't said anything to me. Maybe he thinks I know something about this with my daughter in the middle?"

Jack shrugged. "Everyone's a suspect."

"Well, back to Alex Cranston," Stu said. He turned his attention back to Marie. "Marie, I'm not sure how much you know about your boss and I don't want to go into a lot of it with you, but since you're here and you know so much already I think you should know a little more. I have issues with this guy and I want you to be careful over there. This Tom Wallace thing we just heard has me confused as hell right now. I can't believe things went along like this and no one knew or said anything. Tom told me that night in the restaurant that Alex Cranston was up to his neck in crap at the bank, and he told me about the loan at the bank to Rocco Penza and the Clairmont Hotel."

She nodded. "I'm aware of that, Dad. It's now in bankruptcy. The firm is litigating the case for the bank."

"Wonderful. I forgot where we were with that."

Marie shrugged. "I don't understand."

Hendricks said, "If I may, Stu." He looked at Marie. "The five million dollars Rocco borrowed from the bank should have been two and a half million. The project now sits half-complete and the five million went into the account of none other than Alex Cranston through an elaborate scheme with this guy Wallace using phony construction inspections to make it look like the project was much farther along than it actually was. That, with other stuff we found, is going to put your boss in prison. They're using the Clairmont Hotel account to launder large amounts of money. And who knows? There could be drugs involved in this scheme. They also come into the bank with cash to the commercial note teller and reduce the principal balance of their loans; then, shortly afterward, they take an advance on the line a few weeks later as a new construction advance. Everything seems normal, but its not. There are a hell of a lot of advances and repayments on this account so far, and we still have farther to dig. Cranston also had a secret twenty percent partnership interest in the Bartley Towers project, but it's not a secret anymore." Hendricks stood and slipped on his jacket ready to depart for home.

"Dad, I'm getting the hell out of there," Marie said. "I can't work in a place like that. You're actually scaring me."

"I wish you'd leave there, but I think you'd better hang around a little while longer or they'll be suspicious."

Jack said, "Your father is right, Marie. We'll tell you when things are right for you to leave. We'll hold you blameless for anything that goes on there."

"Okay, but right now I'm scared to death. All I wanted was a job. I didn't know I'd get mixed up in something like this. My father's exposed here too. I'm concerned for the both of us."

Jack nodded. "Marie, don't worry about what you've heard here. Just go to work and do your job. We'll keep you posted on what's going on. Your father's been up front with us, so I believe he'll come out the other end fine."

Marie said her goodbyes and left. Stu was uneasy about the whole thing and Hendricks could see it on his face, but now wasn't the time to be sentimental. "Stu, let's talk about Main Street Investors for a moment."

"What about it? I haven't had a chance to look at the file, but it's on my hit list as one of those loans I should be worrying about."

"Perhaps I can save you some time and tell you what you won't find in any of your loan documents. We believe Main Street Investors was started by Desmond Cain. Somehow I heard you were a general partner, but as of now we can't find anything about that. The group buys properties throughout Florida using funds from your bank. They pay cash for most of their holdings in order to get a deep discount on the price, and they finance it later after the deal is closed at extremely low under-market rates and high loan-to-value ratios in excess of ninety percent. These properties never appraise out correctly."

"You don't have to tell me—Donaldson Associates?"

"You got it! These are the same guys who did the Clairmont Hotel project appraisal, so you know how well off your bank is in these deals. They have about six investment properties.

Condominium units that are rented annually for the season at above-market rents. They get their price because of location and the quality of their clients—mostly clients who don't want any questions asked. These are wealthy people from all parts of the world who spend their winters here in Florida."

"How many units are you talking about?"

"I'm not sure, but I think a few hundred. We think Wallace was trying to get out because he knew what was going on and how the properties were attained. He's the one who kept the lid on this. The payments were always made on time and there were no glaring problems with the loans. They made sure everything was up to snuff so as not to draw any attention to the deals. I'm not sure yet how it worked, but Cain had a direct line to Wallace, who took care of all the details and processed the rental payments."

Stu shook his head. "And I assume the best is yet to come?"

"You're right. Main Street Investors is made up of general partners who are also known as Ocean Beach Properties—you know who that is—plus Walter Dobbs and Hank Stone."

"The mayor and the police chief?"

Jack nodded. "And worse yet, they have a limited partner in the deal who is a United States Congressman—none other than Congressman Donald Zale, Chairman of the House Banking Committee."

"How did you find out about all this?"

"Zale wasn't smart. He was living in one of the units in the winter and cashing checks drawn from the account of Ocean Beach Properties, and a lot of them were cashed at the House Bank, so many checks that someone got suspicious. We started looking back at the activity in his account and traced the checks back. He had dealings with Johnny Mack and Ocean Beach Properties. We just put two and two together."

"So why are people hitting on me and my daughter? I don't understand."

"No one wants you back here. People are nervous. The bank is in trouble and when repairs start to be made things begin to surface. You were not welcome here so they tried to scare you off. They scared your daughter too, thinking that would get your attention. Walking with Tom Wallace wasn't good for your health either. They know you're snooping around, and who knows how many others in the bank are watching you and what part they play in this whole mess?"

"Hey, I'm in the shitter here. I have a brother-in-law who's probably going to do some time and a wife who isn't happy with what I am doing, especially now that the family is involved. My daughter's scared to death of what she just found out when all I really wanted to do here was clean things up, save some of my investment, and get my ass out of here. I don't need any trouble. I'm going back to work in my father's bank."

"Stu, we want to put this whole goddamn bunch away, but we need your help doing it and it's not going to be easy."

"Okay, so what's the deal and what's in it for me? I am not a good Samaritan when it comes to this kind of crap."

"The FDIC and some folks in my department wanted to hang your ass as well. That's not the case now, but it was a few weeks ago."

"Why?"

"You're the executive officer in charge and you were responsible for the lending in the bank no matter how you cut it. What you knew or didn't know made no difference. We could have nailed your ass and you'd never work in a bank again. Let me ask you, Stu, how often have you raised money through your bank customers to support political friends in congress?"

"I raised some money in the past. Des said it would be good for the bank. I never got involved much other than raising the money."

"Still, it's illegal and you know it, no matter who gave the money. This is a bank, not a candy store. Tell me, how much did you raise?"

"I can't remember, but it wasn't that much."

"How about five hundred thousand dollars over the last four years?"

"How do you know what I did?"

"We know almost to the dollar what you collected. Look, Stu, we're putting together a sting to catch all these guys. We can't pull it off without you. Main Street Investments is going to purchase some more buildings at a very attractive price from what we've been told. The details will be explained to you when everything is about to go down. We'll give you all the support you need and you'll know well in advance. Your brother-in-law's going to jail when this is all over. I want you to loosen up your relationship with him. Don't give away the place, but make it easier for him to maneuver around without you questioning his every decision."

"He'll get suspicious. I don't like this. He'll know it's not me."

"It's not a question of what you like. You were brought back here because Des was told to get you back or he'd lose the bank. He knows he has to listen to you. The only reason he's where he is right now is because we're letting it happen. He thinks you can pull this whole thing off and return the bank back to him as soon as the heat is off."

Stu sighed. "I guess I don't have much of a choice, do I? Well, I'm not going to roll over and just play dead. I'm still going to challenge him on the expenses of the bank."

"Just take it easy. Stu, we all have to make choices in life; that's just the way it is. I think you're making the right one here. These shitheads owe you nothing and they're robbing everybody blind. Just look at your stock investment that's in the tube because of what's going on. Do I have to draw you a picture?"

That clinched it. *Hendricks is right. Look what's happened to me,* Stu thought. *My life's been turned upside down. My wife isn't even living with me. What kind of life is this?* Stu nodded. "I'm in."

"Good. We'll take care of you, I promise. Your phone in your office is already wired. We'd like to wire the house. Call Cranston and have lunch with him. He's the kingpin in putting these deals together with Des. Make him feel comfortable. Confide in him. I think you should level with him on some things you know. He's no dummy, so you're going to have to get him to lower his guard."

"I'll do my best."

"We'll keep in touch, and we'll be around all the time."

After Hendricks left, Stu went to bed. As he closed his eyes, he slipped his hand under the pillow where it felt cool. The feel of his Astra .357 Magnum revolver gave him all the comfort he needed for a good night's sleep.

Chapter Twenty-Two

At 6:30 in the morning Stu was sitting at an empty table in the corner of Harry's Café. It wasn't part of his daily routine, but he thought a change would be good. Besides, he wanted to get an early start before the bank filled with employees.

The café was busy with people scurrying in and out, purchasing newspapers, coffee and breakfast rolls. Many patrons had dressed incognito, or thought they had, with hats pulled down tightly and wearing large sunglasses. Stu's scrambled eggs on a hard roll arrived at the table with a bottle of ketchup. He took a sip of coffee when suddenly he recognized a familiar face. "Good morning, Des. Have you eaten?"

"No. I'll just grab some dry rye toast and a cup of java. Let me order and I'll be right back."

When he came back, Des asked, "How's everybody in your family? I haven't heard you talk about them much, including my sister."

"Everybody's fine. I think Becca is coming down in a few days."

"When she gets here let me know and we'll go out for dinner one night."

"I'll let you know."

"Stu, let me just ask you—why did you send me those goddamn memos yesterday?"

"Memos?"

"Yeah. The ones about the non-interest expense items. You know, stationery, landscaping and the goddamn boat. How the hell are we going to get rid of the boat? We use it constantly to entertain clients. If we pull that boat, it's a sign to the people over here that we're in deep shit. Who told you to do this?'

"Des, stay cool. It's called cleaning up a hornet's nest. These things aren't important any longer. Everyone's on our ass right now. Just get rid of the stuff. If things change we can look at them later, but for right now it looks better if we start making some cuts.

You're going to look like a hero if we can pull this off because you took the right steps in controlling these costs."

Des talked through clenched teeth. "You have no right to make any changes without speaking with me first! Who do you think you are? This isn't going to happen!"

"Des, let's just stop the bullshit right now! You've been screwing the bank as far back as I've had time to track. While I'm trying to keep your ass out of hot water, you might start acting like a chairman! Remember, you're the guy who asked me to come back to keep the heat off you. And in the meantime, what do you do? Bill the damn bank for everything under the sun! I hope these guys don't dig too deep into your expenses because there's just no way to disguise them as legitimate. Tell me, how in the hell are you going to explain five thousand poinsettias billed to the bank?"

"They're for a promotion. What's wrong with that? I'm in trouble because I own a nursery?"

"You still don't get it! Or is it just that you don't want to? You're billing the bank for stuff under twenty different companies. That doesn't fly, Des. Something's really wrong when the chairman's pulling this shit. Christ, how much is enough?"

The way Des' eyes were twitching Stu knew his devious brain was racing. Stu waited. Not a word.

Stu decided to jar him out of his trance. "I don't think you're stupid, Des, but I'd sure like some other explanation for your behavior."

"Lifestyle, Buddy. It's a matter of lifestyle, and I'm not planning on any income reduction, hear me? So I suggest you go back to your drawing board and figure somethin' out." He flashed Stu a smile.

"Forget it! I'm not doing anything of the kind."

"Stu, we all make a few mistakes now and then. It's getting caught in the act that separates me from you."

"What the hell does that mean?"

"Let me explain. I've kept my side of the bargain when we decided to look out for each other through this ordeal. I had all I could do to put a lid on the rumor mill around here. You really don't know what I'm talking about?"

"All I know is you're doing your best to change the subject."

'Not so long ago there was a lot of gossip about you and a certain secretary. I heard through the grape vine that you were seeing her quite often."

Stu rose from his chair. "You sonofabitch!" He strained to keep his hands at his sides as he loomed over Des. "Why in hell would you bring that up at this particular moment and in this place? Is this some sort of a threat??"

"Cool it," Des said. "I stamped out that little fire very quickly by passing the word that it was impossible. No one in their right mind would do anything to hurt my sister. Everyone here knows how you feel about Becca. The gossip's over. But if Becca did hear it, your nuts would be hanging from a Christmas tree, brother-in-law, and you know it."

"But none of it's true!"

"Stu baby, now it's your turn to stop bullshitting. Don't ask me how I know. I just do. No matter how you want to camouflage the truth, I know what went on. So before you start pointing a finger at me about some possible indiscretion of mine, I suggest you look in your own camp. Now, get this problem worked out. Just take care of it, like I took care of you. You know I have a personal interest in some of this stuff."

Stu glared at him. "I'm aware of that, and you should have done this long ago. If the word ever got out that you were involved in some of these companies we do business with, you wouldn't be able to stand the wrath of not only your stockholders, but also the bank regulators. You should have known better. I'm trying to protect your ass as best I can right now."

"Listen, I hear you're coming to my party tonight." Des remarked in a questioning tone.

Stu was still seething. "I got a call from Jessica and she told me you wanted me there."

"I did. There will be a lot of important people there and I want to make sure we have ample coverage with bank people. This is an important fund raiser, and I want it to make me look good."

Stu wanted to ask him about the arrows that Jessica told him about, but he thought it best to wait and see for himself tonight.

Des put ten dollars on the table.

"My treat. Any extra goes to the waitress."

"Thanks." Stu reached in his pocket to add a few bills, knowing the ten wouldn't cover it.

Stu parked his car in the rear of the bank and used the side entrance. One of the security guards was there to let him in before the banking floor was open for business. "Good morning Mr. Stuart. Looks like another nice day."

"You bet, Harry. Can't remember a bad one." He hit the elevator button. The door opened and he found himself face to face with Walter Dobbs and Hank Stone. He was stunned for a second to see them in the bank before business hours. "Good morning, Walt, Hank. What brings you here so early?"

"We had a short meeting with Des—real short, because he showed up a little late—to go over tonight's fundraiser at his house. Everything has to be just right. You know Des no hitches right?"

"Yeah, that's for sure. See you guys tonight."

They exited the elevator and went out through the side door. Stu noticed that Hank Stone was carrying a large brown suede briefcase. What could be inside that briefcase so early in the morning? He also couldn't forget the looks on their faces. They not only looked surprised, but also, nervous and uncertain when they saw him standing at the elevator. He pushed the button for the second floor.

Stu grabbed another cup of coffee and decided to review again his conversation with Tom Wallace. He searched for his notes and finally found them among some loan files on the desk. *What was it that he told me?* He was hoping he'd written it down. *Yes! There it is.* One of the loan files had an address written on the outside folder by Tom himself. Des told him specifically to send a copy of the loan documents on Main Street Investors to an address in Washington, D.C. If Stu could just locate that folder, he would know who received the documents from the bank. He thought he knew the answer, but this would confirm the smoking gun.

It was 7:15, and Charlotte would be in at any minute. This was going to be a difficult work day looking through files.

Within a few minutes keys dropped on the desk outside Stu's office and he knew it was her.

"Good morning, Charlotte."

"Good morning. How was your evening?"

"Fine. I hope yours was as pleasant."

"Not really, Sir."

"Why? What's wrong?"

"My phone at home keeps ringing. Every time I pick it up a voice says 'Be careful. Stay away from the bank.' I'm frightened, Mr. Stuart. What does it mean?"

"When did it start?" Stu asked as he headed for her desk.

"Just last night." She sighed. "The phone rang about five times."

"Did you call the police?"

"No. I was going to, but I decided to wait and see if it got any worse. I didn't want cop cars all around my house for a prank."

"Well, if it starts again, call them and call me. I'll be right over."

"Thank you, Mr. Stuart."

"Charlotte, we have a big job to do today. Come with me to the book vault. I'm going to need your help."

The book vault was located in the basement of the bank. It was where all the commercial loan files were maintained. The huge vault door lay open against the wall, exposing its stainless steel ribs as Stu and Charlotte approached the entrance gate. Inside the vault the air was still and had a strong odor of stainless steel polish combined with the musty scent of steel and concrete. The poor ventilation and the lighting needed to be improved. The gray painted concrete floor contrasted with the beige walls. Twelve motor-driven filing cabinets were positioned on rails. They were approximately thirty feet long, took up almost the length of the room, and could be separated from each other by the push of a button, enabling the attendant to retrieve the required files. The cabinets held all the commercial loan files. At the end of the day the cabinets were folded together like an accordion.

"I haven't been down here in years," Charlotte whispered. "I'd forgotten this place even existed."

"It's still here. Unfortunately, it's going to be your home for a while...or least until we find what we're looking for."

"Just what are we looking for, Mr. Stuart?"

"I need your help searching these file folders for an address. I'm sure part of the address is Washington, D.C. I need the rest of the information. Before Tom died, he told me about an address he wrote on one of the loan files. I need that information."

She sighed. "Well, this is going to be a big job. Must be thousands of files."

"I know. I'll get you two or three helpers besides Annie."

Annie was close to seventy-five years old and had spent most of her life in the bowels of the bank. She wore thick bifocals that hung on the edge of her nose. She was a thin, frail woman with silver-blue hair who had lost her hearing in one ear early in life, but made up for her loss with uncanny recall ability for her age. She could remember everyone who had a file out of the vault without writing it down. If the file wasn't returned within two days she would march to the department or person who had the file and retrieve it, leaving a few choice words behind. She was queen of the file room.

"What's going on here? Don't fool with these files unless you want a kick in the butt."

"Annie, I'm Halsey Stuart. You remember me don't you? We worked together several years back reorganizing this place. Remember all those hours and dirty file jackets?"

"Yeah, Mr. Tight Ass, I remember."

"Pardon me?"

"That's what they all called you. I remember, Mr. Stuart. Everything had to be just right or you'd come down on us for not following your orders exactly the way you wanted these files to look. I remember."

Stu laughed... "I didn't think I was that bad of a guy."

"You were no piece of cake, but the files still look as good as they did then, don't they?"

"That's because of you, Annie."

"I do my best. I'm not getting any younger, y'know."

"Annie, I need some help. Charlotte here is my secretary. She's...—"

"I know her. She used to be Mr. D.'s secretary. I know them all... even the one with the big knockers he's dating now. Boy, that man must be real tired during the day. If I were only a few years younger he wouldn't be wasting his time with all those other babes in the woods. Anyway, what do you need?"

"Your help. Charlotte needs to find an address that was written on the outside of a loan file jacket."

"Why did you use a file jacket to write on? Don't they have any paper up there? I know the bank's having its problems from what I read in the papers, but no paper? Christ, next thing will be the toilet paper will be gone."

"I don't know why, but it's there somewhere and we need to find it."

"Okay, I'll help her best I can. It'll be a big job for just us."

"I'll send down some help."

"I've never seen so much activity down here as there's been in the last few weeks. What's in here, gold or something?"

"What do you mean?"

"Everybody's been down here, from Mr. D. to those sneaky, shifty eyed examiners."

"No kidding. What were they looking for, did they say?"

"They told me nothing. I just do my job, but everyone was looking through files."

"Where's your record book?"

"Don't need one."

"What do you mean you don't need one?"

She tapped her temple. "It's all up here... every person, every file."

"Annie, we can't operate like that. We need written records of who comes in here and takes files out."

"You do it your way and I'll do it mine. Now scoot, we have a lot of work to do. Come on, Charlotte, let's get hopping through these files."

Stu left them to their business and called personnel to get some help. He was assured four clerks would be working within the hour.

Shuffling through the papers on his desk, Stu located his phone log and placed a call to Alex Cranston. His secretary answered and told him he was with clients and would call back in fifteen minutes. He decided to use the time to review what he was going to say to him, especially since they hadn't ever had lunch together. Within minutes the phone rang.

"Stu?"

"Yes. Alex?"

"That's me. I bet you can never forget a voice, especially mine."

"You're right."

Alex Cranston was forty-seven years old and a successful lawyer when he wanted to be. He found it was easier to rip off people and companies with his influence with judges and politicians. He used the judicial system for his own good and contributed to the right causes that would benefit him and the firm the most. He was tall and thin with salt and pepper hair and always looked unshaven. For the most part he looked as if he'd just crawled out of bed with his clothes on. Evidently, he relied more on his business intelligence to make a living than what others thought of his appearance.

Cranston hated missing a deal no matter what or where it was. He had to be in on the action. He'd acquired most of his holdings by representing clients and then stealing the deal outright, or taking a minority interest in the investment. Soon he would be running the whole venture to his advantage until everyone was so frustrated that he wound up with most of the ownership out of sheer disgust.

"Des told me you were coming back. I was glad to hear that. You were good for the bank. I know the board is going to be glad you're back too."

"Well, it was something I had to do. We're getting it from all sides and I don't know which hole to plug in the dike first."

"It's not as bad as all that. The economy has been bad down here and we've had a few bad breaks, but I know we'll pull out of it pretty soon." That long southern Mississippi drawl was about all Stu could take. He didn't know whether he could endure a full hour lunch with this good ole boy.

"Alex, how about joining me for some lunch today if you aren't too busy. I'm sorry for calling you so late."

"Well, my secretary has lunch open from what I can see on my calendar. Why not?"

"Good. How about at 1:30 at Nadine's."

"That's as good as any, and they make the best martinis in town."

"See you then."

Chapter Twenty-Three

Nadine's was another popular eatery in Fortune Beach. The corner table was reserved daily for the bank. Tables two and three were reserved for high-ranking political figures who happened to be visiting during the winter. There were twenty two other tables available, and the bank provided the capital along with a healthy seasonal line of credit. The overflow room in the rear of the restaurant was quite attractive and comfortable, but had the feeling of eating in an Amtrak dining car. The room was long and not very wide, but the full windows provided an open feeling that satisfied many of the general clientele.

Stu remembered his first visit to Nadine's on July 4th weekend, 1987. Becca and Stu took Tom Riggins, his old college buddy, out for dinner with Tom's new girlfriend to celebrate his independence. July 4th he was a free man from a marriage that lasted ten grueling years. Nadine's staff, not knowing the party, put them in the back room and treated them as if they were infected with a contagious disease. They ordered a bottle of 1980 Opus One for one hundred fifty dollars that qualified them for extra attention. By the second bottle, everybody employed that evening was waiting on their table. From that day on the name Mr. Stuart was etched in their brain as a person to pay attention to whenever he entered the restaurant.

Stu arrived early and ordered a glass of Merlot. While waiting for Cranston he thought about how he would handle himself over lunch. He had to be careful not to get too comfortable. Stu was about to get the attention of the waiter when Alex Cranston appeared through the door and was heading toward the table with the Maitre D in tow. The room was packed to capacity with the lunch crowd as they wove their way among the tables until they reached where Stu was sitting.

"Hi Stu, ol' buddy. I'm late, I know."

Stu extended his hand. "I'm glad to see you. I thought something had happened."

Cranston looked just as Stu remembered: scruffy. His oily peppered hair needed a comb run through it. He was unshaven and wearing a wrinkled white oxford shirt with the collar tips turned up.

"Mr. Cranston, may I get you something from the bar, Sir?" asked the Maitre D.

"Yes, Zack. A Bombay martini, dry and hold the olive."

"Certainly, Sir."

"Stu, goddamn, you always look so good. What's your secret?"

"I stay away from broads. If anything will age you, they will."

"You can say that again. Unfortunately, I never took that advice." He scratched his head.

"Let me tell you why I'm late. I don't want you to think I just showed up haphazardly without regard for the time. We're representing the bank in a foreclosure. This guy stiffed you for about three hundred grand. We were ready to go to sale today after twenty months of litigation when the sonofabitch pulls a chapter eleven on us. I was so damn mad because I thought we had it all worked out. I called his attorney and one thing led to another before we both were yelling on the phone."

"What's going to happen?"

"It's going to set us back six months or so, but this guy's at the end of the line. We're going to take a hit, but we won't lose it all."

Stu wondered what he was worrying about. His excuse was good, and for three hundred dollars an hour, he should be yelling and screaming all day long.

"Well, they tell me you're kicking ass and sniffing in all kinds of places at the bank. I can't make out what this exam is all about though. Don't get me wrong; I'm glad to see that you're back. We need you right now."

"Well Alex, you're on the board, so you know as much as I do. But you're definitely right, there are a lot of people sniffing around right now, and I want to make sure we're not the ones at the end of the trail."

"I like the way you say that, 'cause I sure agree."

"Alex, I'm doing the best I can to see that your own dealings with the bank are at arm's length. Don't get me wrong, but I'm having a really tough time convincing these federal examiners about that."

Cranston leaned forward in his chair, his arms folded on the table. "You're shitting me, right? What are you talking about? My personal dealings with the bank have always been above board. What's their problem?"

Hmm...must've hit a nerve. "You have to understand, you're a board member, Alex, and general counsel to the bank. You're pulling a lot of money out of the bank. Besides your board fees, your firm is billing us close to two million a year. The examiners are reviewing your billings and I can tell its pissing them off that they have to go through it. The invoices are extremely high and they can't let it pass. In the meantime they're paying a great deal of attention to your overall involvement with the bank and trying to find something they can use to nail your ass to the wall." Stu sat back in his chair, waiting for a response.

"Why those small minded sonsofbitches! Des was right all along! These jerks should get a life! If government can stick it up your ass, they will. They probably read my financial statement and it's driving them crazy because I make more money in one week than they make in a year's time. You can't tell me personalities aren't involved here."

"Well, they might have small minds, but I think if you leave the door open for them you're going to be a goner."

His face turned ugly. His hairy, overgrown eyebrows raised and his eyes narrowed as he glared at Stu.

"Hey, don't get pissed at me," Stu said. "I'm here to warn you. I'm just saying, you should prepare yourself for some heavy questions."

"Like what?" Cranston asked.

"Let's start with the Bartley Towers."

Cranston shrugged. "I know about it. I closed the deal for the bank."

"I know you did, but we didn't know you were partners with the Servin brothers at the same time."

"You're full of shit!"

"Alex, don't make me press you on this because you know I'll win. I'm not the asshole Yankee you think I am. You have a conflict of interest here that can probably get you disbarred. If the bank takes a loss on this deal you might even go to jail if the feds find out you're in on it."

"Go on. You seem to know so much, do you mind if I eat?"

"Hey, I'm just trying to understand you, Alex. You make more money than you can ever spend in a lifetime and you're still trying to find ways to screw your clients."

Cranston looked up. "I resent that remark!"

"How about the Clairmont Hotel project?"

Cranston dropped his French roll into his soup. He leaned across the table and pointed his index finger at Stu. "Listen here, what're you driving at, Boy!"

"Don't 'boy' me, Asshole! You used my daughter and the kid at the bank who died to do your dirty work! Her name is on documents for the firm on the Ocean Beach project, even though you knew full well I worked at the bank. How dare you leave her exposed like that? I ought to take that bowl and smash your goddamn face!"

Cranston hissed, "I didn't involve her! This is the first time I'm hearing this. You think I'm a fool? I don't need this crap or your smartass remarks! I'd never let her sign anything! Besides, what the hell does she know? She's a trial lawyer."

"Well, I'm going to get to the bottom of this. Her name was forged and I want to know why. I'm no Perry Mason, but I'll dog the shit out of your people until I find out what's really going on here."

"Listen, Des and I are involved in lots of things. We grew up together. We lived in the same town for God's sake. What do you expect? We've been close all of our lives. We help each other now and then, and yes we made a lot of money that other people were trying to steal from us. We didn't steal it; we just beat them at their own game."

Stu leaned forward and looked directly into Cranston's eyes. "Does beating them to the punch involve murder?"

"Murder? You mean the kid at the bank?"

"That's the only one I know of."

"That's so far out of my league I can't even comprehend that kind of question. Are you looking for a medal or what? What's your story?"

"I'm looking to come out of this bank crap somewhat whole. We have all kinds of financial problems and the bank can go either way. I can clean up some of your mess, but I want some financial reward. And forget giving me any partnership. It's cash only."

Alex sighed. "For the moment I'm tongue tied. What do you want to know?"

"First. I want this stuff with my daughter straightened out. Find out who is in back of this. Second, I want to know your partnerships and partners along with the companies we have loans with where you have an interest."

Cranston grinned. "Sonofabitch, Stu, I think some of this southern hospitality has rubbed off on you. Let's talk some more as soon as I get this stuff together, but let's not be so goddamn mean, y'hear? I liked you better before you knew all this shit."

"Self-preservation, Alex, that's all it is."

They finished their lunch, Stu paid the bill, and they both walked out of the restaurant. On the sidewalk, Stu lightly grabbed his arm. "Listen, this thing with my daughter... I want to know why her name is on those documents or I won't lift a finger to help you. I suggest you do some checking and give me a call. That's number one for me."

As they reached the corner, Cranston looked at him. "I'll get back to you in a few days. Maybe we can have dinner at the rib place over the bridge."

"Are you going to the cocktail party fund raiser tonight?" Stu asked.

"You bet your ass. Anytime Des throws a party I know I'm going to have a good time. See you there."

Stu watched as he walked across the street with a swagger that was part of his natural demeanor. He believed he had him. Cranston was convinced Stu was going to help him cover his tracks. Back at the bank, Stu spent the rest of the day answering phone calls and putting out fires since Charlotte was on assignment in the basement.

At around four p.m. he decided to work his way down to the basement and give the ladies a well-deserved break and let them go home early.

Stu made his way to the stairway from the executive offices. The elevators were jam packed this time of day with employees heading for home. As he descended the stairs he heard talking on the stairwell below, but he was too far away to determine who it could be. As he approached the bottom landing of the basement, he noticed Des and Gil, the security guard, talking. They looked up and were surprised to see Stu.

"Stu, what's with you and the stairs?"

"I do walk, you know. More to the point, what are you two doing here? Aren't you having a party tonight?"

Des nodded. "I am. I'm down here counting how many round tables we have. I might have to borrow them tonight."

"Isn't it a little late for planning?"

"There were more people than I thought."

The guard said nothing. He just awaited orders for what to do next. Stu felt uncomfortable. It was as though he was interrupting a conversation. As he passed and approached the steel door leading toward the basement, he noticed a cloth gym bag in the guard's left hand. *That doesn't add up. What are these guys really up to?*

"Listen, I know it's late, but if you need any help I'll be glad to give you a hand. My back isn't the best, but maybe I can hold a door or something."

"I'll send someone over from the caterer's people to pick up some tables if there aren't enough. Stu, what are you doing down here?"

"I have a bank project going on down in the book vault. I should be done in a few days. We're just cleaning up some files. I don't want the examiners to get the wrong impression that our file room looks like a shit hole. It's all in the perception, remember?"

"I'm glad to see you're getting on that, but working these people past four-thirty's a little much I'd say. Remember, no overtime."

"It's just a project I want finished and out of the way. There's a lot more to do down here."

Both knew they were bullshitting each other, but Stu wasn't ready to tell Des what he was doing. He hoped Charlotte used her head and told Annie to be quiet about what they were doing.

Stu didn't care much for Gil. He had an eerie feeling that they had met somewhere before. He was a large man with a mean look in his eyes and a scar on his right cheek as if someone had sliced his face open with a knife. He didn't look like a security guard and Stu was uncomfortable being around him.

Stu opened the steel door leading into the basement. As the door closed he could see through the window that the guard and Des had moved up to the next landing and continued their conversation.

As Stu walked into the book vault, Annie and two girls were busy putting files back in the cabinets.

"Mr. Stuart, what are you doing back here so soon?"

"I thought I'd come down and give you some support."

"That's nice, but we don't need any more people working in this place. It's like Grand Central Station. Mr. D and another guy, I think it was the guard, were just in here looking around."

"What did they want?"

"Nothing much. They just looked around and wanted to know what we were doing down here."

"What did you tell them?"

"Not much. Charlotte said this is special work and to keep a lid on things down here. Your orders."

"Good. That's exactly what I wanted."

"I told them we were cleaning out old files. Was that okay?"

"You bet it was. Where's Charlotte? Did she go home early?"

"She left about an hour after her lunch hour. She wasn't feeling well. In fact, she looked terrible. Her face was all sweaty and had that washed-out look, y'know? I think she might have caught the flu."

"It must have come on all of a sudden, because she looked great this morning. Maybe it was the work down here."

"You know that isn't true. She's a hard worker. I worked with her for years before she found fame and fortune with you guys in the ivory tower. She knows what hard work is."

"I'd better give her a call this evening to make sure she's all right. She lives all alone and might need someone to talk to. I think she has some family close by... a sister or something."

"This isn't an easy job, pulling all these files out and inspecting them. We're even looking inside the covers to be extra sure we don't miss that address."

"You're doing a great job. Just what I need, Annie. It's time for you guys to take off now. Go home and rest because there's a full day tomorrow. I'd like to end this soon."

"Thanks. These tired old legs couldn't take much more of this today. I'm usually home by now having a shot of Jack and water to relax me." She herded the girls together, grabbed her sweater and was on her way out of the vault. "Mr. Stuart, the clocks, how are you going to set them?"

"Don't you think I know how to set vault clocks? I used to do all this stuff before I became a big shot, remember?"

She pointed toward a key ring on the wall. "The keys are over there."

"Set the clocks to open at 7:00 a.m. I always open the door one hour in advance to make sure nothing goes wrong. You're going to need fourteen hours on all three of them now. If you leave later, the hours will be less."

"I believe I've got the picture. Thanks, Annie."

"Make sure you sign the log book before you leave."

"I will, I promise."

Stu decided to poke around and pull a few files himself. He started with the letter S. There was no real tactical formula for the decision except for his last name starting with an S and his hope that maybe he might get lucky for once. To get to the selection of files he wanted he had to move several cabinets out of the way. He pushed the buttons on the wall by the vault door. Button one moved the first file cabinet against the far wall. Button two moved the next cabinet and so on until he reached the cabinet where the S's were held. He pulled the first file that read Sabern Corporation and inspected its contents. No address.

He pulled files for the next half-hour looking over each file cover hoping the next would reveal the missing address. *What if Tom was bullshitting me?*

Stu heard a thumping sound coming from the back wall, but when he walked back to inspect the area, nothing had fallen off the shelves. He went back and continued pulling more files. While bending over to pick up some papers that had fallen out of a file folder, he thought he heard the noise again. As he looked around and heard nothing, he assumed he was just tired and it was time to quit the project for the day. He wasn't concentrating on what he was doing. He began shoving file folders back onto the shelves that were stacked on the floor between the cabinets. As he bent down he heard a noise once more, but this sound was different. It sounded like a motor humming. For a few seconds he couldn't quite link the familiar sound to anything he could recall. Then it hit him: *the cabinets! They were moving!*

He tried to run, but he tripped over the files and smacked his head on a steel post. Dazed and disorientated, he thought, *someone had to push the button to close the files!*

As the cabinets closed more quickly, he struggled to clear his head. *What can I do?* Then he looked up and saw a fire extinguisher hanging on the wall in its metal sleeve. He had very little room to move. He stretched, reached out, and grabbed the bottom metal rim of the extinguisher. It didn't release.

Lift up and pull; it has to release! He pulled with all he had left while lifting the bottom of the metal canister with his left hand.

It came loose.

He pulled it toward him, turned it lengthwise, and jammed it between the metal posts of the nearest cabinets.

The motor continued to hum, but the cabinets finally stopped with a crunching, grinding sound.

Stu turned sideways and slipped out from between the cabinets. He was trembling uncontrollably, but he was in one piece.

Someone wanted me out of the picture. Who? Why?

He left everything exactly the way it was, and even decided not to set the alarms. He closed the door and spun the combination dial.

He decided to take a quick look around the bank to see who was still in the building.

The place was empty.

The security guards were not on the grounds. Stu thought for a moment and remembered they must be at Des' house for the party.

Attending the party was the last thing he wanted to do, but he decided to go. Maybe the would-be murderer was there.

Maybe it was Des.

Chapter Twenty-Four

Stu turned down Atlantic Avenue heading toward Des' house. It was close to sundown, and the air seemed somewhat cooler. *Imagine someone trying to knock me off! For what?* He felt alone with no one to talk to. Who could he trust?

Stu pulled up to the driveway. His car was about twentieth in line sitting behind a jet black Mazda. Pete Langworth exited the driver's side of the car in front of him, walked around to the passenger side and opened the door. Out stepped Marie!

He opened the window and yelled, "Hey, is anyone going to help an old man?"

They turned, looked, spotted Stu and grinned.

Pete's smile slowly disappeared as he turned his head looking for a valet to park the car.

Marie walked over to her father's car sporting a beautiful green dress she'd picked off the rack at Burdines's earlier today.

"You never told me you were coming to the party."

"First though, I need a kiss."

She gave him a delightful peck on the cheek and proceeded to wipe the lipstick off with a tissue. "I didn't know I was coming until about three hours ago. Pete called me and wanted to know if I wanted to go. He had two tickets."

"How did he get them?"

"Alex Cranston can you believe it? He bartered the tickets for a golf lesson. Imagine that. Two hundred and fifty dollars a piece!"

"Cranston should be playing scratch golf for that price."

"I'll say. But I'm glad I came since you're here.."

"Whose car is that?"

"Pete's. Isn't it beautiful?"

Stu nodded. "It is. I guess golf is treating him pretty good lately."

"Not really. I'm helping him out with the payments."

"You're what?"

"Not much, just a little. It's for helping me when I needed him, remember?"

"I'm not so sure I like that idea."

"Oh Dad. Come on. Let's walk up or we'll be here for an hour."

Stu retrieved his suit jacket from the back seat.

"Dad, what's wrong? You don't look right. I can tell something isn't right."

"I'm fine. It's been a long day. I had lunch with Cranston today."

"No wonder you don't look so good."

"I leveled with him on a few things."

"And?"

"He didn't deny them."

"I'm not sure what you're talking about specifically, but do you think what he said makes him guilty of any of this stuff?"

"I'm not sure. Time will tell."

They walked up and met Pete. Stu admired his car. "I guess the tour days are over since your new addition here." Stu said as he rubbed a hand over the smooth front fender.

"I gave it lots of thought and decided to stay at the club. Moving around would be difficult for me right now and this car just overpowered me."

They all walked up the circular driveway together admiring the color-splashed flower beds that lined both sides of the winding driveway. The landscaping was a sight to behold with sculptured gardens and strategically placed cascading fountains. There was no doubt that Camelot was alive and well in this magical mansion. The soft yellow halogen flood lights projected an evening image of the mansion almost too beautiful for description. Night turned into day at *1400 Tierra Del Mar*. The sanctuary of Desmond Cain was upbeat with music and the smell of garlic and wine sauces tantalized the nostrils, drawing them closer to the activity in the rear of the estate.

Elegant façades of manicured fichus trees lined the entire perimeter, ensuring privacy. The shrieking voices of cockatoos and macaws filtered out of two large Australian pines.

People were wandering on each of the levels, drinking and talking in small groups while waiters in white cotton gloves and silver trays offered hors d'oeuvres.

"Dad, how did Uncle Des get all this money? The gardening alone must cost thousands a month."

"It's complicated. Besides, the bank picks up a good portion of all this stuff. You know the story, Maire. Your grandparents were broke and living from hand to mouth. Your grandfather was so distraught for not being able to provide a better life for his family that he took his own life. Your grandmother started drinking, and one night she took the car out and headed straight for a tree full throttle, and died at the scene. Your mother and Uncle Des went to live with their grandparents. When your uncle became of age to inherit his share of a life insurance policy that your grandparents had, he went to college. He's very smart. He did not want to end up like his father. He could detect a business having problems before its owners could. What might seem like a poor investment to some returned him millions just from looking at a balance sheet, profit and loss statement, and chopping heads to reduce expenses. He can buy a poorly performing company, return it to profitability and voila! He finds a buyer and it's off to the bank."

"That's some story, but I'll bet it wasn't as bad as you just portrayed it."

"Pretty close. He screwed a lot of people along the way and most likely did a lot of things that I really don't want to talk about. But look at him now; he's on top."

"For now."

"You're right."

They were finding it difficult to continue talking, with people weaving in and out and stopping to say hello. Pete and Marie were being tugged away by some friends.

Stu said, "I'll see you later. It's getting crazy here. Let's try to find each other before we leave."

"Okay. See you later."

Stu moved through the crowd, finally reaching the bottom landing near the waterfall. It seemed cooler here and easier to get a drink from the bartender. He glanced around for Des and saw him up on the patio talking with Dobbs and Cranston. *Bet they're tearing my ass inside out after today's luncheon... maybe planning my funeral.* Whatever it was, there was a lot of finger pointing going on, and nobody was smiling. Stu decided to work his way through the crowd, rather than break-up the intense discussion. He knew the subject would quickly change if he edged any closer.

The aroma of different foods permeated everywhere. He made his way up to the pool on the second level where a display of marvelous creations took center stage with the finest chefs from all over Florida doling out small dishes to taste. *Des, Dobbs, and Cranston can wait a little while,* Stu thought. He decided to try the sliced rare prime rib. He took a plate and sat down next to Peg Neff.

"Stu, is this something? He sure does it with class, huh?"

"Yeah, he sure does. I guess he's the star tonight."

"I hear around town that the star might be losing its glow."

"Is that so? What do you mean?"

"Well, from what my sources are saying, the locals are upset about the bank and all the publicity it's getting. Almost every day something is in the paper about the bank."

"You can control that, can't you?"

"You know better than that. I'm not the only paper in town."

"You're right."

"The killing of that employee on a Main Street has a lot of people very nervous. It's hurting their business." Peg took a sip of her drink.

"That may not be Des' fault."

"Even so, he's created too much attention around here and I see big trouble coming for him. I don't want to speculate, but he isn't the only powerful man around here. And I do know one thing for sure: things will be different around here next year. I can feel it. You should have been president of the bank, but Des wouldn't give up anything. He had to be in complete control of the bank, the town and anything else he could get his hands on. Stu, greed is going to ruin him, and I don't care how much money he has or who he knows. Many of us here wish you were in control because you do what's right and fair, and you don't try to squeeze the last drop of blood out of everyone with whom you come in contact."

Stu decided to change the subject. Peg was the owner of the local powerful newspaper and he had enough problems to deal with. He rose from his chair. "So is this affair a success tonight?"

"How about two hundred thousand dollars."

"Wow! I should say so."

He said goodbye and left, talking with some locals he hadn't seen for some time. He stopped for a refill of his drink when suddenly he felt an arm around his waist from behind. He turned, surprised to see Jessica standing next to him. Stu smiled. "Well, hello. The last person to grab me like that was the woman I married. I remember you told me you were going to be here, but this is a little over the top. Where is Des; with his buddies?"

"I have no idea at the moment. What are you doing down here? You should be up there where the action is. I was just on my way up. I need a friend right now. I hear all this talk behind my back. I know what they're saying about me around here. It's all coming from those old bitches who on their best day couldn't fit into an outfit like mine no matter how much money they have."

Hmm, Stu thought. *She's probably right, but she shouldn't have said it. Maybe she's had a bit more to drink than she should have this early.* She was dressed in solid black cotton knit dress that ended at the middle of her thighs and certainly caused more than the average number of stares from both genders. The stiletto high heels didn't help either. She was in excellent physical condition and her upper body was somewhat muscular, giving definition to her breasts and contrasting with her extremely trim waist. He couldn't help but admire the magnificent opal necklace that hung around her neck and dangled where her cleavage began. "I can't argue with that," Stu said, smiling.

"Stu, you know what I mean. I'm tired of these jerks spreading rumors that I screwed everything I saw, that I'm a tramp and don't belong on this side of town. The old bitches can't stand young people around them. I give them too much competition, and they're all afraid their husbands might look at a nice piece of ass now and then."

She paused for a moment. "Stu, I'm sorry I'm dumping on you. Maybe I've had a little too much to drink, but their smart-ass remarks just set me off."

"Like what?"

"Ah.... if I had an ass like that I'd put it in a museum.... with a pair of legs like that, who has to work.... or how about..., Des is the only guy we know who can eat his cake and have it too."

"Well, you sure give them the opportunity to talk. Why didn't you dress the part and put on an evening gown with some diamond earrings or something?"

"I just didn't feel like it. Des isn't happy with me either. He doesn't like to be embarrassed, especially around here."

"Then why did you do it?"

"I'm bored. I'm just goddamn bored!"

He gestured broadly with his arms. "With all this?"

"Yeah, I didn't know that money dictated your life every minute of every day. I wanted a chance to be me for once instead of kissing ass every single time I'm with him. I just wanted to do my thing. What's wrong with that?"

"It's probably the wrong place to do your own thing, if you're going to get serious with Des. I don't know where you stand on that."

"I think I'm in pretty good shape in that category. That's why everyone is so nervous. Do you think I screwed up?"

"It looks that way, but don't worry just roll those big blues of yours and shed a few tears and you'll weather the storm."

"Thanks but I don't think it will be that easy. Hey, how about a tour of the inside? You game?"

"Sure. Let's do it."

She took Stu's hand and they were off up the stairs to the top level and through the servant's entrance, which led into the kitchen.

"Have you ever seen this part of the house?"

"I've been here a few times before."

"Well, it's a really beautiful kitchen. I'm told that Des added it a few years ago. You can tell by that huge skylight overhead. The old mansion was dark and didn't have much life to it I'm told, but the skylight really adds dimension to the room and makes the black marble floor looks absolutely great."

The room was marvelous. Under the skylight in the center of the room was a black Corian counter ten feet in length balanced on a mahogany pedestal where three chefs and a dozen waiters, give or take were bustling around. All the cabinets were made of the same wood with black Corian counters surrounding the outer perimeters of the room. The ceiling was painted light gray to match the grout that joined the marble flooring.

They moved on to the Great Room. It overlooked the pool and entire back yard with its twenty foot solid tinted windows that stretched from floor to ceiling. Three televisions were built into the black lacquer cabinets so guests could watch different events at once. Hundreds of tiny pinpoint lights in the ceiling adjusted automatically with the time of day and gave the illusion of thousands of stars lighting up the night from the inside. The red lacquered coffee and end tables added balance to the black-on-black silk wrap-around sofa.

Stu really didn't care what the place looked like. He wanted to see the crossbow arrows she spoke about that he never seen before.

Stu walked around the room. "The place really looks great. But this is not where Des spends most of his time? This is too... you know, perfect."

"You're right. You'd never find him in here unless he had company. He spends his evenings in the den next to the library, over there."

They were about to enter the den when Des came in. He smiled. "Hey, guys, I've been looking for you. This place is buzzing. What are you doing in here?"

"Hi Sweetheart. I'm just showing Stu around the house."

"Are you kidding? He knows more about the place than you do."

Jessica looked somewhat puzzled, but decided to blow it off.

"Stu, I knew you were around somewhere. I ran into Marie outside and she told me you were talking up a storm. I wanted you to say hello to Congressman Don Zale who just showed up."

The last thing Stu wanted to do right now was to go and shake hands with a congressman. He wanted to go into the next room and see those arrows Jessica had mentioned. In a way he hoped she was wrong. But the evidence was adding up. Des could be the killer, and he could have been the one who almost struck again earlier tonight. Stu's mind raced. *But how could he have done it? He was here at the party... or was he? The bank's only a few miles away, and the only way in at that hour requires a key. But why would he do it? What did I ever do to him? My God, I'm even married to his sister!* He smiled, trying to maintain his composure. "Des, I believe I've met him on more than one occasion don't you remember?"

"Where?"

"You and I took him to Duke Ashley's in Washington, remember? We passed him the twenty thousand on behalf of all your Democrat buddies over here through your efforts as state campaign chairman. If it wasn't for you his ass would be out in the cold right now. I know you contributed a lot more than that, but that particular time I was with you it was only twenty thousand."

"Yeah... that's right I do remember now. Jessica why don't you go out and greet some of the guests? I'll be out as soon as I finish up with Stu here."

She smiled and left through the den, exactly where Stu wanted to go.

"Let's go out and say hello to the congressman. Hey, how do you like that outfit of hers?"

"It's a heart stopper. She must have broken a few in her day."

"Well, the only thing she's breaking right now is my balls. I told her how to dress before this party and she decided to do it her way. Having good looks and a tight ass gets you nowhere here in this town. One must look the part and act accordingly to fit in. She's having a tough time understanding that's the way it is. If she keeps it up, she can do it somewhere else. It's tough enough for me living here. I don't need this shit."

Stu believed she was smarter than that.

They moved onto the patio to join the others and spotted the congressman talking to two reporters. Don Zale weighed about three hundred seventy-five pounds, and most of it showed right up front in his stomach. His hair was ashen white, which made him look much older than he really was. He graduated from Notre Dame, and he looked more like a monsignor than a congressman. He had a holy presence about him that mystified most who met him for the first time. He spoke softly, and listened carefully, absorbing thoughts like a sponge. He wasn't quick to respond, but when he did reply, he was direct. He was also crafty, cunning and knew the political game better than most anyone.

Washington had treated him well, and he would serve four more years as Chairman of the House Banking Committee. It was a powerful position and he ruled it with an iron hand. Bankers, lobbyists, lawyers, and colleagues had to kiss his ass every day and he loved every minute of it. He was loyal to his supporters, and made sure his district received their fair share of pork barrel projects. He could call in plenty of chips when he needed to, but he used them wisely because you only get so many to use before it's payback time.

"Don, say hello to Halsey Stuart, Vice Chairman of the Bank and family member."

The congressman offered his hand. "Hello. Is it Hal or...?"

"It's Stu, Congressman. We've met before. I'm sure you don't remember. It's been awhile, but—"

"Wait... wait a minute.... How about Washington... dinner at Duke's. I'm sure it was at Duke's... Duke Ashley's place." Snapping his fingers. "Am I right?"

Stu laughed. "Well I'll be damned. How did you remember?"

"I always remember things that impress me. That night we discussed a lot of banking matters. As a matter of fact I used some of your material on the House floor. I recall one of our discussions where the sons of bitches on the other side of the aisle slipped in a bill that the FDIC could charge you state chartered banks' examination fees. Imagine, you guys pay insurance premiums based on your deposits and the condition of the bank, and they also want you to pay for examinations? I know you guys pay separately for state exams, but this was just out of control. I'm glad we put a stop to that."

"Thanks. We needed your help. No one else was listening."

"Well, it's not entirely over. In fact the battle is that the FDIC tells us their insurance fund is decreasing rapidly because of so many banks going under and naturally they have to bail them out. That's why they need a sizeable increase in premiums, to replenish the fund. It's the only way to completely stabilize the banking industry. Of course, they actually see it as their money. They don't give a shit where it comes from, but they know exactly what they are going to do with it and it's not just to bail out the banks. It's to keep their asses working. Downsizing government isn't easy.

Des seemed interested. "So where do we go from here, Don? What can you do for us? You know our little talk before?"

The congressman laid his hand on Des' shoulder. "Listen Des, when you open your bank tomorrow, I think life will be a little different than usual."

"What do you mean?"

"Well, I just delivered a message to Mr. DuPree over there."

Des nodded. "I know him. He's the head of the regulators. And?"

"Well, he isn't as happy as he looks right now. I just gave him a letter from Washington, from the Director of the FDIC."

Des was growing impatient. "And?"

"It tells them to pack their bags and move on."

Des' eyes grew wide. "You mean they have to get out?"

Zale nodded, smiling. "I'm serious. I managed to convince the Director that there were more serious problems elsewhere. Screwing up the Fortune Beach economy down here and making our international friends nervous while they're trying to relax on the beach isn't what he should be doing right now."

Des slapped Zale on the back. "You're a genius!"

Zale shook his head. "It wasn't easy. In fact, it was difficult. Remember, we all have a limited number of chips and I used mine here. I agreed to support the bailout fund to the tune of ten billion dollars. So that's the price of the negotiation." He shrugged. "Of course we're sticking it up the ass of the American taxpayer, but it's either them or us."

His face glowing with delight, Des grabbed Zale's hand. "Donald, you did it again. I knew you'd come through."

Stu glanced over at DuPree, who definitely was not happy about what had just happened.

Stu excused himself. "Well Congressman, thanks for your support and help. I'll leave you two to talk."

"Nice seeing you again Stu."

Stu walked around and worked the party crowd for a few minutes so it wouldn't look too suspicious when he headed for the mansion again. He took a glass of seltzer and made his way back up through the servant's entrance, walking through a few rooms until he reached the den.

The lights in the room were dim. This was Des' private office, where he came to relax and conclude many of his business deals. The art of the deal was always better on home turf, and Des always made sure his meetings outside the bank were here.

The room had the ambiance of the old mansion. The twenty foot high Italian hand painted ceiling lent a softness to the gold-painted oak leaves etched in the molding and beginning to lose their luster. A capacious Italian marble fireplace was nestled in the opposite wall, and 15th century Flemish tapestries hung loosely over the windows that stood tall on both sides behind the inlaid cherry desk where Des did most of his work. The coral and blue Persian rugs gave the place a feeling of opulence. Two glass bookcases bordered the entrance to the room. They held Des' private collection.

At the far corner of the room was an arched blue, red and green Venetian stained glass window. To the right of the window was a framed plaque upon which Stu fixed his gaze as he crossed the room. There, encased in a gold frame under glass, two arrows approximately one foot in length lay parallel to each other. Each sported a blunt steel tip with a blue stripe around the center of the shaft. Stu's face flushed as memories of that night flooded back: blood all around, Tom gasping for each breath.

Now he knew. Des was the killer.

He read the inscription through the tears welling up in his eyes:

DARTMOUTH COLLEGE PROUDLY PRESENTS TO
DESMOND CAIN
THESE COMPETITION ARROWS USED IN THE 1964
NATIONAL COLLEGIATE CROSSBOW CHAMPIONSHIP
FIRST PLACE NATIONAL CHAMPION

There it was. Stu had been played for a fool and had almost wound up dead. He was startled at the slight, sudden pressure of a hand on his right shoulder.

"Hey, you look like you are in a trance," Peg whispered.

I'm in shock is more like it. I'm trying to put two and two together. I just can't believe that my brother-in-law could be mixed up in a murder."

"Are you talking about those arrows up there and the bank employee who got shot?" Peg pointing to the wall.

"Yep." Stu answering with tightness in his voice.

"That's going to be difficult to prove. Let me offer you some advice." As she walked over to the window to be sure no one was coming. "The power of the press Stu is amazing, and if you really want to bring him down and hurt him in his bulging pockets full of cash let me help you. Give me a little time. Be patient. This can happen if you let me develop the plan I have in mind."

"Look Peg I know how you feel about Des, but I don't want to get you involved in my fight."

"No. It's our fight. He's ruining the town and destroying the bank, and something has to be done."

"Look, I see people making their way up the steps. I don't want to be seen here. I'll take your advice and see your plan. I'll be in your office in a few days. I have some ideas myself."

"Good, I'm not going to let you down. See you in a few days. We better go."

Chapter Twenty-Five

Marie decided to get up early and walk the beach before the sun peaked over the horizon for the start of another hot and humid Florida day. Walking early in the morning cleared the cobwebs out of her head. She could think and plan for the day as she walked along the sandy beach. She was becoming more concerned over the eventual confrontation between her boss and her father.

Alex Cranston was powerful. He had lots of connections besides having a lot of money. He was always well mannered at staff meetings and treated her just like the other associates in the firm. His slow southern drawl was difficult to understand at times, but she put that and his personal wardrobe preferences aside. He didn't seem as bad as Hendricks had tried to make him out to be.

Marie's life hadn't been complicated until the evening she'd found her father's home trashed, and then someone following her on that miserable, rainy night. Her father had come back to the bank to straighten out some problems. The bank was in trouble and it was no secret. *What problems, though?* She thought. *What problems could warrant the things that have happened to him? What did he do?*

She was sure the incidents were related somehow, along with the matter concerning her signature on those documents. Then there was her relationship with Pete. Up until a few weeks ago it was great, but suddenly, for some unknown reason, he seemed to get irritated over little things that would have never bothered him before. Also, she'd known him to be fairly conservative in making financial decisions, but recently he'd gone on a spending spree, buying new suits, a silver and gold Movado watch, and two pairs of Bally shoes at two hundred and fifty dollars each, all while she was helping him with the payments on his new car. What's going on here? Did someone in his family die and leave him a wad of cash that he wasn't telling anyone about?

Also more than once when she was meeting with Cranston in his office, Pete would walk by the door and stick his head in to say a quick hello, suggesting that he was there on business. What had started out to be a few golf lessons had taken on another life somehow. Both Cranston and Pete had graduated from Dartmouth College and Alex was responsible for getting Pete the job at the club, but she didn't like the way he was changing. That, and the recent meeting with her father and Hendricks gave her some cause for concern. She decided not to involve her father with this—he had his own problems—but now wasn't the time to interrogate Pete. He'd been really upset when she'd questioned him about his finances.

She came to the end of the beach where a huge rock jetty protruded into the ocean approximately three hundred feet. The waves splashed up against the slippery, mossy surface, lapping at the feet of a few early morning fishermen. The sun peeked out above the horizon as she plopped herself down where she previously set her sand chair; digging her feet into the cool sand. She could not put aside what was really on her mind.

Chapter Twenty-Six

Stu made another morning stop at Harry's Café to get a container of coffee with the morning paper. The Fortune Star gave a great review of the party last night. Peg Neff made sure her paper got picked up first. The front page pictures looked like a who's who. A smart businesswoman always knew how to sell the sizzle, and with color.

Desmond Cain received all the credit for the success of the party, which raised $250,000 for cancer research. Stu was surprised to see one of the pictures on the front page was Hendricks talking to Congressman Zale. He wondered what they could possibly have in common and why Hendricks hadn't come over to see him. He must have known he was there. He paid for the coffee and paper and was about to leave when Johnny Mack waved to him from the corner of the room. He was sitting at a table with his back to the wall, finishing his breakfast with a newspaper folded neatly beside his plate.

Stu went over to see what was on his mind.

"Stu, hi! I heard through the grapevine that you were back. You probably don't remember me, but we met a couple of times with Des. I think you came out to my project once in Ocean Beach, but I never saw you after that."

He was right. Stu always made sure that he stayed at arm's length from Des' accounts.

"I believe you're right. It was when you had the first five models open and you threw a cocktail party to kick off the project."

"Can you believe that was almost five years ago?"

"It's amazing how time moves on."

Johnny was thirty two years old and had a manner about him that made everyone around him feel somewhat uneasy. His jet black hair was combed back and lay flat against his head. His eyebrows were thick and bushy and contrasted with his powder-blue eyes, which appeared almost cat-like and pierced right through you when he talked. His deep voice had a raspy sound, but left no misunderstanding what he was saying. Except for being extremely loud, he would have made a good bass singer in a quartet. His mob connections were rumored throughout South Florida, but he was never connected to any crimes, or had any misfortunes with the law. It was the back room gossip that made people fear him. His large, muscular frame shored up the heavy gold chains that hung around his neck like the inner workings of a grandfather clock. One chain in particular stood out from the rest, supporting a powder-blue opal that matched the color of his eyes. He was dressed like he was ready for work. He had on khaki pants, a tight-fitting tee shirt with the bank logo that sponsored the Fortune Five Mile Run. A pair of tattered leather gloves that were once tan in color but now had a blackish look to them protruded from his pants pocket, indicating that Johnny wasn't afraid of hard work.

"How are things going over there?" Stu asked.

"We have about twenty-two houses left to build with twelve sold, so we're just about finished. I'm working my ass off to get out of there. I want to start a new project. This one has been a winner for me, but it's time to move on. Hey, I hear rumors that my loans are being pulled apart at the bank because the examiners think I'm in cahoots with Cain. I wanted you to know, Stu, that's bullshit. He helped me out in my early years, but everything I do now is strictly on my own."

Stu thought Johnny was hoping that the examiners were not going to dig too deep because they might discover what he was really into.

"Johnny, I'm really not sure just where they are with your files. Just keep building the project out and pay off the bank. That should be your major concern right now."

"You're right. I'm just glad they're getting the hell out of here and leaving us alone. Everything was fine before they got here."

"Did you go to the party last night?"

"No, I had some things I had to do. I'm sorry I missed it. The papers said it was great."

Stu left Johnny at the café and drove back to the bank. *How in the hell does he know the examiners are leaving?*

At 7:30 a.m. there wasn't much activity at the bank. Harry was walking around the parking lot picking up deposit receipts and currency envelopes.

"Good morning, Mr. Stuart. Just leave your keys in the car as usual and I'll have it looking brand new when you come out later."

"Harry, you're the best. You always take care of me. Thanks."

"I think you beat everyone in this morning."

It was just what he wanted to do. He told no one about what happened last night. Stu wanted to go back down to the vault before anyone else got there to see whether there were any clues left behind. He opened the metal door at the bottom of the stairwell and entered the vault area. The door was standing open. *That isn't the way I left it.* He'd closed the door and spun the combination, but hadn't wound the timers.

Stu flipped on the light. All the file cabinets were pushed together rather than apart as he'd left them. He wondered who had come back. Had whoever it was expected to find him dead?

The fire extinguisher! Where is it? He looked around, but it wasn't to be found.

He turned off the light and decided to get out of there. Anne would be in for work in about fifteen minutes and he didn't want to answer any questions as to why he was down here so early. He would ask Charlotte later to find out whether anything unusual was going on in the bank last night. Then again, he couldn't trust anyone, especially Des. Stu knew what had to be done. His plan had to be perfect. He needed more time.

He took the stairway back up to the executive offices and decided to call Becca while he finished his morning coffee. She should be up by now, back from her morning walk with the dogs. The phone rang three times before he heard that familiar "hello."

"Hi Hon. How are you today?"

"Stu. I didn't expect you to call so early."

"I got into work early and thought I'd give you a buzz before the day got started. How's Alice? I haven't heard much about her."

"She loves college and has some friends. Somehow she managed to make her way to the varsity tryouts for cheerleading. Once they saw her, she was a shoo-in."

"That's great! I hope she gets a chance to get down here over the winter."

"I'm sure she will, but I thought you'd be finished by then."

"I thought so too, but who knows? Everyday down here is another adventure. Something's always cropping up."

"Well, I'll be down this weekend with your parents."

"All the arrangements have been made? What time and what airline?"

"We arrive at 3:30 p.m. Saturday on American. Will you be there to meet us?"

"With bells on! Are you kidding? Well, I have to run. Lots to do today. I'll see you at the airport on Saturday. Say hello to everyone for me."

"I will," Becca whispered softly. "Love you."

"Love you too."

Stu hoped they would change their minds before the weekend, but they had no reason to. After all, they had no clue that things really were not going well here. He was afraid they would be in danger if things got any worse, but he didn't have the heart to tell her to stay up there, and besides she would have put up a fight about it and he would lose that battle. He had to make the best of it and just be very careful. As he tossed his empty coffee cup into the trash basket a soft knock sounded at the door, which was partially open.

"Come in please. Charlotte?"

"Sorry, it's not Charlotte."

It was Lionel DuPree and not in his usual attire, but sporting tan pants, a blue button down oxford shirt, and a blue blazer.

"I thought I'd come in and visit with you before you get too busy this morning."

"Lionel, come on in and grab a chair. You look very relaxed today."

"It's because I have on my traveling outfit. Cecile and I are being transferred to another job in Atlanta." DuPree shrugged. "I really don't mind, because it's closer to home, and I haven't been home in weeks. I can use the break."

"I'm sorry I never got back to you on those few matters that you wanted cleared up, but one thing led to another and you know what happens."

"I sure do, and don't worry about it. I have all the information I need. I'm sure you've heard that a bunch of us will be leaving today, and it's not our decision that this is happening."

"Does this happen often?"

"Not really. Sometimes there are bigger problems elsewhere and we go with no questions asked, but here that's not the case... or at least that's not the way we see it."

"I did hear you were leaving." Stu confessed.

"I'm not an asshole. Stu. I know the program. Zale thinks he put one over on us. He went to his buddies in Washington to get us the hell out of here and that's fine, but we'll have our day."

"It sounds like a revenge thing to me."

"Call it what you want. We know the place is infested with shitty loans, a thief is at the top, and even your lawyer board member is a crook. Why do you think you're back here? Because Cain asked you?"

"I originally thought so."

"Well, think again. You're back here because when we came into this shit hole we told Des, your brother-in-law, that if he didn't bring you back or if he didn't have another competent number two in place within a few days, we were going to close down this bank. He thought it over and decided he'd rather take his chances with you than a stranger." DuPree shrugged. "Sorry, but I had to say it."

"So you're the reason why I'm back here. If it weren't for my stocks I'd never have come back. They're all I have. How come you didn't close the place down anyway when you found out how things were here?"

"When I look back on it now, we really should have. Your boss was doing stuff you'd have never found out about. There are tremendous pressures from the Hill to keep these places open as long as we can because they have no more money to bail out banks, or at least that's what we're being told. We thought with someone solid in here and with an understanding that the bank would raise some new capital that you could probably make it. We were the ones who wanted you back. We looked at your track record and it's been good over the years. We're not blaming you for what's happened here, but we believe you should have been more attentive about what was going on around you. The people you trusted were out for themselves. Against our better judgment, we left Cain in place hoping he could gather the locals up to raising about thirty million in new capital. We think he could have pulled it off. There are a lot of people who believe in him. They just don't understand his big picture, but we did. As soon as the capital was raised, he was going on a long vacation."

"Did he know that?"

"He's no fool. I'm sure he figured it out, but for the moment his trump card was bigger than ours. Zale has been around the Hill for a long time and he's made millions sniffing out deals from his vantage point. He and Cain go back a long time. Cain spent a lot of money getting him elected and it paid off for him, but both of these characters are going to be in for a big surprise down the road. I'm here today to tell you to watch your ass. I think what's going on here is bigger than some of the bad loans you've got. I can smell it. Why do you think Hendricks is kissing your ass and being your buddy? It's because he wants a trophy. He has a chance to nail Cain and Zale, together along with some other politicians that are up to their eyeballs in illegal crap around here."

"Why are you telling me all this?"

"I've been in a lot of banks, Stu. You're the kind of guy who gets hurt when things come down. You're not such a bad banker; we looked at your accounts up and down. We investigated your loans and you're clean. You can be trusted; you're a down to earth family man. We ran you through credit bureaus and did FBI checks on you, and you came out okay. We did all that before you were asked back. I'm just letting you know we might need you later to put all these characters away, even if it might be family."

"Lionel, I'm sure my life is in danger to some degree. I almost got it last night in the book vault in the basement before the party. I'm sure Des is behind this in some way. I know we all have to sit in death's chair sooner or later, but I'm not ready for that now or in the near future. Let me tell you what happened." Stu told him the story.

"Did you see anyone in the vault?" DuPree asked.

"No. It all happened so fast."

"Christ! Well, you'd better be careful. And watch this guy Cranston. He's up to his neck right along with the others. We have a hell of a lot more information than you do, but I'm not at the liberty to share any of it with you right now. I can tell you this, though: we found money laundering going on and you can only guess where that's going to lead."

"Cocaine?"

"Congratulations! I guess I don't have to draw you a picture. Oh, by the way, you know Hendricks' assistant? Docker... Dave Docker?"

"Yeah?"

"He's missing. Hendricks sent him out to get some information on Cranston over at his golf club. I think he was going to do some snooping around, but he never returned and it's been a few days now."

"Has Hendricks called the police?"

"No, he wanted to keep a lid on things right now, and besides he doesn't trust Dobbs."

Stu still looked surprised at the news. "He never told me about any of this cocaine stuff."

"I'm sure he didn't or you'd have been scared off.... and keep an eye on the golf pro over there at your club. There's more to him than you think. I saw him last night at the party with your daughter."

"How did you know it was my daughter?"

DuPree smiled. "I asked."

"We've been quietly checking him out. His living habits are a little high and there has been some unusual activity in his bank accounts lately."

"He banks with us?"

"Yep."

"Look, I've only known him for a short while, but I think he's a good kid. I can't believe he's mixed up in anything with these characters. He's a golfer. I wish we'd have had this talk earlier."

"We wouldn't have if I were still on this job. I'm leaving, and I'm pissed off. I don't like to be pulled off any job before I'm done, especially one like this."

Stu looked at his eyes and knew that he was visibly upset for being taken off the examination. The tall black man stood up and Stu shook his hand as he limped out of the room holding on to the brass handle of his cane.

When he called Annie at about 10:30, to his surprise, Charlotte hadn't shown up for work. He put two calls into her house and there was no answer. It wasn't like her. She always called if she was going to be out.

Annie told him that Charlotte hadn't been feeling well late yesterday afternoon. He was becoming concerned and decided to see whether she was all right. He decided to take a ride over to her house.

As he drove on the Dixie Highway heading toward Lake Worth, the air conditioner was going full blast just to keep it bearable. Stu thought back to his earlier conversation with Lionel. Des should be removed from the bank. He was robbing the place blind. But Congressman Zale had owed Des, and Des had called in all his markers. Zale had really handcuffed the FDIC.

The market price of the stock had dropped way below the book value of the bank. He was sure there were a lot of concerned board members. The drop in the stock price was killing them. Luckily, he had Peg Neff who had a plan, and the power to expose the Chairman. He was glad he'd gone back into Des' house a second time last night.

He turned onto Vine Street. Stu knew he had the right house because the driveway sported a 1960 white two-door Thunderbird. The car belonged to her deceased husband, and she could never give it up. She was the envy of the bank employees when she pulled into the parking lot each morning. Charlotte had a corner piece of property that she and her late husband purchased thirty years ago. It was situated right on the lake and had a splendid view of the water and the bridge that separated the mainland from the island, but the house was in desperate need of repair: the house needed a coat of paint; the screen door on the north side of the house was torn; tall weeds were everywhere. Stu decided when he got back to the bank that he would send two maintenance men over to clean the place up. His secretary wasn't going to live like this.

Stu walked up to the entrance door and rang the brass bell beneath the nameplate. Inside, what sounded like a small dog barked. He rang the bell again and wiped perspiration from his forehead. Still, there was no answer.

He tried the door handle, but it wouldn't turn.

He went around to the side porch, pushed aside the torn screen door and tried the door handle. The door opened and there on the floor, next to the end table, lay Charlotte. Stu ran over and bent down to examine her when he saw the telephone on the floor next to her with the cord wrapped around her neck.

Her eyes and mouth were wide open. He felt for a pulse, but there was none and she was cold to the touch. A contusion on the side of her head indicated she'd been hit with something before being strangled.

Stu was overcome with grief and frustration. He looked around the room. Apparently there hadn't been much of a struggle. Everything seemed to be in order except for newspapers that lay scattered on the floor. *She was probably reading the paper when someone walked in on her. Was it someone she knew?*

Stu couldn't think anymore. He bent over and closed her eyes and mouth. He decided not to touch anything else. He used the phone in the kitchen to call the police and had gone on his way to the porch to wait for them to arrive when he spotted a notepad under the couch. He picked it up hoping for a clue, but the pad was clean of any handwriting. He decided to tear off the top page and hold it to the light. There was a slight impression on the paper but couldn't make out what it said. He found a pencil in a kitchen drawer and began to rub over the pressed area. As he rubbed it became clearer.

He couldn't believe it. *What's my phone number doing on that pad? Was she trying to reach me last night? I was at the party. The answering machine! I didn't check it last night. Could she have left a message?*

Suddenly, the sounds of sirens drew nearer. It was the police.

He stuffed the paper into his pocket just as two police cars pulled up in front of the house along with an unmarked car.

Out stepped none other than Chief Walter Dobbs.

"Walter goddamnit, my secretary's dead!"

"She's dead? I wasn't sure what happened. I heard the name over the Plectron and came over to see if I could be of any help. I have to be careful because this isn't my jurisdiction, but anything I can do to make things easier... that's why I'm here."

The two police moved them aside and began their investigation, asking Stu basic questions about Charlotte and what he was doing there.

"Walt, what the hell is going on? Why did she have to die like this?"

"It could have been a robbery and she spotted the thief. They've had their share of incidents here by the lake over the past several months from what I hear. And most of it's drug related."

"I don't think this has a damn thing to do with any robbery. This is murder and someone wanted her dead!" Stu paced around the front yard. "This is the second killing involving people at the bank. What did she know?"

"You're speculating."

"Like hell I am, and you had better get your detectives off their asses. I haven't heard one piece of news about Tom's murder. That wasn't robbery. It was a cold-blooded, calculated killing, and you know it!"

"Just hold on there. I know you're upset right now and rightfully so, but we've been working our balls off day and night trying to find some shred of evidence that would lead to something real other than that crossbow arrow. No one at the bank knows very much. Believe me, we've been asking questions, and lots of them Stu!"

"Well, my friend, you're asking the wrong people."

"Okay, so why don't you tell me, who have we missed?"

"How about starting at the top?" Stu said.

"What do you mean by that?"

"Des, Walt... Desmond Cain."

"The Chairman of the Board? Your boss?"

"Yes. My boss, brother-in-law, and your partner. I know more about Main Street Investors than you think. I'm not back here because I love this goddamn place."

"What would he have to offer the investigation?" Dobbs asked.

"Well, for starters, ask him what he knows about crossbows and exactly where he was at the time of Tom's murder. He drove me home that night after the ambulance left, but where was he before that?"

"You're kidding! You think Des had something to do with the kid's death?"

Stu gestured wildly with his arms. "Who the hell cares what I think? It's your job to investigate! Did you know he was a National Crossbow Champion? Wouldn't you naturally want to ask him a few questions? It's not every day someone gets shot through the neck with that kind of an arrow."

"This is the first we've heard of it. You're damn right we're going to ask. How did you find out he knew about crossbows?"

"Jessica told me. Go to the den at his home and see for yourself. I'm surprised you didn't already know."

Two more police cars pulled up in front of the house. A photographer and fingerprint crew moved through the crowd that had assembled along the walkway, gawking to see what was going on. One of the officers told Stu to be available later for some additional questions. It was time for him to leave. He couldn't do anymore here. He turned to Dobbs. "Walt, I suggest you start paying attention. Fortune Beach is your town. Soon you're going to be asked questions as to why you haven't turned up any leads. Let me give you a piece of advice. As you can see I'm very upset here. This was a good woman. Nobody had to kill her, but somehow this senseless killing is tied to the bank. Make no mistake about it. If you don't do something about what went on here today, even if it's out of your jurisdiction, rest assured that I will, my friend."

"I'll make it my business. I still believe you're wrong. Des is a money maker and entrepreneur, not a murderer!"

"Well, then convince me. Show me I'm wrong."

Stu drove back to the bank, gripping the wheel tightly. *Why did she have to get involved and what did she find out?* He decided to march straight up the stairs and into Des' office. As he passed through the secretary pool everyone sat at their desks, not moving a muscle, watching him. He opened Des' office door and barged in.

Des had two board members in his office: Preston Clark, a local jeweler who couldn't tell the difference between a diamond and a piece of charcoal but had gobs of money, and Jeffery Justin, the local art dealer. They all looked surprised as he pushed open the door.

"Gentlemen, Des, Charlotte has been murdered."

"What?"

"You heard me, murdered! Someone killed her. I think last night during your party."

"Christ, that's hard to believe," replied Clark. "She was an old woman. Who would want to kill her?"

Des' eyes opened wide with surprise as he looked back at Stu. "She was a gentle woman and my secretary for years. How did you find this out?"

"I went to the house and found her lying on the porch floor with a telephone cord wrapped around her neck. She was strangled."

"That's insane!" Des said. "And why? Who would want to hurt her?"

"That's what I want to know. The trail of deaths is leading right back here to this bank."

Justin stood. "Des, we can't stand much more publicity. Every time I open my store the locals want to know when the regulators are putting the key in the door. This isn't good for the bank."

"Don't worry about that. It's the least of my worries," Des said, then looked at Stu. "I'm sorry she's dead, Stu. I liked her a lot. What can I do?"

"Nothing now, Des, but rest assured the investigation is going to get much more intense than what you've experienced so far."

Des glanced at Stu, then the others. "I get the feeling you think I'm at the center of all this. Don't you guys?"

Stu said, "Hey, nobody's judging you but yourself. I suggest you make sure you aren't part of any of this. Beyond that, I don't care what you or anyone thinks. I'm sick of my life being turned upside down. There were almost three deaths around here."

"Three?"

Stu stared at Des. "Yes, three. Someone tried to do me in last night."

"At my party? Who would want to make an attempt on your life, especially with all those people around?"

"It wasn't at your house. It was in the book vault in the basement, right here at the bank!"

"What happened?"

Stu told them the details except what he was doing down in the vault. They all seemed shocked. Even Des looked surprised. "How come you didn't tell me at the party?"

"It wasn't the place!" Stu shouted. "But I'm pissed now and I can't stand it anymore! Consider this a warning, Des! You have the power, so call the wolves off or I'll ruin you!"

Their eyes fixed on each other and neither blinked. After what seemed like an eternity, Stu backed out of his office. "Call them off, Des. *Now!"*

He slammed the door and left them looking at each other, wondering whether this was a bad dream.

Stu entered his office and was surprised to find Jessica there. She stood and gave him a hug. "I'm sorry for what happened to such a nice lady."

"So I guess you heard."

She nodded. "I saw the look on your face and knew something was wrong, and besides, Walter called and gave me the news. He said you were very rude when he was only trying to help."

"Screw him! He's a lazy, fat sonofabitch who's just waiting for his pension to kick in and some of his investments to pay off and he'll be gone from here. He doesn't give a rat's ass about anyone except himself. I don't trust him one bit, the bastard. He should be out there trying to find out who killed Tom instead of kissing Des' ass."

"Do you trust me?" Jessica asked.

"Trust you, for what? Jessica, please, sit down." He pulled out a chair for her.

She sat in front of his desk. He believed she really wanted to know where she stood with him, but he wasn't quite sure. He also didn't know what her motives were or who had sent her, if anyone.

"You're a beautiful, ambitious twenty-two year old woman who will probably wind up getting what you want out of life one way or the other. I like you, but your allegiance is to the guy who's been taking care of you, and I understand. I don't have to draw you a picture to tell you what's going on around here. I really can't say much more about it right now."

"Do you need some help down here? Is there anything I can do? You do need a secretary, right?"

"Yes. I think I'll have to hire a temp to get me through the next few days anyway."

"How about letting me handle that for you?"

"Thanks, but I'll manage."

She smiled and squeezed his hand as she rose from her chair. "Okay, but if you need me just call, please?"

"Fine. Thanks."

At 4:00 p.m. Stu turned on the television to hear the local news. Just as he thought, Charlotte's death had made the headlines with somewhat skimpy information about the murder. He heard his name as the one who'd found her body. He would be getting calls soon from the local news agencies. He decided to take care of a few details and get out of his office before he was flooded with phone calls. He'd picked up the phone to dial Becca when he remembered the paper in his pocket with his phone number on it.

He hung up, then dialed his home number, then the two digit code to retrieve any messages. To his surprise there were no messages. Not one. Nothing. He thought that was strange.

Why my phone number? Did she find out something?

Perhaps, but Stu wasn't getting anywhere now. He picked up the phone again and dialed Becca. This was a call that he wasn't thrilled about making. He spent the next half-hour pleading with her not to come to Florida. The danger that she and his parents would put themselves in was just too great. As he surmised, she wasn't happy. She wanted to come down more than anything, and Stu missed her dearly, but from what he'd experienced over the last few weeks, he wasn't about to let his family be put in harm's way.

Stu told Becca he would call his father and tell him to cancel the plane reservations. He knew he would listen to him. The reality was that he never enjoyed coming to Boca Raton in the first place and it was as good an excuse as any.

Becca wanted Marie and Stu out of Florida, and he knew that he had only a short time before she would listen to no more of his reasons why he should be there. It was just a matter of time before she would jump on a plane and come get Marie and him personally. Reluctantly, she agreed to stay put for the time being.

Stu hung up feeling empty.

Chapter Twenty-Seven

Making his way down to the musty book vault again was no treat, but Stu had to question Annie before the police arrived. He found her sitting in a chair with two other workers, wiping tears from their eyes. Bunches of Kleenex were rolled up in a ball on the table nearby.

"Annie? Girls, are you all right?"

"Mr. Stuart, we can't believe this. She was here the other day. Right here. It's hard to believe she was murdered. She had no enemies."

"I know it's hard to understand who could have done such a thing. Annie, think back, please. Do you remember anything about that day that might help? Did she eat something that didn't agree with her? Why all of a sudden did she get sick and leave early?"

"I'm not sure. I didn't go to lunch with her. When she left we had to put her work away. It was very unusual. She must have been pretty sick because she would never leave the stuff sitting around the way she did. That wasn't like her."

"What do you mean?"

"Well, she had ten or twelve files out all at once. That was really unusual. We only took out one or two files at a time."

"So?"

"Well here, let me show you."

She walked over and pushed two buttons to separate the cabinets. As they moved through the aisle Stu began to get nervous. He checked to see that no one was near the buttons. Annie pointed to a group of files on the shelf. "Here... here are the files she left out. See, we put a rubber band around each one in case she came back and forgot where she left off. If anything other than food got her sick it had to be here in one of these files. I'd bet on it."

"Annie, you think of everything. Let me take them out of here and look them over. I'll bring them right back. I want to look through them before some other people decide to do the same thing." Suddenly an odd thumping sounded on the other side of the room. "What's that noise?"

"I don't know," Annie said. "I hear it a couple times a day. It sounds like something in the walls."

Stu walked to the last cabinet, which was against the wall where the noise had come from. It was stationary and couldn't be moved. He looked to see whether there was a button that would move the cabinet away from the wall, but there were no other buttons.

He began to pull some files out of the cabinet, but found nothing. Suddenly the noise sounded again! *Where's it coming from? Annie's right... it's in these walls.*

Stu bent down to the bottom shelf and removed more of the files, which now lay scattered on the floor everywhere. He lay on his side and looked through to the wall on the other side. "Jesus, mother of God!" It was a safe built into the wall. He tried the handle but it was locked. He needed a key and the combination.

What could be behind those doors?

Suddenly, the noise appeared again.

Thud.... thud

Someone was dropping something down a chute and it was landing in the safe. *Is this a night depository? But how could it be? It's on the other side of the building.*

"Mr. Stuart, what's going on here? You got the whole place a mess!" Annie knelt and began picking up folders.

"Annie, did you know there was a wall safe down here?"

She stared, then shook her head. "I've never seen this before."

She peered through the shelves at the safe. "How are you going to open the door? The cabinet's in the way."

She was right. Somehow the end cabinet had to move in order to open the door. Stu felt around the outside of the frame. There was nothing. He slipped his hand around the back where there was just enough room for a hand to fit. Still nothing. He felt down further and there it was, a latch. Stu flipped it up and pulled on the huge cabinet and it began to move away from the wall. It slid on tracks, easily and without much energy. He looked at Annie. “Who would have known this was here?”

"Well, if that doesn’t beat all. Who would ever have thought this cabinet could move? So what's the safe used for?"

"I don't know right yet. Did you ever see anyone down here who didn’t belong here?"

"Sometimes, now and then, but only once in a while."

"Like who?"

"Jesus, I can’t think right now in this hell hole?"

"I just need to know if you saw anyone down here who didn’t belong."

Annie thought about it. "Well, once in a while I see the security guard from upstairs, and sometimes I’d see Mr. C down here, and a few others now and then."

"Okay, Annie. I’m going to push this cabinet back now and take the files Charlotte was working on with me. You'll get them back later. I want you to keep quiet about all of this. It's between you and me, you hear?"

"Mr. Stuart, I won’t utter one word. Do you think this has something to do with Charlotte?"

"I’m not sure."

"If you need to know anything about the building, ask Harry, the doorman. He knows and remembers everything around here."

"Thanks. I'll do just that."

"Christ, Mr. Stuart, you left me with a mess here. I’m getting too old for this. I’m going to need three shots of gin tonight."

Stu smiled. "Enjoy them."

He took the files Charlotte had been working with and made his way back up to his office. He began to review the files for any clues that Charlotte might have found: Lacey Limited Inc., nothing unusual; Lamount Apparel Shop, everything in order; Labor, Jack, good bank customer and long-time Fortune Beacher. Langworth, Pete—Pete Langworth? *What’s he doing borrowing here?*

Stu reviewed his file. There was very little in it. A loan application for a car. Des had approved a twenty-five thousand dollar loan for a car two months ago. It must have been for the

Mazda. Pete's financial information was sketchy at best, but that didn't matter since it had Des' signature on the approval. Stu was surprised to know that Des knew Pete that well that he would personally approve the loan. On the back of the application Stu found a yellow Post-It with a short note to Des:

Des, please approve this car loan for Pete Langworth. You'll have no problems with him. He banks with us now and I personally recommend him. He's one of our clients. This is all the information I have on him.

Thanks!

Alex

Cranston! Cranston got him the loan! Then again, there was really nothing unusual. Everything seemed okay. There wasn't much to go on, but the loan was recommended by Cranston, who was also a board member, so Des had approved it. As he turned over the file and grabbed the next one to review, Stu saw another Post-It on the back of Langworth's file. It was upside down, and he had to turn the file around to read what was on it.

Bingo! This is it! An address was written in pencil. *Tom was right. He wasn't bullshitting me. The Post-It must have attached itself to the back of the file.* It read

Send copy of Main Street Investment file to Mr. Z.
Rayburn House Office Building, Room B340Z
Independence Avenue & South Capital Street
Washington, D.C. 20003

It had to be Zale. He wanted a copy of the documents to make sure he knew what the deal was all about. Things were starting to tie in now, and not only in the loan area. If Stu looked further he was sure that he would find that Zale had a lot to do with some of the decisions that went on around the bank. All Stu had to do was to make sure the address was Zale's. The next step would be to trace back through Main Street Investors' transactions to see how the funds were disbursed, even if it meant looking through multiple accounts. Stu had to find the truth in black and white. He needed some help in Washington, someone who had enough influence to get into the House Bank where Zale's congressional account was maintained. It was either Dad or Hendricks and he wasn't completely sure about Hendricks just yet.

It took Stu all of five minutes to confirm the address of Zale's congressional office in Washington, D.C. and it was just as he thought. Stu gathered the files together to return them to the vault as he promised, but before doing so he jotted down Pete Langworth's account numbers. He decided to do a little homework and review Pete's bank accounts and their activity over the past months. This would be a priority project for him since Pete's name kept coming up and he was dating Marie. He returned the files and left for the day.

Outside the main entrance Harry was preparing to leave. He was folding the last of the towels he used to clean the cars that stopped at the bank. "Long day, Mr. Stuart."

"Every day is long around here, Harry," Stu replied.

Harry's old eyes just glistened beneath his thick bushy white eyebrows. "I just take 'em as I can. Each day for me is a blessing, so I'm grateful."

"Harry, I need some history on the bank. Maybe you can help me."

"I'll try, Mr. Stuart."

"In the book vault in the basement there is a safe, like a night depository, like the one over there by the front doors. I can't find where the other one in the vault leads to."

"Well, you have to remember that the bank had an addition put on about ten years ago and they were to seal up the old night vault, but I remember Mr. Cain not letting that happen."

"Why not?"

"I don't know. I think he thought it might be useful some day. And why ruin a perfectly good piece of equipment just because we got a new one?"

"Well, where is it?"

Harry pointed toward the end of the bank building. "It's over here. Let me show you." They walked around the south side of the building near the employee parking lot and he pointed again. "Over there... next to the brick chimney going up the side of the building. That's where the original night depository box is located. There, you can see a sign in front of it now that tells customers when we're open for business. It's hardly ever used anymore."

"What do you mean hardly? Is it or isn't it?" Stu asked.

Harry cleared his throat. "Mr. Stuart, I'm probably going to wind up getting my ass beat because this is none of my business, but you're asking me all these questions."

Stu put his hand on Harry's shoulder. "Harry, listen, just tell me what's going on here so I can deal with it. This is just between me and you."

"Well... only a few people use it during the day, but late at night when I come around just to check up on the place now and then, things start popping around here because a lot of people use it at night."

"No kidding. I never even knew this was here until today."

"Yes Sir."

"Thanks Harry. This is our secret. And thanks for cleaning my car." Stu passed him fifty bucks for his trouble.

On his way home Stu finally figured it all out. The bank was the drop site. The money bags were dropped each day or night at the bank from the sale of drugs. This was how they were laundering the money, and what better place than at the bank vault. Someone had to know their way around the federal regulations about cash transactions, but this was how it was getting into the bank. He wondered who was making the drops. It had to be hundreds of thousands of dollars a week coming into the bank. There were some very rich people around here, and killing someone was small potatoes when a network like this was alive and working around the clock.

Chapter Twenty-Eight

Des sat in his high-backed leather chair in the corner of his den drawing slowly on the long, sweet-smelling Macinuto cigar. He fumed over the incident in his office as he watched the smoke forming small circles above his head.

Who the hell does Stu think he is, busting into my office and embarrassing me in front of the board members? Every time he thought of it he puffed more rapidly, filling the room with the lingering smoke. *Who's he trying to impress, himself? Stu has to go.*

Des had to think about his partners too. Cranston couldn't stand Stu no matter what anyone thought. He wanted him out of the bank before he brought the whole thing down around their necks. And Zale had told Des he wanted Stu out also, even though he had no official say in board matters. A few years ago, Des had asked Stu to raise campaign contributions through his borrowing customers. Stu raised twenty-five thousand dollars in two weeks and donated all the cash to the Fortune Beach Humane Society. That really pissed off Zale.

Des sighed. Zale had done a good job of getting rid of the examiners, but it was just a matter of time before they'd be back with a larger army than before. It was time to put an end to all this. Des would call a meeting of the partners and start slowly liquidating their holdings. Perhaps with planning they could leave Stu holding the bag while they all quietly slipped away with wads of cash.

He tapped his finger on his temple. *How can I pull this off? How can I successfully implicate Stu?*

He rose from the chair, stretched his arms and yawned. Jessica wouldn't be over tonight so he could get some much-needed sleep. As he glanced around the room he noticed the crossbow arrows in the frame. He was the National Crossbow Champion at Dartmouth and he was proud of it, but Stu's accusations really upset him. After all, he wasn't the only one who knew how to use a crossbow.

Chapter Twenty-Nine

Sleep didn't come easy for Stu. Someone had been in his house because the tape in the answering machine was missing, but there were no signs of a break in. All the doors were locked just as he'd left them, and the windows were still shut because he checked every one of them since things began to get out of control around his home. *How did someone get in here? And what did Charlotte want to tell me? Did she leave a message?*

The Astra .357 Magnum revolver lay beneath his pillow, ready for anything. He'd had enough. He welcomed someone to come through the doorway because it would be their last house call ever.

Stu's pillow was hot against his head so he turned it over. The coolness helped for a minute, but he still couldn't get comfortable. He sat up in the middle of the bed and took off his pajama top, then lay back down, leaving his feet outside the covers. Slowly he drifted into a calm sleep.

A noise. In the darkness his eyelids flew open. *Am I dreaming?* Turning his head slowly, he blinked at the clock. 4:35. *There... by the window. Is that a shadow?*

Stu reached for his gun.

Something moved by the bedroom window. He rolled off the bed and crawled into the living room. He waited in the center of the room, crouching low with sweat dripping from his forehead.

Nothing. All was quiet.

Someone's outside... the front door... a shadow! There! The silhouette of a man!

Stu raised the gun again with both arms extended and took aim. He cocked the hammer and—there was a knock on the door.

He stood motionless and didn't move a muscle.

"Stu, open the door! It's me, Ray. Are you in there?"

"Ray?"

"Open the door before the mosquitoes carry my ass away."

Stu ran to the door and flipped the lock. There in the doorway stood his friend.

"Hey, ole' Buddy, sorry for the early morning call"

"Ray, what the hell are you doing here? You scared the crap out of me. I could have killed you."

Ray glanced down at the Magnum in Stu's hand. "Yeah, I'm seeing that. I tried to leave a message on the phone but that didn't work, and I wasn't sure this was the right house it's been awhile. I wasn't sure if you were home, so as a last resort I gave a tap on the window in the back and that didn't work either. The rest is history."

"Come on, get in here. I'm not sure if I'm still dreaming."

"Boy, how can you sleep with all this shit going on down here?"

"Don't believe it. I just fell asleep about an hour ago. I haven't slept in days."

"Well, from what I can see the place hasn't changed much since I was here last. I can't understand it. This set up is beautiful, and you want to come back to Jersey? You're outta your mind."

"Try living here year round and tell me that."

"I guess the grass is always greener somewhere else."

"Ray what are you doing here at 4:30 in the morning? I mean, I'm glad to see you, but what's up?"

"Put on some coffee and we'll talk. From the looks of you, I'm glad I'm here. Not everyone answers the door with a .357 Magnum in their hand."

"I'll concede that." As Stu was putting on the coffee, he looked at Ray. "So really, what are you doing here?"

Ray shrugged. "I had 315 days accrued leave, so I decided to use some of it, that's all."

Stu turned on the coffee maker and sat at the kitchen table, where Ray joined him. "That was your early retirement and besides, you were up to your neck in a murder case up there. Becca sent you down here, didn't she?"

"Well, she had a little bit to do with it, but I've been hearing stories lately that frankly I don't like. I was concerned so I thought you might need someone to talk to down here."

"Thanks. I can't believe you did this. You must have left the house at 10:00 last night to get here. Do you want to get some shut eye?"

"I'd rather have some coffee." He pointed to the pot on the stove.

"Just a few more minutes."

"Well, what's going on? It sounds like the wild west down here with all these people being knocked off."

"I'm sure you heard some of this in bits and pieces, but let me tell you the full story. As you know, I came back down here because at the time I thought my boss and brother-in-law, the Chairman of the Board, wanted me to come back. Since then I've found out differently. But I also came back because I have a lot of stock holdings that I wanted to protect. The bank was close to going down the tubes, and if it did I'd lose my investment. There was also a good chance I could have some personal liability also in the event the FDIC had to liquidate the bank and take a loss. As an executive officer and a board member, I don't think I have much of an excuse if they really wanted to get me. To tell you the truth, I should have put my foot down a long time ago, and maybe things would have been a little different."

Stu got up and poured them both a cup of coffee, then sat back down.

"But this guy Cain... he runs the show and is the one responsible for what's going on, right?"

"Pretty close. He has holdings in several partnerships. Some are fairly open but others are silent, depending upon who he's doing business with. He's involved with some shady characters, and a few are on the board of the bank. They all use the bank as if the place was theirs personally. The bank gets charged for everything he does, and most of the time it's one of his companies that's doing the work. No one even knows it unless they do the leg work to find out."

"From what I read in the papers and what you tell me sounds like the place is being run by a bunch of crooks. Quite frankly, you might be better off getting the hell out of there before you're left holding the bag. What's this about all these murders?"

"The young kid in the bank had all the dope on everyone."

"I remember you telling me about the kid who got killed with a crossbow arrow. Do they have any suspects?"

"We'll get back to that later. Anyway the kid, Tom, met me in a restaurant one night and told me what was going on. There was stuff I never knew about."

"Like what?"

"Like construction fees that were supposed to be paid to the bank that never got to the right accounts. Loan proceeds in some instances going into the personal account of one of the directors, who was the attorney representing the bank and the borrower at the same time. You wouldn't believe it. The guy even had deposit tickets doctored to make it look like the money was being deposited into the right account. I found out that the checking account numbers didn't match up with the borrower's account."

"That's not good."

"No shit. The funds were going into the personal checking account of the lawyer who closed the loan. Can you believe it? And that's only a small part of what was going on here."

Stu shook his head and continued. "It's a shame they haven't nailed the kid's killer. The police are doing absolutely nothing. I had a run-in with the police chief because nothing has happened yet. Can you believe this? The kid is killed on the streets of Fortune Beach, which is hard to believe in the first place. He's killed with an arrow from a crossbow, which isn't your everyday murder weapon, and nothing has been done. And wait till you hear this: Des Cain was a national crossbow champion in college, and no one even questioned the guy!"

"How come?"

"The chief didn't know that Cain knew anything about crossbows, or at least that's what he told me. Dobbs knows everything there is to know about Desmond Cain."

"Sounds like a shitty excuse to me."

"I know. Dobbs is in a number of partnerships with Des and probably some other stuff that I don't know about, but you can see how far this investigation is going to go."

"Man, Cain doesn't miss a trick. He even has the police chief on the take, huh?"

Stu nodded. "And the same chief, who I think has some shady dealings with Des, tells me he knows nothing about his past as a crossbow champion. As of now Des isn't a suspect, but I believe he killed Tom."

"Can you get any evidence to back up your hunch?"

"No, but just listen to what I told you. I originally thought the arrow was meant for me, but Hendricks told me Tom was involved in some of the funny business that was going on, and that was the reason I assume he was killed; however, I also think I could have been the target. Anyway, evidently, the kid was getting nervous when the bank examiners came. Sooner or later he would crack under pressure, so I guess they had him killed before he started to name important people around town who were robbing the bank blind. And a couple of days ago I almost got it down in one of our vaults. I was lucky. I could have been crushed to death, but I found something to wedge in between me and one of the moving file cabinets that holds our bank files."

"Was there someone down there with you?"

"Obviously there was, but I didn't know there was someone else down there. I'll tell you about it later when I take you down there to take a look for yourself."

"Well, from what you told me, I think you're getting in the way. How come you never knew anything about this before? This stuff didn't just happen over a few weeks."

"You're right. I knew Des had his own agenda around the bank. What the hell, he's the Chairman of the Board. It wasn't any of my business. Remember, it was always his sandbox, but I never knew about all the partnership deals, the kickbacks and the money laundering stuff."

"Money laundering? Tell me are these characters moving stuff down here?"

"Well, I don't know, but there's something going on and I haven't had the time to check it out, but I think that's what it is. I'm glad you're down here because this thing is getting bigger than I originally thought."

"Okay, so tell me, what's the program? What do you want to accomplish here? Are you going to get a medal when all this is over?"

"No. No medals. My secretary was killed yesterday—I'm sure Becca told you the details—and that was the last straw. I found her with a telephone cord wrapped around her neck on her porch. She had to have found out something that got her killed. What was strange is that I found a notepad under the couch at her house. The pad was blank but the top page had an impression on it like someone was writing something on the top sheet of paper. Let me show you."

He went into the bedroom and tore through his pants, then returned to the kitchen. "Here it is. I used a pencil and rubbed out what was on it. It's my telephone number! I think she was trying to get in touch with me before she died. And I'm carrying this Magnum because someone got into the house and stole the message tape out of my answering machine. There was no forced entry so either someone has a key to the house or they're just really good at getting into places. I'm not taking any chances."

"Well, whoever killed your secretary probably killed the kid also, so you aren't far behind. You'd better watch your ass, friend."

"I know. I worry about Marie. She works for this law firm I was telling you about, the one where the lawyer, Cranston, represents the bank and the client at the same time?"

"Yeah."

"Well, he's also a member of the board. Anyway, I found out that my daughter's signature is being used to sign bank documents that she knew nothing about. I'm still checking into that, but we've been so tied up with other crap I didn't have time to follow through. I did manage to confront Cranston though."

"Christ, what an incestuous group you're involved with! We'd better keep an eye on her or she's gonna get hurt."

"I really want her out of here."

Ray nodded. "That'd be a good idea."

"One more thing—remember when I called you about doing some checking. I was hoping more would turn up on Hendrick's. I'm just not comfortable with him, and I can't put my finger on it. I need to be careful of him."

"Stu, as I said to you before, I never found the guy to be a problem, but let me do a little more work on him. It's been a number of years and you never know."

"Okay. He stood and stretched. Hey, we probably should try to get a couple of hours' sleep."

Ray stood as well. "I'll use the couch if that's all right. I just want to lie down for a while; we'll talk some more later."

Lying in his bed looking at the ceiling, Stu felt some relief now that his friend was with him. He wasn't alone anymore. *It's time to put these bastards out of business. I'm taking control of the bank.*

Stu closed his eyes and finally drifted into a quiet sleep.

Chapter Thirty

Stu filled Ray in on the rest of the facts before leaving for the bank. They discussed Jessica, and her magnificent body, and what role she played to the best of his knowledge in all this besides her working on a degree in matrimony with Desmond Cain.

They talked about Johnny Mack, who gave everyone the impression that he was the kid with talent that Des took under his wing and made something of himself. It was all too neatly packaged for Ray. He wasn't buying that story. Anyone that successful got a taste of the action at the top, and there was more to the guy than was being told.

Pete Langworth came with his own set of baggage. Ray was very skeptical of him and his association with Cranston, and most of all his dating of Marie. Stu had to agree even though he didn't have enough facts to go on. He was more suspicious though of Pete's new-found wealth and who he was hanging around with.

They also discussed the mysterious Morecom Data Corporation and Hank Stone, the Mayor of Fortune Beach. His name didn't come up very often, so Ray would do some extra checking on the mayor's activities to see whether he was for real or just another one of the silent boys who stayed in the background.

Ray Collins was an executer, an organizer and no one to screw with. He wasn't going to sit on the sidelines and wait for Stu to make decisions on what should be done. Ray wanted Marie and Stu out of there. Becca had given him his marching orders. He would move very quickly once the pieces to the puzzle became clearer. He decided to visit two old buddies who were detectives in Ft. Lauderdale who might have some connections that would lead him to the information he desperately needed. Trying to find out anything locally was impossible and might get someone else killed. On his way back from Ft. Lauderdale, he would stop and see a state trooper he'd known in his earlier days when both of them had pulled the night patrol at the Wakefield police headquarters. The trooper was assigned to the Florida State Police Organized Crime Task

Force Unit and should be able to give him the skinny on some of Des' friends and activities.

Stu finally arrived at the bank at 11:00 a.m., rebounding from a sleepless night filled with plenty of surprises. He expected another hectic day. Just as he expected when walking through the bank, he sensed a solemn mood among the staff. They were heartbroken, concerned and scared to death. He went down to the book vault to tell Annie that the project was over. He also wanted to take a look at the trap he'd set the last time he was down there. "Annie, where are you?" Stu shouted

"Here, second row. Who's there?"

"Mr. Stuart."

"Oh, great. We have to have a talk." Annie replied hastily.

"Sure. What's on your mind?"

"I can't do this crap anymore. I'm not a spring chicken and the activity of moving these files all around is just too much for me. I'm going to quit."

"Wait a minute. Don't get all hot and bothered. I'm down here to tell you to stop. The project is over."

"Over? Complete? Finished?"

"Yep."

"Damn, you're the greatest, Mr. Stuart. I really was at the end of my rope. These old legs were wobbling more than ever."

"Well, you won't have to worry about it anymore. Just finish putting these files back and it's done." He left her and moved to the back of the room to the filing cabinet against the wall, and sure enough someone had been there within the last twenty-four hours. The invisible tape that he'd placed from the file cabinet to the wall was broken, indicating that the file had been moved. Someone was getting in and removing the contents out of the safe, but how were they getting in?

"Annie, can I see you a minute?" Stu asked.

She came right over.

"Annie, tell me your schedule down here. Is the place ever left alone, even for a minute during the day?" He asked.

"A minute? Are you kidding? Sure it is."

"Tell me."

"Well, the vault opens every morning automatically at seven o'clock. I don't get in until eight in the morning. I always set the vault clock as you know, one hour before I get in like I told you. All you need is the combination and it will open. I close the vault door at noon, but I don't lock it when I go to lunch, which is about an hour. Every afternoon at three o'clock I go to the dumper, and by then I don't have time to close any doors. It's everyone for themselves."

"So those are the only times the vault is left unattended each day?"

"That's right."

Someone has Annie's time schedule down, he thought. *When the vault was left unattended, the safe was being emptied.*

"Thanks Annie. Keep up the good work!"

"Did you find anything new about Charlotte's death?"

"Nobody has gotten back to me yet."

"The cops were all over this place earlier, asking me all kinds of questions."

"They're only doing their job. I assume you told them she was only helping you out down here?"

"Exactly right. They couldn't understand why the vice chairman's secretary was working in the file room, but I told them I was behind in my filing and being the person that she was, she was helping me get caught up."

"Boy, Annie, you're fast on your feet."

"Thanks, but I hope to be off them soon."

Stu made his way back up to his office thinking of the next plan. When he reached the executive lobby, he saw Des standing by his door waiting. At Charlotte's desk was a new secretary shuffling papers and trying to look busy.

"Who are you?" Stu asked.

"I'm Louise. Sir. Louise Tallmount. Are you Mr. Stuart?"

Stu smiled. "Yes, I am."

"I’m your secretary... well, if you want me for the next few weeks. I was sent over by personnel. I hope I can help you. I know you’re a busy man and I’ll do my best if you want me here."

"Thanks Louise. Yes, I can use you. I'll see you a little later."

Des looked at him. "Stu, can we talk for a few minutes?"

"Sure."

As soon as the door closed behind them, Des said, "What got into you the other day? I was completely surprised by your actions, and quite frankly, so were Preston and Jeff."

Stu held up one hand. "Please, Des, don't start with me. And quite frankly, I don't give a shit about Preston and Jeff."

"Your attitude goddamn stinks. Don't forget I was the one who brought you back here and I can—"

"Just hold on a minute! If you think for one goddamn minute that I believe that story, then you’re a fool. The only reason I'm back here is because if you didn't toe the line you’d be on the unemployment line by now and a For Sale sign would be hanging in the front window, so don't bullshit me!"

"I think it's time for you to go. I can see we’re not going to see eye to eye here. I’m still the boss around here and don't you forget it.” Des opened the door and grabbed the sleeve of Stu’s jacket. “Let's go." Stu didn’t move and Des grabbed him with both hands.

Blood rushed to Stu’s face and he thrust the edge of his hand into Des’ Adam’s apple. Des dropped to his knees, his eyes bulging as he gasped for air. Stu glared down at him. “That’s probably a fraction of what Tom must have felt when that goddamn arrow pierced his throat!” As Des struggled to stand, Stu shoved him up against the wall. "Listen, pretty boy,” Stu growled. “Don't make that mistake again. The only one who’s going to be leaving this place is you. You’re a thief, an embezzler, and a murderer. You prey on the less fortunate. I watched you cheat people out of their fortunes with your scams. Your business interests do nothing but siphon-off the capital of this bank. There are people here who have given their lives to this organization to make an honest living and to do something good for someone else. But you, with your filthy money, think it's the cure-all for your deceit and that people don't know about you. Well, guess again because if they don't know by now, they're sure as hell going to know soon. Now get out of here." When Des rushed through the door, Stu flipped the lock.

After he'd thought for a few minutes at his desk, he decided to take a walk just to get out of the bank. Before he left he stopped in to see Dennis Swayzee who was in charge of the bank's central filing system. "Dennis, I need you to merge all deposit account information into a readable form on Mr. Cain's and Mr. Cranston's accounts. I need to see all transactions over the past year, including the account balances."

"No problem, Stu. I should have it within... oh, say three hours or so. I'll put it in a sealed envelope marked to your attention."

As Stu went out the front entrance of the bank, his mind was racing. *I should've punched Des square in the jaw. He's the one who should pay the ultimate price if this bank doesn't survive. His selfishness and greed put everybody's job in jeopardy. He's a bastard who doesn't care about anyone. Most of the employees know it, too.* Stu needed the employees behind him. He would need their strength to weather the coming storm. He was about to do something that was going to make front page news.

Before he realized it, Stu had reached the door of the *Fortune Star,* which was about three blocks from the bank. The rush of cool air refreshed him as he opened the door to walk in—and he caught a reflection in the glass. Someone standing across the street. He'd had a feeling that he was being followed. He closed the door and quickly looked behind him. Standing near the post office was Gil the bank security guard. It appeared he was mailing a letter, but Stu knew better.

He approached the receptionist who was sitting at a drawing table pasting together advertisements for a local store's ad. Stu decided to find his own way around to Peggy Neff's office. He walked past room after room through a center hallway, admiring the framed headlines on the walls that had made local history over the years. He was about to stop and read a few lines when a familiar voice came from the end of the hall.

"I expected you here but not quite so soon." Peg smiled, her hands on her hips and her glasses hanging on the tip of her nose. "I guess things are moving a little faster than I originally thought. You'd better get in here because you aren't going to believe what I have to tell you. And for starters it's not what we talked about at Des' house."

Stu didn't understand what she was talking about as he walked down the hall to her office, but one thing for sure: he was glad she'd been in Des' den the night of the cocktail party. Stu knew he wasn't alone when he was looking at the crossbow arrows. It was Peg who had come in behind him that evening. Her tap on his shoulder had surprised him, but he had been glad she was there. She had no use for Des and she traveled with a crowd that felt the same way.

A small grin appeared on Peg's face. "I thought you'd like to hear the latest."

"Please, spare me. I don't think I could stand another murder."

"How did you know?" Peg said surprisingly.

"Get out! You can't be serious!"

"Sure am. I have, right at this moment, two investigative reporters on the scene at the golf course."

"Golf course? Where?"

"Pointe Royal Golf Club."

"My club? What the hell happened?"

She picked up her note pad and began to give him the story. "It seems that Mrs. Kirkman—"

"Mrs. Kirkman? That old bitch finally got it."

"No. Will you listen? Mrs. Kirkman's golf ball landed in the sand trap on the twelfth hole near the green. She went into the trap to hit the ball out and missed a few times. Finally she swung real hard and out came the ball and landed on the green next to a finger that also came out of the sand trap. People heard her screaming and yelling and began to gather. Naturally they looked in the trap, and lo and behold, they saw a hand with a finger cut off. So they called the police, who came out and dug up the sand trap and found a body."

"So who was it?"

"Well, I'm told it was a guy named Dave Docker. His head was bashed in with a seven iron. The club was buried with him."

"Docker was a Federal agent. He worked for the Department of Justice and was investigating the bank. His boss, Jack Hendricks, told me a few days ago he hadn't seen or heard from Docker for two days. Hendricks sent him over to the golf course to snoop around trying to see what he could find out. I can't believe those bastards would kill a Fed. Government agents are going to be all over our ass at the bank."

"What in the world was on Hendricks's mind to send him out to a golf course?" Peg asked.

"Beats me. I think they wanted to do some checking on Pete Langworth, the golf pro. Well, him and Alex Cranston.

"Cranston? The lawyer? Well, they had to have their heads up their asses because nothing goes on anywhere without one of Cranston's buddies getting back to him. They had to be crazy."

"You're right, and besides, Marie works for Cranston."

"I know, and I don't know how you live with that," said Peg.

"Not only that, she's dating the golf pro, Langworth."

"This is going to make headline news you know," Peg said. She walked over to her drafting table where she flipped on a lamp that hung from the ceiling. There, lying side by side, were two feature stories ready to go to press as soon as Stu gave the word. "Well, what do you think? If this doesn't get the bank depositors shitting in their pants, nothing will." She smiled.

Stu looked at the two press releases. The headlines read *MILLIONS IN BANK FUNDS RISKED TO AMBITIOUS DEVELOPERS and FLORIDA CONGRESSMAN CALLS HALT TO BANK INVESTIGATION.*

A sense of satisfaction flooded over Stu. "You did a marvelous job, Peg. You were really serious that night at the mansion."

"You bet your ass I was, and I knew you'd come to your senses sooner or later. I went to work on these soon after our talk. Stu, if you fool around with this bunch much longer you're probably going to wind up like some of the others."

"Thanks," he said.

"Hey, it's better them than you. Besides, I like you."

"From the looks of these feature stories, thank God you do."

"If you want to create a run on the bank you have to make people nervous that their money isn't safe. These are only the first two articles. I'll have two more ready in another couple days.

Chapter Thirty-One

The walk back to the bank seemed different. Not only had the weather cooled a bit and it was raining, but Stu was relieved that something good was about to happen. Finally, Des would get his due: a heavy dose of customer rage, enough to bring his plans of getting richer to an abrupt halt. The pressure would be on him for a change. Stu figured it would take about a week before Des would be gone with some unexpected help from his so called Fortune Beach friends.

When he reached the portico of the bank, he was drenched. The rain was coming down in buckets. Storm clouds were looming overhead and it looked like Fortune Beach was in for a good soaking. Harry looked him over. "Hell, Mr. Stuart, if I knew you were walking I'd have sent a car for you. You're drenched."

"It feels great. I'm glad you didn't, Harry."

Harry handed him a dry towel. "Whatever makes you happy, Sir."

Stu walked into the lobby and approached the bank's security area. The guard was on duty behind the desk.

"I thought there were two guards on duty at all times. Am I wrong?"

Gil looked up, surprised. "No Sir, Mr. Stuart, you're not wrong. Jason is on break for fifteen minutes. It's 3:00 p.m. and each day we take our break at this time, leaving only one of us on duty for a half-hour." Gil replied.

"Well, you must have taken your break earlier, I assume."

Gil shook his head. "No Sir."

Stu looked into the guard's eyes as he spoke. "I believe I saw you earlier at the post office. It looked to me like you were either mailing a letter or following me, or maybe both."

The guard didn't know what to say. He fumbled with his pencil and sputtered, "Mr. Stuart, I mail a letter to my daughter every day. My wife and I split-up and they moved to San Diego. I miss the kid a lot so I write her every day. I wasn't following you, Sir, but I did notice you across the street. I wasn't supposed to be away from the station, Sir."

Stu looked at him for a moment. "Tell me, do all these cameras constantly monitor all the areas shown on the monitors?"

"Twenty four hours a day, Sir. They shoot the areas frame by frame. If we see anything that looks unfamiliar or suspicious, we just push this button here and the camera runs continuously on the area."

"What do you do with the tapes after they're used up?"

"We mark them with the current date and place them in these cabinets below the desk for a month. Then they're transferred to one of the vaults for about a year."

"I see. Thanks." Stu tossed the towel back to Harry and headed toward the stairwell and the book vault.

He was too late.

He reached the second landing and Jason was on his way back up to the lobby via the stairs. He was carrying a blue sports bag. He saw Stu and nodded nervously. "Good afternoon, Sir."

Stu returned the nod and said nothing, but he turned and watched as the guard continued up the stairs. The bag seemed full of something as Jason was supporting it from underneath. *The sonofabitch is picking up money in the vault.*

Stu continued down the stairwell and entered the vault area, and sure enough it was left unattended. Annie was off doing her daily routine in the ladies' room just as she'd told him. It was the perfect opportunity for anyone to get in and out of the vault without a soul being the wiser. Except him. *Now isn't the time to expose anyone. This is only half the story. I need it all.*

On the way out the vault Stu looked up and sure enough in the corner was a security camera. Before the end of the day he would pay another visit to the security monitoring area for another discussion.

Entering the executive area Stu saw that Louise looked like she was in way over her head. Phones were ringing, her basket was full of incoming mail that hadn't been opened, and a slew of reports were lying on her desk. Apparently she had no idea where they belonged.

She smiled nervously. "Ever since you left, the place has come alive. Is it always like this or did I just hit a bad day?"

He smiled. "A little of both."

"I have your father on line one." She cupped the phone with the palm of her hand. “I also have an irate customer on the line. I left a bunch of messages from him on your desk. I’ll do my best to get his number if he wants to leave it. Also, there’s a sealed package waiting for you downstairs from Dennis Swayzee. Mr. Cain came back to see you, but he got tired of waiting and left for the day with Jessica.” She tapped her lip with a pencil for a moment. “I think that’s it.”

“Thanks, Louise. When you finish your call, please go down and pick up the package for me. I’ll take that call from my father now.” He walked into his office.

"Hey Dad, sorry to keep you waiting, I just walked in."

"Sounds like you’re really busy. You out of breath?"

"No, not really. I have a new secretary and it's hard to get used to the system around here. It's her first day."

"I heard the news about Charlotte from Becca. I'm sorry I didn't make it down; I think I need some time away from this place. You know, a different environment."

"How are you feeling? Any better?"

"Yes, much better. I slowed down a little at the bank and I’m spending a little more time at home with your mother. That's why we were looking forward to coming down."

"I know, and I’m sorry for the change in plans. Ray Collins is down here at the moment."

"Becca told us."

"I’m glad he’s here. I think I can use his help. You haven't heard about this yet, but they just found another body buried in a sand trap on the golf course down here."

"What course?"

"Pointe Royal. Guess who found the body?"

"Can't think of a name, it's been too long."

"Mrs. Kirkman."

He laughed. "That fat old bitch who cheats and steals golf balls?"

"You got it," Stu said. "I'm just glad Becca's home, away from any danger. And Dad, I really didn't want to involve you, but I don't think I have a choice. I'm going to need your help and pretty fast."

"What can I do?"

"I need access to a congressman's bank account at the House Bank. What can you do for me?"

"What do you want to do? Look into Don Zale's account?"

"You're always one step ahead of me dad."

"That's one of the reasons I called you. The word around the Hill is that Zale is on the take down there and they're about ready to pounce on him."

"Dad, before they pounce, can you get a hold of someone to do you a tall favor?"

"What do you want done?"

"I need the last six months of bank statements that will show any deposits made to his House bank account. I also need a copy of the checks he deposited. I'm sure everything is on image or microfiche."

"Boy, when you want a favor you sure ask for a big one." He chuckled. "Actually, I know the guy who runs the House Bank. He's been there for the past forty-something years. I guess he's milking it for all he can get. I'll tell him forty eight hours maximum."

"Thanks, Dad. How did you find out about Zale?"

"There isn't much that I don't find out around the Hill. I still have a lot of buddies hanging around who keep their ears close to the ground. I've always kept in touch and, as you can see, it pays off when you need it."

"One more thing is bothering me. See whether you can find out anymore information on a guy named Jack Hendricks. I was going to ask you earlier but I had Ray do the job for me. I need someone to look into this a little further. The guy who got killed down here was his partner on the job, a guy named Dave Docker. They both work for the Department of Justice. Something just doesn't feel right with Hendricks."

"I'll do my best."

"You never answered me straight about Zale."

"I knew his old man. He was a pain in the ass, but a good politician. His father was also a congressman, and also from Florida. He was a good Republican. There's a picture hanging in my office of all of us sitting around a dinner table at Jack Dempsey's with Ike during the convention."

"Dad, you amaze me on how you remember all this stuff."

"It comes with age son. Hey, your mother's looking for a free meal, so I'm taking her to dinner at the Black Orchid on the square up here. She loves the place, and quite frankly, so do I. You'll be hearing from me soon. I'm glad you're all right. Watch out and don't try to be a hero. Understand?"

"I'll be careful, and thanks Dad. Give my love to Mother."

The messages were piling up on his desk. Becca, Marie, Ray and Hendricks had called. He decided to grind out the calls before he left for the day. He called Ray first, only to hear a message that he couldn't be reached and would call back at about 5:00 p.m. He called Becca next. The phone rang six times before she answered. The dogs were barking in the background.

"Becca is everything all right up there?"

"Sure. We were just lugging groceries in from the car when I heard the phone ringing. I ran in to get it and got the dogs all worked up."

"It's good to hear your voice. I miss you, Honey."

"Same here." A lighter tone filled her voice. "Did you get some unexpected company?"

"Yes I did. Was that some of your doings?"

"Not really. Ray wanted to go. He didn't like the situation down there and it didn't take much to get him on his way after I told him some of what you told me."

"He came in the middle of the night and scared the hell out of me. He was lucky I didn't shoot him. I'm a little nervous down here. By the way, there was another murder here this afternoon. I just found out about it an hour ago." He told her about the sand trap killing and the plans he had with the local newspaper.

"Well, I'm just glad Ray's down there with you now," she said. "I've tried to call Marie about three times and there was no answer. Have you heard from her?"

"Not in awhile."

"Well, why don't you try getting in touch with her at the office and tell her to call me."

"How's Suzanne doing?"

"She's as nervous as I am. We both want our men back here, and soon!"

"Believe me, we both feel the same way. I'll have Marie give you a call, and I'll call you again tomorrow. I love you."

He called Marie next at the law office, but she was out. He left a message for her to call him as soon as she returned, then decided to get back to Hendricks.

"Hendricks here."

"It's me, Stu. Where have you been? I haven't heard from you in the last few days."

"I had a couple of important errands. What's going on with you? We should sit down and update each other. I did see in the newspaper that your secretary was killed. Any ideas?"

"No, I'm at a loss. I can't figure out why anyone would even want her dead unless she stumbled across something."

"Like what?" Hendricks asked.

"I'm not sure, but she must have known something. I just don't know what it could be. That poor woman wouldn't hurt a fly. By the way, I'm sorry about your partner too. I know it hasn't hit the wire service yet, but I'm sure we're going to get a lot of visitors around the bank very soon."

"Yeah, I got the news a short while ago. What a sick bunch of bastards, burying him in a sand trap like that. We're going to have a full court press to find out who did this."

"We'll have to get together soon. There's going to be more than one full court press going on at the same time. Hey, I'll talk with you later, Jack."

“Later, Stu.”

Louise brought in the sealed envelope from Swayzee and dropped it on Stu’s desk just as he hung up. Tracing back the activity on the accounts he’d asked for wouldn’t be a fun job, but it had to be done.

He was looking for large deposits and transfers between accounts, how were they being made, and by whom. He pulled out Pete Langworth’s bank statement and was very much surprised to see a current balance of $142,000 in his checking account. *No way is that from golf lessons or heavy Nassau bets with some of the club members.* Most of the transactions in his account were regular deposits and expenditures except for a large wire transfer every Monday to his account for the past few months. *What would a guy like Pete be doing with this kind of money in his account, and why the wired money?* Before he could approach Marie with the information he needed to know for sure where the money had come from. He called Louise to order up a microfiche reader to the room in order for him to look at back account transactions. Lucky for him Swayzee did most of the hard work. Stu had all the dates and transaction codes, so it was just a matter of finding the actual entries.

"Mr. Stuart, I have Mr. Ray Collins on line two. He says he knows you."

"Thanks, Louise.” He picked up the receiver and punched the button for line two. "Ray, I got your message. How’d you make out?"

"Well, better than I expected, but I have to tie up some loose ends. I’m going to stay overnight; I’ll be back sometime tomorrow. You aren’t going to like some of the stuff I found, but I'll tell you about it when I see you."

"Why not tell me now?"

"I don't have it all yet. I need to do a little more checking with my buddies down here, but I can tell you one thing. There isn’t much that goes on around the state that these guys don't know about."

"How can I reach you?"

"I'm staying at the Holiday Inn tonight off Interstate 95 at the Powerline Road exit, Ft. Lauderdale, North. I don't have the number, but it's room 202. If I'm not there, just leave a message and I'll get back to you."

"Great, I'll see you tomorrow."

The fiche reader and the appropriate microfiche made its way to Stu's office and he began looking up transactions. He flipped through hundreds of deposits, checks and debit and credit slips until he came upon the transaction he was looking for. *There it was. Transaction number 271055-3: July 27, 1992.* A wire transfer was received from the New York correspondent bank Chase Manhattan via Goodwill Trust Limited, Cayman Islands, from the account of C & M Financial Group. Fifteen thousand dollars was deposited into the account of Pete Langworth. Stu checked the next wire-back deposit the week before on July 20, 1992 and found that twenty-three thousand dollars had been wired to Langworth's account. He checked every wire back that appeared on the statement. The amounts ranged from fifteen thousand to thirty thousand dollars per week being deposited in his account on Mondays. Stu leaned back from the microfiche reader. *Langworth's up to his ears in something that isn't kosher.*

Damn, Stu thought. *Marie will be devastated when she hears the news.* He suspected Langworth was connected with Cranston and Des doing drug deals. *Marie could be in real danger hanging around this character.* Stu picked up the phone and called his New York correspondent representative Jerry Pote, whom Stu had known for years. Stu gave him the transaction information, then said, "Jerry, I need a favor. I need you to trace back through Goodwill Trust Limited to find out who originated the wire. I know it's almost impossible to hope for the actual names behind the company, but I figured asking couldn't do any harm."

"Hey, Stu, glad to do it for you it should be on the original wire. Who knows? Maybe I'll get lucky. I'll call you back if I find anything to report."

Stu cleared off his desk. He gathered up the bank statements to take with him to review later that evening. Then he remembered the security guards and the downstairs book vault. *Can't let that go until tomorrow.* He made his way to the elevator, descended to the lobby and walked over to the security desk. There sat Jason, adjusting two security monitors that were giving him problems. Stu watched him adjust the monitors until they were clear again.

Jason looked up and smiled. "Mr. Stuart, we thought you were still here working, but we weren't sure until you walked down the hall and we picked you up on the monitor. How late are you going to work tonight, Sir?"

"Not too long. Tell me, I saw you on the stairway earlier. Looked like you were coming up from the book vault. What were you doing down there?"

"Well, when you saw me on the stairway I was feeling much better than I was when I went down there. I had an upset stomach and made my way down to the bathroom in the basement. I was on my break at the time and wasn't feeling well. I keep a bottle of *Pepto-Bismol* in my bag at all times and it has been my savior more than once. But thanks. I feel a lot better, Sir."

"Ahh, I see. Well, I'm down here because I need some of the video tapes from the past month. I'm not at liberty to discuss my reasons, but I can tell you that I'm working on a project involving traffic flow in the main lobby area. If I'm right, some changes have to be made."

"We don't let these tapes out of the security area, Mr. Stuart. Mainly we keep them in the event we need to go to court on a matter and produce evidence that the person was actually here in the bank."

"I understand your concerns, and I'll bring them back in a few days exactly the way you gave them to me. I'll sign for them and take full responsibility."

"I'm sorry, Sir, but Mr. Cain gave us explicit instructions that these tapes aren't to be removed from the area or taken out of the bank."

"I understand, and that's a good idea—after all, we don't want just anyone coming down here and pulling tapes out of the security area—but my reasons are different and you'll get them back right away."

Jason shook his head. "Still, I'm sorry Sir, but—"

Stu leaned forward. "Listen to me carefully. Get your ass off that seat and give me the tapes I need before I throw you the hell out of here. I'm not taking any shit from you. So what's your pleasure? Are you going to get me the tapes or am I coming around there and get them myself?"

Jason put his hands up. "Yes Sir. No problem, Sir. I'm sorry I upset you, but that was the instruction I was given by Mr. Cain."

"Well, when Mr. Cain isn't here I'm the boss, and I need those tapes now!"

"Why don't' you come back here and pick out the ones you want, Sir? I'll copy down the numbers and you can sign for them. I'll even give you a bag to put them in."

"Good decision!"

Stu came around the desk and slipped open the cabinet. He picked out a dozen tapes, staggered throughout the month. Jason recorded the numbers and Stu signed the log. Then he was on his way upstairs to lock his office and leave. If his assumptions were correct, Jason would be seen leaving the downstairs book vault every day at about 3:00 p.m. Stu knew his story wouldn't hold water because Annie was in the bathroom every afternoon at the same time and there was only one restroom on that level. Reviewing the tapes carefully would tell him what was going on and who was telling the truth. He also wanted to know where Jason was going after he left the stairwell. Where was the money going in the bank? He knew he was the messenger boy making the deliveries, but to whom? Stu exited the elevator and heard the phone ringing in his office. He rushed, hoping it was Marie.

"Hello? Marie?"

"How did you know?"

"A father's intuition. Where are you?"

"I'm sitting in a shopping center off Palmetto Hills Boulevard. I tried calling you a few minutes ago, and I decided to give it one more try. Where were you?"

"I was just out of the office for awhile. Your mother's been trying to get in touch with you for the past few days at home. What's been going on? Why haven't you called her?"

"I've been doing some detective work on my own at the firm. I believe you were right. Something smells."

"What do you mean detective work?"

"I needed to know if I was working for a bad guy, a thief, or someone who did just what he pleased with total disregard for the law. I admired Alex. I thought he was just a smart, good lawyer who knew his way around the legal system. There's been a lot of talk about what side of the legal system he's on, so I had to find out for myself. No one else could help me.

"I went into Cranston's office looking for some clues, just snooping around to see what I could find out. He keeps hundreds of briefs in his office that we all prepare. They're all stacked up on his round table in the corner of the room, so if I were caught in there I could just say I was looking for a brief."

"Marie, you're fooling around with the wrong person. These are rough people, and you could get yourself in serious trouble. Three people have died and—"

"Dad, it's all right. Maybe it was stupid, but I did it. I remembered the last time Pete was in the office with Cranston. I walked in not knowing he was there. I never liked their relationship, but I never said anything about it. Alex smiled because he knew we were seeing each other and he asked when the big day was coming. We just blew it off, but he had this black leather book on his desk, and he was writing things in it while he was talking to us. He never looked up; he just kept jotting things in that book. I decided to find out what was in it."

"So what was in it?"

"Well, I looked around the room at first and went over to the table to make sure the brief was there in the event someone came in. Lucky for me it was there. Then I went over to his desk. When I looked in the right top drawer, there it was! It was filled with all kinds of writing and initials with numbers. Then I heard a noise outside and I got scared, so I hid in bathroom linen closet."

"And?"

"Cranston came into his office. He was talking in the next room. I couldn't make out the other voice at first, but then I realized who it was."

"Who?"

"I hope you're sitting down: Hendricks!"

"Jack Hendricks? Justice Department Hendricks? What was he doing there?"

"They were speaking so quietly it was hard to hear until they came into the office. I was scared to death. They were talking about someone who'd just gotten killed, but I couldn't make out the name. Then they started yelling at each other because of where the body was found. On a golf course?"

"Let me bring you up to date. Dave Docker, Hendricks' assistant, was killed and his body was found at Pointe Royal."

"Oh boy! I was so scared when they raised their voices. Hendricks was mad as anything at Cranston. Said he's finished with him, and he's nothing but a low life sucking the last drop of blood out of everyone he touches. He said the killing was the last straw and if he tried anything with him he would have his "ass cooked." Those were his exact words. Dad, do you think Cranston had this Docker guy killed?"

"It sure sounds like it from what you just said."

"I'm glad to be out of there. I was sitting in the closet when Hendricks came into the bathroom and turned on the light. I could see him combing his hair in the mirror. He went to the bathroom while talking to Cranston in the next room. He even washed his hands and put water on his face, but he couldn't find a towel to dry himself. I saw him fumbling around, squinting, looking for a towel. Then he came toward the door. He opened it and felt around until he found a towel. I was hiding in back of the towel hamper."

"Where did you say you are right now? I can't take this much longer."

"I'm at the Palmetto Shopping Center off Palmetto Hills Boulevard. I have the black leather note book with me."

"What? You took the book out of the drawer?"

"When they left I waited a few more minutes, then grabbed the book and slipped it into my pocket book. No one saw me leave. I wasn't hanging around there any longer!"

"Listen, get out of there now. Do you hear me? Stand inside the doorway of Publix and I'll be there in twenty minutes to get you. Stay where there are people around you and keep your eyes open. I can't believe you did this."

"Sorry, but I knew you needed some help from the inside and there was no one better than me if everything was true about Alex Cranston. The stuff in the book is a little like Greek to me, but there are lots of account numbers and bank records."

Stu hung up and went to get Marie. As he exited the elevator and headed for the front door he noticed no one was behind the security desk. A cigarette was still burning in the ashtray. *Where are they?*

A tiny red flashing light was blinking on the control panel. *Is there a problem in the bank?* The phone receiver was off the hook. He picked it up but there was no dial tone. He pushed the button on the receiver but still no dial tone. He hung up and the blinking light went off. Stu picked it up once again and the light started to blink again.

He slid back the panel doors below the counter to trace the wire from the phone through the top of the counter. Built into the counter behind the paneled doors was a reel to reel tape recorder. He slid back one of the panels above the counter top and found toggle switches to every room in the bank including the board room. Below each switch was the name of the room. Below the name was a small button with a tiny red light, which he couldn't quite figure out.

He went back to the tape recorder and turned the machine on, but heard nothing. He picked up the phone and still heard nothing, but the blinking light was on again. He tried flipping a switch labeled *Tape* next to the phone, and a scratching and humming sound came through the receiver. He pushed the *Reverse* button on the tape recorder, put the receiver to his ear again, then pushed *Play:* "Listen, get out of there right now. Do you hear me? Stand inside the doorway of Publix and I'll be there—" Stu slammed the receiver down and raced out of the bank. *They know where she is! They went after her! They know she has the black book!* In his car he sped toward the shopping center on the mainland. He raced over the Emerald Bridge at eighty-five miles an hour. *About ten more minutes....* He reached under the seat for his .357, preparing himself to use it in the next few minutes.

Chapter Thirty-Two

Marie waited for her father for what seemed like an eternity. She paced back and forth in the doorway of the Publix market. It was dinner time and the store was bustling with shoppers trying to get home. She decided to walk next door to the liquor store and buy a lottery ticket while she waited. In the store, she searched her pocketbook for ten dollars. *I just used the bank ATM this morning and got money for the rest of the week. Where is it?* She stepped aside to let others be waited on while she looked through her pocketbook for the third time. Wait a minute! *I put the money in the inside pocket of my blazer!* As she paid for the tickets and stepped aside, she kept watching through the window for her father's Lincoln to appear in front of the Publix next door. Suddenly a car pulled up in front of the liquor store and two men got out. She recognized them as the security guards from the bank. They looked as if they were looking for someone. *What would Jason and Gil be doing in this part of town so far from the bank? Maybe Dad sent them? No... he was coming to pick me up himself.*

The men ran into Publix, and a few minutes later they came out, then split off and scoured the area. *They must be looking for me.* She was glad they'd come so fast. Her father would breathe much easier now that she was safe. She opened the door and walked out of the store.

Jason looked up and stared at her for a moment. Then he smiled. He whistled to Gil and they both came running toward her. She'd started walking across the parking lot to meet them when a car horn sounded at the other end of the shopping center. It sounded as if the horn was stuck, and the car was coming toward her with headlights flashing.

Gil recognized the car. He turned and ran toward Marie.

Marie looked at Gil, then the car

Suddenly her father was yelling out the window. "Run! Run!"

Marie turned and ran toward the market. Glancing back, she caught a glimpse of Jason pulling a handgun from his holster as he ran toward her.

She headed for the store entrance at full speed, but the electric eye didn't react fast enough. She grabbed the edge of the door and shoved, then ran past the cashiers. She stopped, turned and watched as her father rammed Gil. The security guard landed, limp, on the hood of a garbage truck that was parked in front of the store with a flat tire.

The other security guard raced toward the store entrance, his gaze fixed on the store window through which he could see Marie.

She saw him coming, turned and ran down one of the aisles as fast as her legs would carry her. At the end of the aisle was a large metal door. She hit against it hard, pushing it open, then fell to the wet, dirty cement floor. The dimly lit room was cold and filled with large, dirty cardboard boxes that smelled of rotten food. She felt along the nearest wall, kicking boxes out of her way until she found the corner, then knelt down under a sink and pulled a large box over to hide her. She was shivering, and she began to get sick to her stomach from the smell of the rotten food as she lay motionless on the floor. *Dad was right. I shouldn't have gotten involved in any of this. It's definitely out of my league*. Seconds passed, seeming like hours.

Two shots rang out! Four! Five! The door slammed open. *Oh God!*

She was about to scream when a familiar voice called, "Marie, where are you? It's all right. It's Dad."

She was so scared she couldn't talk. Boxes shifted, as she moved her legs. "Dad?"

Then she felt warm hands as two store clerks pulled her out from under the sink and helped her stand. She ran to Stu and fell into his embrace. He held her, rocking her gently back and forth.

As they walked through the store the employees and shoppers applauded.

Marie smiled slightly as she walked along with her father holding her. She was dirty, her dress was torn, her stockings were ripped at both knees, and blood had found a path to both ankles. The doors at the front of the store swung open, and for once the warm air felt good. Two police officers came over and helped. Paramedics bandaged Marie's knees and cleaned her up.

A boy of about 12 came over and slapped her pocketbook on her lap. "Here, Lady. You dropped this when you went into the store. I held it for you. I'm glad you're okay."

Marie produced a soft smile. "Thanks, Sweetheart. That was very nice of you."

Stu couldn't believe so many cops were on the scene. He was happy they'd caught Jason and it was finally over.

A man in a suit approached. "Hi, I'm Detective Santora... Lou Santora. Glad to see you and the woman are all right."

"She's my daughter, Marie Stuart. I'm Halsey Stuart, Vice Chairman at Fortune Beach Bank. I believe we met a few weeks ago. Those two guards work there too."

"They're both dead."

"How did Jason get it?"

"He shot an officer in the arm and killed the police chief."

"Walter? He killed Walter?"

"I didn't know you knew him. He never felt a thing. He got it right above the eyes, dead before he hit the ground."

"I can't believe this. How did something like that happen? This isn't even his town. It's unbelievable!"

"The chief evidently knew the guard. He said he'd handle it. We told him to stay with his car and we'd take care of it, but he insisted. He walked over with his arms at his side calling out to the guard to take it easy, that everything was going to be all right. He told the guy he wasn't going to get hurt, that he should just put the gun on the ground and they'd walk together back to his police car. As he got closer, without any warning the guard shot him at point blank range."

"Unbelievable!"

"The next thing we knew, the guard shot himself in the head. Why were they after you?"

"They were after my daughter. I think they were trying to abduct her. Somehow they knew I was picking her up and they beat me over here." He gave the detective all his personal information and turned to Marie. He wasn't going to tell him anything more, but wanted to make sure Marie knew his story. It was now time to leave. He grabbed her pocketbook and they both walked to the car. Marie unzipped the pocketbook and took out the black leather notebook. "Thank God something went right today. Here's the notebook."

"You're something. This should make interesting reading."

When Stu made an odd turn, Marie asked, "Where are we going?"

"We're stopping off at the house to get a few things. Then we're leaving."

"To where?"

"To your grandfather's condo in Boca. No one will get a good night's rest here."

"I have no clothes."

"You have some stuff at our house. Just get whatever you can. Your mother should have some pajamas in a drawer. Tomorrow you can pick up some things at your house."

"What about my car?'

"We can pick it up on the way to Boca and you can follow me."

Marie fell silent. She began flipping through the black notebook. Suddenly she stopped when she saw the name *Pete Langworth.* She wished it were not true, but there it was in black and white. In columns marked *Date, Gross, Net* and *Langworth,* the log confirmed that Pete was making daily cash drops and being paid handsomely to do so. She was devastated. Hundreds of thousands of dollars were changing hands and it wasn't from golf lessons. She loved Pete, but this confirmed that he was up to his neck in dirty business with Cranston. *I have to convince Dad not to turn him in. Not yet anyway! I have to hear it from Pete first. Maybe somehow there's an answer to all this.* Her eyes began to fill with tears.

They pulled up in front of the house.

Marie decided that her father couldn't see some of this material. Not just yet anyway. "Dad, please hurry and open the door. I think I'm going to be sick."

When he opened the door she flew through the living room and straight for the bathroom. Once inside she closed the door and pulled the black notebook from her purse. She began removing the pages involving Pete As she tore the pages out one by one, she began to cry. She felt betrayed. *I thought we loved each other. How could he do this to me? Was he just using me?* She had to find out for herself. She had to see him face to face. She wanted to hear from him that he'd sold out to Alex Cranston.

Thirty minutes later the car was packed and they were on their way to the Boca condo. They stopped at the shopping center to pick up her car.

Chapter Thirty-Three

The Ocean Dunes was the best that Boca had to offer in ocean-front living. It had all the amenities: a club house, a pool, tennis courts, a theater, the Tower Shopping Center, underground parking, a private beach and a spectacular view of the Atlantic Ocean.

Stu slipped the plastic security card into the slot next to the double glass doors, then opened the door and proceeded toward the elevator. He inserted the card again and the red lobby light illuminated above the elevator. The two brass elevator doors vanished between the walls and they entered the small cubicle.

He pressed the *PH* button and they went to the top of the building within seconds. On the twenty-second floor there were six penthouse units, one of which was owned by his father and mother.

They reached the front door of Unit 2001, which had a shiny brass plate and the initials HJS engraved in Old English letters. He opened the door with the same security card. They both recognized the familiar smell. Janice loved pine and made sure that the cleaning maids used a pine-scented disinfectant everywhere. Stu turned on the light. They dropped their belongings on the sofa and began turning on the rest of the lights and opening the electric storm shutters.

"I don't know why Grandpa ever bought this place," Marie said. "They never use it and it's so beautiful."

"He has a lot of other things on his mind. This wasn't important to him, but I think shortly the place will become a big part of his life. I can tell when I talk to him, he's almost ready to let loose and smell the flowers while he still can."

"That's good. It'll be nice seeing them down here."

They stood on the terrace overlooking the ocean and the illuminated homes below.

The rooms were large and flowed into each other with pastel Floridian colors of coral, blue and white. The three bedrooms were off to the back of the living area with the master bedroom exiting onto the terrace.

Harrison had spared no expense in decorating, and he'd left the task up to his wife. He wrote a check for one hundred thousand dollars and told her to go to work. The result was absolute elegance.

An off white tweed carpet covered the living room floor. A huge beige leather couch hugged a large portion of one wall. Matching end tables complemented the oval marble coffee table with its swirls of tan, light blue and gray. Pictures of egrets and flamingos adorned the walls, showing Floridian nature in all its beauty. The room was tranquil and relaxing as the sound of the ocean filtered up from the shoreline below.

Stu placed a call to the residential services department and ordered a pizza, as well as enough food for the next few days.

Marie was exhausted. A shower would do her good before the pizza arrived.

Stu searched the phone book for Ray's hotel. He remember it was Room 202. He found the number and called him.

"Hello?"

"Ray? Stu. I'm glad I caught you."

"I just got in from dinner. I was just about to call Suzanne. Is there anything wrong?" Ray questioned.

"Nothing's wrong now. In the short time since we last talked, Marie was almost kidnapped, and two bank security guards and Police Chief Walter Dobbs are dead."

"Jesus! What are you talking about? Where are you now? How's Marie?"

"She's a little shaken up and has some cuts on her legs and arms, but she weathered it like a trooper. We're at my father's condo in Boca. We decided it was safer here. Nobody knows about this place."

"Do you have an extra cot there?"

"I have an extra bedroom if you want it."

"I'll be there in half an hour. I have some things to tell you that you're probably not going to like."

"Like what?"

"See you there."

Marie came out and sat on the couch, combing her hair and deciding whether to call her mother. "Who was on the phone?"

"I was just talking to Ray. He's on his way up from Ft. Lauderdale to stay with us. He's taking over one of the bedrooms."

"Ray Collins is down here? When did that happen?"

"Yesterday. I didn't get a chance to tell you with all that happened. He's the only one I can trust who can help us."

"I'm glad he's here."

"It's going to get very busy around here the next few days, so I suggest you call your mother and tell her you're all right. Don't tell her about what happened today or she'll be down here on the next plane. Tell her I'm not here right now. I'm out with Ray or something. I can't talk to her right now."

Marie picked up the phone to dial.

Stu raised one hand. "Wait. Before you do that, call security and tell them Ray will be coming and to escort him up. Where's that black notebook? I should start looking at this stuff before he gets here."

"In my purse on the table."

Stu began assembling the video tapes he'd brought with him in date order. He counted twelve tapes taken from the security area of the bank. He'd be spending the next few hours looking at the tapes between 7:00 to 8:30 a.m. and 2:30 to 4:30 p.m. daily. If his assumption was correct, he'd see a pattern of how the cash was collected and by whom.

"Marie, why don't you use the bedroom phone? I need the VCR in the living room. I want to look at these tapes from the bank."

"Sure, but I'd like to see them too."

"You will. Just finish your call to your mother first. She's worried as hell about you."

Stu inserted the first tape, dated Monday, June 15, 1992. The monitor displayed the date, time and camera number of each frame. There were ten security cameras placed throughout the bank. In order to get back to camera one, the monitor cycled through all ten cameras, which took about a minute. Stu noticed that camera five monitored the book vault. He fast forwarded the tape until it reached 7:00 a.m., then viewed the tape for a few minutes. When nothing appeared on the screen, he advanced the tape to 7:37. Sure enough, Jason was in the frame, turning the combination to open the vault door. A large bag hung loosely over his shoulder. Stu tried to tell whether the bag was empty, but the monitor flipped to another camera. When it returned to camera five again the door was open and Jason was gone from the scene.

Stu advanced the tape until camera five came into view once more. Nothing. He advanced it again. Jason appeared again, this time coming out of the vault with the large blue bag bulging in front of him. The picture was clear. He waited for another pass of the camera, but by the time it returned to camera five the door was closed and Jason had disappeared.

Stu couldn't wait to reach 2:30 p.m. Jason had to be there. He just knew it. He spent the next fifteen minutes forwarding through the tape trying to find the right time. Annie had said she went to the ladies' room every day at 3:00 p.m. There was Jason again with the same blue bag, again opening the door to the book vault. The timing was perfect. Stu looked through a half-dozen more tapes before he felt comfortable. As he viewed the tapes he noticed the guards switched off every other day. *This isn't about loans,* Stu surmised.

As he continued to flip through the tapes, Stu thought his mind was beginning to play tricks on him. Cameras eight and nine, with their wide-angle lenses, covered the entire lobby. In the center of the lobby floor was a large round carpet with the bank's name inscribed around its borders. In its center a bald eagle held two one thousand dollar bills in each talon. When reviewing the frames from different periods, he noticed that the eagle in the center of the carpet wasn't always in the same position as it was previously. Whatever the reason, it was enough for a watchful eye to pick it up on the tape. He'd had enough TV for the moment, so he grabbed another slice of pizza and started to look through the black notebook.

Marie came out of the bedroom all smiles. "Don't worry about Mom. After she ranted for a few minutes about my not calling she calmed down. She said she was glad to hear my voice and wanted to know if I was all right. I didn't know I'd be on the phone so long."

"I told you that's all she wants."

"I know. You're right. Anyway, she sends her love and hopes you call her tomorrow."

"I'll do that without fail." He passed her a paper plate. "Here... grab some pizza."

"You looked at the tapes already?"

He nodded. "I marked the counter number from the VCR so you can see what I was looking at. Just push fast forward and you should get to the spot."

"Did you see those guys going into the vault like you mentioned?"

"You bet I did!"

"Great! I can't wait to see them actually doing this. Didn't they know they were on camera?"

"They probably didn't care because they had all the tapes. Who was going to notice? Anyone would naturally think it was part of security procedures."

As Marie turned on the VCR, Stu began looking through the notebook. There was page after page of account numbers with foreign letters that were in code. There was a page titled Combos, which he assumed were combination numbers to something. Many of them he didn't understand, but one group of numbers caught his eye. It read *R-45 L-22 R-16 L-0 bv. I know that one. It's the combination to the book vault.* He was almost sure of it. *How in the hell did Cranston get this information?* All bank combinations were under dual control and the numbers are kept under tight security. There was another combination: *R-29 L-14 R-33 L-2 bv2. That must be the inside safe in the back of the sliding cabinet!*

He flipped through several more pages in the notebook. The more he flipped the more interesting it got. He couldn't make any sense of all the coded numbers because they weren't even close to the banks numbering system. He would have to do some cross checking with Dennis Swayzee. Maybe they could find a match and where the accounts were maintained.

The intercom buzzed.

"Marie, get that, will you please?"

"Hello?"

"This is security. I have a gentleman here to see—"

"That's fine, we know he's coming. Please show him up."

"We'll be glad to, Ma'am."

"I guess Ray finally made it. I guess he got the directions right."

"I guess he did. It seems about the right time for him to be here." Stu said.

"Dad, these tapes are really something! I see what you were talking about. These guys were really bad news."

The doorbell rang and Marie headed for the door with Stu following close behind. She opened it and there stood the security guard and Pete Langworth.

Marie's mouth fell open. Stu grabbed her by the arm and pulled her back. "What are you doing here and how did you find us?"

Pete reached into his jacket and Stu was on him like a bear. He took Pete to the floor, then pinned both hands. The security guard stepped on the hand that was holding an object.

Pete writhed angrily. "Please, goddamnit, I can explain! What the hell is wrong with you people?"

"Don't ask me what's wrong with us, you sonofabitch! What are you doing here and what's going on with you and my daughter?"

"Dad, let him explain."

"He isn't getting up unless he has a really good story."

Pete glared at the security guard. "Get off my hand, you jerk!"

The guard shook his head. "Not a chance."

"My ID is in my hand. Look at it!"

The guard knelt and retrieved the ID. "Mr. Stuart, I think you better let him up. He's a DEA agent. The picture here is the same guy on the floor. There is no mistake about it."

"What? You're shitting me!"

Marie glared down at Pete. "Pete, what's going on?"

Stu grabbed the brown leather case from the guard and looked at it, then shifted and let Pete get up. "Hey... sorry."

Pete shook his head. "Not necessary. In fact, it makes me feel good that you didn't have the slightest hint. That means I was doing my job. Believe me, there were many times when I wanted to tell you or give you some hints."

Stu glance at the security guard. "Thanks. Sorry for all the fuss."

"That's all right. We're going to change some procedures around here."

Marie pushed past her father and threw her arms around Pete. "Why didn't you tell me what you were doing? How could you have lied to me all these weeks?"

"I had no choice in the matter. I just couldn't say anything."

Stu asked, "Well, what's all this stuff about you being a golf pro. Do you really work over at the club?"

"Yes I do, but I'm not a professional golfer. They think I am, and I want to keep it that way for the time being."

"I don't understand? How did you pull that off?"

"I've always been a pretty good scratch golfer. I've been playing since I was seven years old. My father was the golf pro at the Knoll Country Club in Boonton, New Jersey during its hay day in the fifties."

"Get out! Boonton?"

"Yeah, in fact, he died on the golf course. Anyway, I play pretty well. When I joined the DEA, it wasn't long before they wanted me down here. Cranston is our man, and it seemed that my background fit the best, especially since we both went to the same college. We don't care about his other activities at the bank except for his drug involvement and where all the money is going. If we can get him on anything else it only makes our case stronger. I don't have any real proof that he killed Tom Wallace, but the evidence seems to be there."

"What do you mean?" Stu asked.

"The jerk keeps his crossbow and arrows in the trunk of his car. I saw it once when he opened his trunk to put some golf clubs away. I knew he used a crossbow, and there it was in plain sight. Wallace was killed by a crossbow, right?"

Marie put her arm around Pete's waist. "Let's go into the living room and hear the whole story. We need to tell you what happened today, too."

They walked into the room. Marie brought over the pizza box and soda, and the phone rang.

Stu answered. "Yes? Hi. Please send him up." He hung up. "Ray's on his way up."

Within a few minutes the guard and Ray appeared at the door. Ray put his arms around Marie and squeezed her tightly, kissing her on the forehead. "Am I glad to see you! It's been a long time. Are you okay? I want to hear what happened today."

Stu came up and shook his hand. "It's good to see you too, Ray." He led Ray to Pete. "I want you to meet Pete Langworth. He's DEA."

They shook hands.

Stu finished the introduction. "Pete, Ray's chief of detectives in Wakefield, New Jersey. He's down here helping me out of the mess I'm in."

Pete nodded. "Stu and Marie just found out I'm DEA. I'm supposed to be the assistant golf pro at the club. Marie and I met and became close awhile back."

"How did you pass off the golf pro stuff?" Ray asked.

"The agency paved my way through the PGA and got me the necessary credentials. That's how I met Cranston."

"By coincidence?"

Pete shook his head. "Hardly. We had our eye on him for the past fifteen months, but no one could get close to him until we started looking into his past. We tried to find something that could get us closer to him without looking suspicious. We knew he liked golf so we followed him for months to just about every golf course in south Florida. We needed something else other than golf and that's where I came in to the picture. Cranston graduated from Dartmouth. He was a marksman and state champion with the crossbow."

Stu raised one hand. "Are you sure you're talking about the right person? Don't you have your facts a little mixed up here?"

"Not at all. I know you think I have him mixed up with Cain, but there's more to the story. They both went to the same college. They were both on the crossbow team and were both champions. Des won more titles and competed on a higher level than Cranston, but they both knew how to use the bow better than most. They graduated together and came here to Florida. They've known each other all their lives."

Ray issued a low whistle. "So you don't think Des killed Tom Wallace?"

"No, I don't. Des is a thief and an embezzler, but he isn't a killer from what I can see."

Ray shook his head. "So where do you come in?"

"I'm also a crossbow champion from Dartmouth, but in a different league, and I'm from the class of 1988. I was on both the golf and crossbow team and if I hadn't gotten in a car accident and broken my wrist I'd have made the U.S. Olympic archery team."

Stu was amazed. "You too? This is unreal!"

"This association just didn't happen. We ran Cranston's background through a computer with thousands of agents trying to find a complement and they lucked out. I was the match."

"How did you work the golf thing out?" Ray asked.

"Cranston was an avid player and they were always looking for new assistant pros at the club. He was chairman of the search committee, so when any new club pro came to town to be interviewed, Cranston always did the interview. I'll never forget the look on his face when he interviewed me and found out I was from the same college and knew how to fire the crossbow. Telling him I'd just missed making the Olympic team was icing on the cake. He hired me that day. I had to play a few rounds with some of the other pros at the club, but I blew them all away except for Dave, the head professional. He's exceptional."

Ray was rapt with attention. "So what's the situation with Cranston?" asked Ray.

"Well, I got pretty close to him. He trusted me a lot and always made sure I remembered who got me the job at the club. I pretended to be very thankful so he would let his guard down and perhaps use me for some of his other dealings. I got a break about three months ago when he asked me if I were financially all right. I told him I was having problems making ends meet, but I was getting by. He told me he had something he wanted me to do and would pay me enough money so that I wouldn't have to worry about any more bills. I hesitated a little to make him think I was really green and wouldn't consider anything illegal, I finally called and told him if it was anything risky I wouldn't be interested. I continued to convince him that I did need the money. I was running a pick-up service. Once a day I was responsible for picking up a night depository bag from six convenience stores here in the county."

"Six?" Stu asks.

"That's right."

"I'm surprised we have that many stores," Stu said.

Pete nodded. "And don't forget, I'm not the only guy doing this. There were five more just like me doing the same thing in contiguous counties. All of them are depositing these night bags, and guess where?"

"At the bank in Fortune Beach," Stu replied.

Marie looked at Stu. "Dad, you knew about this?"

He shook his head. "Not until a couple of days ago. I knew something was going on down in the basement vault, but I couldn't put my finger on it. I just found out that the guards were taking money from a secret safe in the vault. The video shows the whole thing and how they did it, but I never knew how much money was involved."

"Well, let me open your eyes a little," Pete said. "If everybody deposited the same amount I did each day that would be thirty-six pickups every twenty four hours. If each bag held about five thousand dollars, that would be one hundred eighty thousand dollars a day, or about five or six million a month. Not bad for a little extra business cash, huh?"

Ray was stunned. "They're moving that much cocaine down here?"

"Are you kidding? They can't get enough of it. What I can't understand is how they're getting the cocaine the hell in here and where all the money is winding up."

"Well," Marie said. "Since everyone else is contributing, I can tell you that the daily deposits were close to five thousand dollars per store."

"How do you know anything about that?" Ray asked.

She then told Pete and Ray what had happened to her earlier at Alex Cranston's law office and at the shopping center.

Stu said, "She's lucky to be alive. I'm lucky I got there when I did. Just a few seconds more and who knows what would have happened"

Pete paled. "Jesus! How did they even know she was at the shopping center?"

"All the phones in the bank were tape recorded. You should see the system in back of the security desk. They knew everything that was going on. I'm surprised I'm still alive." He pointed toward the VCR tapes. "Take a look at those tapes and you'll see some very interesting stuff going on inside the bank."

Marie looked at Pete. "Pete, how did you know we were here?"

"I just put it together. You weren't at home or at your father's house, and then I remembered you telling me about your grandparents and their condo in Boca Raton. You drove me by the place, remember?"

Marie nodded.

He shrugged. "I walked up to the security gate and you know the rest."

"Marie how do you know so much about the deposits?" Stu asked her.

"Dad, you aren't going to be a happy about this, but I removed some of the pages from the notebook because they had Pete's name in them. I wasn't sure and I was confused and wanted to know what his relationship was with Cranston. I had to talk to him before I let you know what he was doing. I was hoping there was an answer, but it's all spelled out in the pages."

"It's all right. I understand why you did it. Can you get the pages for us now, please?"

"I can't wait to see this," said Pete.

As Marie left the room to retrieve the torn pages, Stu started the VCR and showed Ray and Pete how the two guards made the pickup each day. After reviewing a few of the tapes they were convinced that was the method used to get the money into the bank.

"That has to be right," Pete said. "Each day I started my pickups at 4:00 a.m. and 12:00 p.m. Some afternoons Cranston would have to get someone else because I was out on the course, or we'd have to leave it till the next morning. He never liked these stores holding too much money at any one time."

"I can't believe all these stores were selling cocaine to their customers," Ray said. "I'd have thought someone would have gotten caught by now. The distribution system not only had to be huge, but they had to be careful of blowing their cover and selling this stuff to the wrong person."

Pete nodded. "After a few pickups I got how the program worked. Everything was done through the lottery machine in each store. If you wanted a bag of coke you went to the lottery machine and purchased a one-dollar ticket. The lottery card you gave the attendant had to have a small yellow dot in the right hand corner. For twenty-one dollars you got a lottery ticket, a bag of cocaine and your card back in a nice packaged insert. No yellow dot, no coke. The yellow dot program worked. There was no talking or discussion with the store clerk. You gave your money and you got your ticket and package. If you were not recommended by a current user, you could forget it. The rules were strict and the system was efficient. Each store owner got one thousand dollars a day. It was up to the owner how the shifts worked, but the system didn't tolerate any mistakes or shortages of money on the pickup. Five stores burnt to the ground this year alone in southern Florida and two owners disappeared six months ago and haven't been heard from since."

Stu asked, "What did you make as a runner?"

"We're called Smurfs. Alex paid me through wire transfers, and every dime is accounted for. Cranston wires money to my account every Monday and it's at least fifteen grand a week."

"Why does he have to wire the money?" asked Ray.

"Beats the hell out of me, but the money comes in from offshore banks in the form of a wire."

Stu said, "I have been following some of those wires. I don't have all the answers yet, but there's a great deal of money leaving the bank going to offshore banks. I also think it's Cranston sending the wires. If you take a look in the notebook on the table over there, you'll see some security code numbers and letters used in the bank's Trust Department. I can figure that much out, but I don't know yet how this is being done and through what accounts. I'm now waiting for a call from a friend of mine in our correspondent bank in New York. I'm hoping he has some answers for me."

Ray went to the table, picked up the black notebook and started flipping through the pages.

Marie said, "Pete's bank statements show about $240,000 in the account right now."

"Pete, how did you get so much in the account?" Ray asked. "I thought you were only doing this the past three months?"

"Before I started, he gave me $75,000 and told me to pay off all my loans except my car. He doesn't like anyone working for him that owes money."

"Nice guy."

"He was buying some loyalty; at least that's all I could imagine. I think he might have had some other plans for me down the road. I never found out what they were."

Stu said, "Guys, I want to show you something else that I found on the tape. Maybe I'm over reacting, but I'd like to know what you think about this." He fast forwarded the tape until it reached the frames showing the main bank lobby. "Here, take a look at the carpet in the center of the floor. Watch the position of the eagle in the carpet." Stu forwarded another tape almost to the end and stopped at the lobby.

"There... there!" He pointed to the carpet. "The goddamn eagle has moved from its original position. See?"

"I see that... but why?" Ray asked.

"I believe, and it's only a hunch, that there's more going on under the lobby floor than in the lobby itself. Something is not right there."

Pete's eyes grew wide. "Under the lobby floor?"

Stu shrugged. "Hey, that's my hunch."

"Let's assume you're right," said Ray. "If there's any money down there it's either gone by now or will be gone soon. When the news gets out, everyone who's connected to this scam will be scrambling for the money."

"I have a half-dozen agents on call. We would have shut this operation down long ago, but the problem was we could never find the money. We needed some more time to flush out the other characters in this drug ring, but we're pretty sure we know who they all are now. We've been on this for months, but we just couldn't seem to crack the damn thing. I think we should go tonight, right now, before it's too late and grab any money that's left. If Stu's right about this there won't be anything there by tomorrow morning."

Ray said, "Call your men and have them get over to the bank. Make sure no one gets involved or goes into the place until we get there."

Pete placed the call.

Marie handed Pete some papers as he passed by her in the kitchen.

Pete dialed a number and hung up, then waited for the call back. "Hey, the guy keeps good records. It's all here... every cent he gave me, including the dates. The jerk even has my name in the damn book! I don't believe it!"

Stu frowned. "A lot of the entries in this book are in code."

The phone rang and Pete spoke to someone.

Ray got Stu's attention. "Before we take off, I'd better tell you some of the things I found out in Lauderdale. A lot of people down there know a lot about what's going on up here. They know Des, or know of him, and he's not well liked. He's screwed a lot of business men down there over the years."

"Doesn't surprise me."

" Well, I found out some other stuff that will rock your socks. Des has a sweetheart by the name of Jessica?"

"Yeah."

"Well, that little sweetheart is giving him the ultimate screw and he doesn't even know it."

"Like what?"

"She's engaged."

"Engaged? To who?"

"To the one and only Johnny Mack."

Stu's eyes grew wide. "What?"

Stu tried to think. What did she have to gain by sleeping with Des if she were engaged to Johnny? Stu didn't trust her, but he didn't think this was possible. "So what's the deal?

Ray shrugged. "I'm only telling you what I heard. Nobody trusts Des. They weren't taking any chances with him calling the shots at the bank. Mack and Cranston wanted to know his every move and the only way they could tell what was going on was to have someone very close to him." He shrugged again. "Some people view relationships differently than others. What can I say? Cranston set the whole thing up. This Johnny Mack character could be telling Cranston what to do. I'm not sure yet, but it's beginning to look like that from what I hear. I'm getting a rundown on him. We should know something by morning.

Stu thought back to the other day when he'd met Johnny having breakfast at Harry's Café. *He seemed to know a hell of a lot more about what was going on than he should have known*.

"Hey, Hendrick's the guy from the Justice Department?"

"Yeah."

"Well, you're not going to hear much of him anymore."

"Why?"

"I thought I knew him better than I did. I hear he got suspended from his job. Seems he walked into a house somewhere down here that agents had under surveillance and blew a fifteen month undercover investigation. The DEA had him yanked off the job here."

"What was he doing there?"

"I hear he had a hooker with him that's all I know."

"Well, from what Marie told me about him, his curtain was about to come down anyway."

Pete said, "Stu, my guys will be there in ten minutes. Let's get out of here."

"I'm going too," said Marie.

Stu looked at her. "No. You're staying right here and security is going to be put on full alert. Just relax and take it easy. You've already had a tough day."

"Well... okay, but be careful, please. These bums aren't worth dying over."

Chapter Thirty-Four

They decided to take the Mazda because Pete's agents would know the car.

As the car headed north, Stu thought about all that had happened in the last few weeks. He wondered whether he would ever find out who really killed Tom and Charlotte.

Ray interrupted his thoughts. "It's a little late to be asking you this now, but do you have a key or something? Isn't the bank on some type of security?"

"Well, we used to have the guards, but I don't know what the situation is now." He glanced at Pete. "Here, Pete, let me have the phone. I'll find out what's going on over there."

Pete looked at him. "Who can you call?" asked Pete.

"I'm calling Des."

Pete stared. "You're what? You're shittin' me, right?"

"Why not? I'm not going to let him think that I'm running away from anything. A lot of shit happened today and it would be interesting to see how he reacts when he hears my voice."

The phone rang twice.

"Hello?"

"Jessica? It's Stu."

"Stu, where are you? We have been trying to call you all evening. Are you all right?"

"I'm in my car. I can't tell you exactly where I'm because I'm not sure if the line is tapped in some way. I'm on a cell phone."

"Hold on. Des wants to talk to you." Stu detected concern in her voice.

"Stu where in the hell are you? What's going on?"

"Des, I don't have much time to talk, but I'm sure you know what's going on. Your two security guards are dead. They tried to harm Marie."

"Marie? You've got to be crazy. I heard something about a woman being involved, but not Marie."

Stu ignored him. "And not only are both guards lying in the morgue right now, but Walter Dobbs is lying right next to them."

"I heard. The cops were here earlier questioning me as to what I knew about those guards and my relationship with Walter. Walter was a good friend and did a few investments with me, but that's the end of it. What about you?"

"Me? I don't know, Des, but I can tell you one thing: I'm not going to wind up like those characters."

"Stu, I had nothing to do with any of these unfortunate killings. You have to believe me. I'm not a murderer. You can call me whatever you want, but murder isn't my style."

"Tell me, how did you let all this shit go on in the bank? You're just as guilty. Listen, I don't want to talk about that now. I'm more interested about the security of the bank. The guards aren't around anymore so what's going on? Who is watching the place?"

"This all happened so suddenly. We couldn't get anyone on short notice who knows the systems, so I instructed operations to put on all the alarms and we'll work it out in the morning."

"That sounds like a good idea."

"Stu listen, I'm sorry about the altercation earlier. I wanted you outta here, but I've had time to rethink my decision and I was wrong. I'll be the first to admit my mistakes. You have to believe I had nothing to do with what you just told me about Marie. You have to know I'd never hurt her."

"Someone had it in for her. Tell me, did you know that your phone was bugged in your office, and that there was a tape monitoring system throughout the bank?"

Dead silence. "What.? Tape recorded conversations? People listening to my personal phone calls?"

"Yes, and I have some of the tapes."

"That's hard to believe, but if it's true I know who's behind it. Goddamnit! I never knew—the sonofabitch... I'll see you later."

Ray looked at Stu. "Well, what did he say?"

"He's not a murderer and the alarm system is on."

"Do you know how to disarm it?"

"We're going to find out soon enough. I haven't used the alarm system in years, but I know my code number like the back of my hand. Remembering all the other shit is what bothers me." He glanced at Pete. "Pete, while we have a few minutes, tell me what the hell happened to Dave Docker. You know the guy from the Justice Department?"

"I thought his name was Hendricks?" asked Ray.

"No, Docker was his assistant. He was found dead on the golf course. They found him on one of the holes buried in a sand trap with a seven iron embedded in his skull."

Pete said, "It was funny though... Docker spoke with me a few days ago in the pro shop. I'd never seen the guy before. He was skinny as shit and wore this cheap suit that was too small for him. The guy was really out of date and he certainly wasn't there to play golf."

"What did he want?"

"It was strange. He asked me if I'd ever been to Australia."

"Australia? Why the hell would he think that?"

"I don't know what he thought. He asked me about places there like *Lightning Ridge, Sydney* and *White Cliffs*. I really didn't know what the hell he was talking about. The conversation was going nowhere and made no sense to me at all. I got busy with customers and didn't know what happened to him until I heard about finding him on the course."

"This is the exit coming up," Stu said. He grabbed the black notebook off the seat next to him and turned on the overhead light in the back. He fumbled through the pages looking for the area where Cranston had copied down the offshore account numbers. Something Pete had just said clicked in his mind and he had to satisfy his curiosity. *There it is! Sidney and an account number. I thought it was a guy named Sidney. Instead it was an account number that would lead to a bank in Sydney, Australia.*

As they approached the bank, the parking lot lights cast a dim glow over the area. There in the corner of the lot sat two black cars side by side with their lights off. Pete pulled in front of the cars and turned off his headlights. Four agents emerged cautiously from the vehicles and approached.

"Good timing. It didn't take you very long," said the agent.

"What's going on?"

"Nothing unusual. There's a lot of night deposit activity, but that's about it."

They were going over plans to enter the building when a car pulled into the lot and proceeded toward the night deposit drop.

Pete said, "Watch. Here's one of the drops taking place right in front of us. Cranston has this thing figured out where everyone doesn't merge on the bank at once. He's staggered the drops so nothing seems too unusual."

Ray said, "The fact that someone's still dropping cash tells me that the word didn't get around to all the Smurfs and stores about what happened today. And the guards are dead, so who's picking up the money from the safe in the morning?"

"We'll have to take care of that later," Stu said.

They left one agent outside in the car just in case any cops showed up and saw activity inside the bank. Pete carried a radio with him in case there were problems outside once they were in the bank. Once Stu inserted the key into the lock he would have sixty seconds to reach the Wells Fargo alarm system and shut it down. If he failed, the place would be crawling with cops within minutes. Of course, that wouldn't necessarily be a bad thing. As he opened the door slowly, a soft buzzing sound came from the security area. He ran behind the desk, pressed the Activate button, and inserted his five-digit code number: 12212. The green light went on and the buzzer stopped.

To gain entrance into the main lobby floor, they had to pass through the double glass security doors. He inserted his access card and the doors opened. As they approached the carpet in the center of the bank lobby, he thought, *What if I'm wrong? All this for nothing.*

Pete, Ray and Stu looked at each other as the agents stood watch at the bank entrance. They all bent down and grabbed a section of the carpet that was inlaid below the floor level.

It lifted quite easily along with a solid slab of plywood below the carpet. Stu pointed. "Oh my God!!"

A stainless steel safe, approximately eight feet in diameter, lay at their feet. On the surface two black dials lay opposite each other. Above each dial was a red light and a green light. The red light was shining brightly. In the center of the door, an amber-colored glass compartment housed digital buttons, and that had them totally confused.

Ray said, "Stu, we have major problems here. How are we going to get past these combinations? How are we going to get this thing open?"

"Hold on. Let me think this out." Stu swiped his lip with his forefinger.

"I don't like the looks of this," Pete said.

Stu nodded. "Me either, but take it easy. I think I have some of the answers. I'll let you know in a minute." He reached for the black notebook wedged in his hip pocket. "This book holds the answer to this safe." He flattened the book on the floor. He peeled through the pages until he found what he'd seen before: two number combinations. "Pete, come over here and hold the book open for me."

Pete scooted over next to him and placed his hands solidly on the notebook.

"On the left side, those two sets of numbers... read them to me slowly, one set at a time."

"The ones that end with the letters BV?"

"No. I think those are for the book vault. Read the ones underneath."

"I see them. Okay, ready?"

"Yeah."

"Right 5... Left 8... Right 42... Left 51."

"Nothing."

"Do it again!" said Pete.

Stu spun the dial to exactly the numbers Pete called out.

Nothing!

"Give me the next set of numbers, quick!" Stu said.

"Here we go... Right 7... Left 28... Right... 16... Left 30."

"Got it!"

As the last number clicked into place the red light went off and the green light flashed on.

Pete pumped his fist. "Yes!"

"Give me the other number, quick!" Stu said.

"Here we go... Right 5... Left 8... Right 42... Left 51."

"Got it."

The red light went out and both green lights were now glowing. Ray said, "Okay, where do we go from here?"

Stu was at a loss. He stared at the amber glass in the center of the safe knowing this was the fail-safe. He stared at the numbers.

Ray shook his head. "Stu, we're dead. No way are we going to open this."

"Let me think!"

Stu could feel them staring at him. He just had to concentrate on the glass. Five digits.... Just below the glass Wells Fargo was etched in the stainless steel. *I only know one number that carries five digits.* "Well guys, cross your fingers because this is probably not going to work." Stu pressed each number slowly, watching the amber glass project the numbers he'd just pressed

1... 2... 2... 1....

"Put in the last number, Stu!" Ray said.

Stu pressed the number 2 ever so slightly.

A laser light beam shot from overhead, piercing the amber glass.

"Jesus Christ, what's happening?" cried Ray.

Stu yelled, "We did it!"

The door of the huge safe began to retract ever so slowly. In a few seconds a huge hole appeared. They all stared into the dark entrance below.

Ray said, "Check it out! A stairway. There's a room down there!"

As Stu proceeded down the stairway he could feel the change in the temperature.

The cool and musty smell reminded him of his adventures in the book vault. It was dark and he had no flashlight. He had to feel his way down the stairs while holding onto the stair railing. He finally reached a cement floor.

Pete lit a match, trying to find a light switch.

"There, above you, is the switch," said Ray.

Stu flipped it on and the darkness disappeared. He gazed about the room in amazement. It wasn't what he expected as compared to the elaborate systems needed to get into the place. The room was rectangular, approximately 8 x 20 feet. From the looks of things there hadn't been any activity down here in years.

"Boy, what a shitty looking dump this place turned out to be," Pete said.

They all stood looking at the bottom of the stairway fixing their eyes on the faded gray cinder block walls, which supported the metal shelving. Hundreds of cans of food rations, bottles of water, and medical supplies were gathering dust in the silent tomb. Six fold-up army cots were leaning against the wall in the far corner of the room.

Ray shook his head. "This is nothing but an old civil defense air raid shelter. Look at the signs on the wall. They've got to be fifty years old." said Ray.

"This place was probably used during WWII and probably around the time of the Cuban missile crisis," said Pete.

Stu looked around as frustration began to build on his face. "This is bullshit. Something's wrong with this picture. They wouldn't create such an elaborate, *Star Wars* combination system for this vault if it were only an air raid shelter. What are we missing? Keep looking guys. The answer has to be here."

They searched everywhere tearing through cabinets, shelving, and old drawers. Wherever there was a space they searched. Finally, they stood in the center of the room trying to put the pieces together. If no money was here, what was this place used for?

"Are you guys all right down there?" said one of the agents. "Do you need help down there? How much longer are you going to be?"

"We're okay. We'll be up in a few minutes." Stu looked at the clock on the wall, which read 12:55.

Ray stared at the clock. Something wasn't right.

Stu noticed the look on his face. "Ray, what's wrong?"

"That second hand... on the clock over on the wall. It's not moving." He snapped his fingers. "It's the clock! What would a clock be doing in a place where there are no people?" Ray lifted the clock off its support. Behind it was a silver toggle switch.

"What did I tell you? *I just knew it!"* cried Ray.

Stu flipped the switch and a low, grinding noise came from the far end of the room. They all looked in the direction of the noise. The cinder block wall at the end of the room was sliding to the left, retracting into the wall.

The room was about the same size as the room they were in, but recessed lighting in the ceiling and white walls made it look much larger than it actually was. The floor was white-ribbed ceramic tile gave the appearance of a hospital operating room. A ventilation system brought in fresh air. A small bathroom with a toilet and a sink sat off in a corner of the room. On the wall to the right of the entrance a black marble counter ran the full length of the room and four swivel chairs were neatly arranged underneath. Several money counting machines, large buckets of rubber bands, pens, pencils and note pads sat on the counter. There were also several magnifying glasses, tweezers, small plastic containers, a microscope and jeweler's glasses. On the opposite wall were two sets of fan-fold doors.

Ray walked over and opened the first set of doors and stared. "Now boys, this is what I call a bank. Could you imagine having a closet like this in your house?"

Bags of money were stacked on top of each other, leaving very little room for the door to close.

Ray said, "There must be millions here. How were they ever going to get rid of all this money?"

Stu said, "By the looks of the equipment, I'm sure they knew what they were doing."

Pete and Stu pulled a number of canvas bags out and dumped the money on the counter.

Stu issued a low whistle. "Check it out. It's counted, wrapped and recorded. This bag of twenties contains one hundred and sixty thousand dollars, and that's only one bag. Just imagine what the total inventory is worth."

Pete said, "What pisses me off are the millions that must have left here already. Cranston must have wired the money the hell out of the country by now and I know we'll never see it again. I'm glad at least we were able to get this stuff. But how in the hell is he getting the cash outta here?"

"We're going to find that out. It's going to be interesting to see who comes for this loot in the next day of so," Stu said. "I wouldn't be surprised to see someone here in the next few hours."

"You're right," Ray said. "We'd better get our asses moving if we don't want to blow this. Are we taking this stuff with us or not?"

Pete shook his head. "Let's leave it here and call for an armored truck as soon as we find out who comes for the money. Let's wait outside and see who shows up. It can't be any safer than here in the bank right?"

"Hey, you're right but Pete, check out the other door there and give me a quick count on the number of bags you have."

Pete opened the folding doors and was stunned. "I think you guys better get over here fast!"

Stu looked. "Man alive! Did you ever see anything like this?"

Ray shook his head. "It's the most beautiful sight I have ever seen."

Each shelf was encased in its own glass. A white satin cloth draped the base of the glass cabinets, allowing the gemstones in each of the cases to radiate their beauty before them.

"Look at them," Stu said. "opals... thousands of beautiful opals."

Each case contained so many opals they were too numerous to count. Stu took out a few from each case, and went over to the counter where a more intense light afforded a better view the gems. Both Pete and Ray came over and started inspecting the stones as well. Every color of the rainbow was represented in one form or another. Pete spotted a beautiful black stone the size of a quarter that had flashes of fire red throughout changing to a more brilliant crimson as Pete moved his hand under the light.

"How in the hell do you value these things?" asked Pete.

"By carats, like they do with diamonds," Stu said

Pete pointed to the gem in Stu's hand. "How many do you think that one has?"

"I don't know, but I'd guess somewhere around forty to fifty carrots. I wouldn't be surprised if this stone brings $250,000. Hey, let's get this stuff the hell back in the glass and get out of here. Tomorrow's another day. I'll leave a couple of guys outside until the morning. If nobody shows up, we get the money and gems out of here. Boy are Cranston and his shitheads in for a big surprise."

They began to gather up the stones on the counter to put them where they belonged. Suddenly a loud shrieking noise echoed through the room.

Ray grabbed Stu's arm. "What the hell is that?" he said.

The stones flew in all directions. "I don't know," Stu responded.

Ray glanced up. "Oh my God! The safe door is closing! Let's get the hell out of here!"

Then another noise—something was being dropped into the ventilation system from above. Clouds of white smoke billowed into the room.

"What the hell is that?"

"Run! Get into the other room and close the door!" Stu said.

Stu was headed for the bottom of the stairs when he looked back for Ray, who was lying face down on the floor.

Chapter Thirty-Five

Stu awoke lying on his back. The cement floor was cold and hard. The room was pitch black. So this is what it's like to be at the abyss of death... dead silence, cold and dark. He stretched out his arm and felt the bottom of the stairs that led into the air raid shelter. Now he knew where he was. He rolled onto his side and rose slowly. He felt for the stairway again and decided to sit a moment on the bottom step trying to clear the cobwebs from his head. Whatever had come out of the ventilation system hadn't given him a chance to respond. It was instantaneous and complete. *Death was that close and I didn't even get a chance to say goodbye to Becca. What's a banker doing in the midst of all this? What am I trying to prove? Screw the FDIC!*

Then another thought came to mind: *Ray and Pete! Where are they?* He reached up and fumbled for the light switch, then flipped it on. Ray lay face down on the floor. Stu eyes darted the floor for Pete, but he wasn't in the room. He turned on the light in the other room, but Pete was nowhere to be found. *Where the hell is he?* Stu thought.

He moved over to Ray and turned him on his back. He was alive, breathing. He began to stir, then blinked his eyes and looked at Stu standing above him. He rubbed his face with his hands.

Stu said, "Take it easy, Ray. This isn't going to go away all at once."

"What the hell happened? I remember following you out the room and that was it."

"Same here. Whatever that stuff was it sure was potent."

"Is Pete all right?"

"He's gone."

"Gone? Dead?"

"No, not dead. He's nowhere to be found."

"Help me get up," Ray said.

Stu extended his arm and pulled Ray's big frame up as he steadied to his feet. "Take it easy."

"You're right... this shit really hits you hard. My head feels like a soccer ball."

"You'll be all right in a few minutes."

"How long do you think we were out?"

"I don't know... seemed like only a few minutes to me."

Ray walked steadily to the top of the stairs and tried to push the safe door open. "What the hell are we going to do? How are we going to get out of here? And where the hell is Pete?"

"I'm not sure, Ray... I'm not sure." He walked toward the other room. Something hadn't felt right in there before. "That sonofabitch Cranston beat us to the punch, Ray! Look! Everything is gone! It's all gone! He cleaned the place out!"

Not only were the money and gems gone, but all the equipment had been removed. There was nothing left.

"How could we have been such fools to let something like this happen? We let our guard down and stayed in here too long."

Ray wondered what happened to the agents who were watching the place.

Stu noticed a sheet of paper lying on the counter at the far end of the room. It was a note addressed to him. He read it aloud: "Stu, This isn't your business. Take your daughter and go before you're both dead. You're alive because of a friend. Langworth wasn't as lucky. Forget us. We're gone forever. Hank." He turned the note over, then back. "That's all it says?"

"Hank! Who the hell is Hank?" Ray asked.

"The only Hank I know is the mayor," Stu replied.

"The mayor?"

"Yeah! The mayor of Fortune Beach... Hank Stone. The one you've not quite figured out."

"I knew he was in this damn thing all along!"

Stu shook his head. "I can't believe it. He's an average guy, has a great house on the ocean, and lots of people like him. He was always low key. He retired years ago and made most of his money from op—Jesus mother of God!"

"What is it?"

"It's him! Stone! He was an opal dealer! How could I have forgotten? When I first came to the bank, I met him through Des, and Peg Neff, the newspaper lady. She was pretty close to him. He used to bring in these opals wrapped in tissue paper to show me what he'd just bought. I couldn't believe the things were so valuable."

"So that's how you knew so much about these stones before?"

"I really don't know that much about them. Just what I've heard over the years. Stone's father used to live in Australia. He was a lapidary, a person who works with precious stones. He made a fortune back around 1915 in Australia mining opals. He found some of the largest in the world in a place called *Lightning Ridge*. That's the place Pete was talking about. Docker, the government guy was asking all those questions at the pro shop. Didn't he say that? *Lightning Ridge?* How in the hell could I have forgotten this?"

Ray nodded. "You're right. That was the place he mentioned."

Stu shook his head. "Stone... I can't believe it. He was one of the guys behind this whole charade. He seemed so different. I would never have put two and two together."

Chapter Thirty-Six

Marie had fallen asleep on the leather couch in the living room, but a nightmare had awakened her. When she realized she was safe in her home, she was determined to think of more pleasant thoughts than her near kidnapping. She adjusted her head on the pillow and slowly closed her eyes, hoping to dream of the day she would marry Pete. Her dream was short lived, however, when she heard a whistling noise. She sat up for a moment in the darkness of the room and listened carefully. She'd left the sliding glass door over the balcony open a few inches. The wind off the ocean was howling and whistling through the crack in the door. She was cold and scared. The temperature in the room had dropped. She wondered what time it was. It had to be close to morning. The men weren't back yet. How long has it been?

Marie closed the sliding door and went over to the kitchen to look at the oven clock, which read 5:05 a.m. *Where are they? It's been five hours. Something's very wrong.*

She got dressed and told security she would be back later.

The guards were stunned by the activity so early in the morning. "Can we be of some help, Miss Stuart?"

"Not really. I'm looking for my father and his friends. They've been gone a long time and I'm worried."

"Where did they say they were going?" asked the guard.

"I think they were going to the bank over in Fortune Beach. They had some business there. I'm not too sure exactly. Listen, thanks for your offer, but I'll just drive over there. Maybe they're having coffee or something at Harry's Café."

"Okay, but watch your step. It's busy as can be over at the bank right now."

"What do you mean?"

"Well, it's been on the early news radio. It seems the paper came out with an article about the bank and I guess a lot of the customers are waiting for the place to open so they can get their money out of there."

"What?"

"Yeah. The place is going under, or so they say. There are cops all over the place because of the crowds so early in the morning. Can you believe it at five a.m.? So be careful."

"Thanks, I'll do that."

Twenty minutes later Marie made her way over the bridge heading for Fortune Beach Boulevard. Flashing red and blue lights illuminated the area in front of the bank. Two police cars were blocking traffic one block away. An officer approached her car and she rolled down her window. “What’s going on, Officer?”

"Sorry, Miss, but we’re not letting anyone down there. If you want to park your car and walk that's all right."

"What's going on?"

"Have you seen the *Fortune Star?* I guess the news wasn't so pleasant. Some congressman is involved along with the guy who runs the bank. They say the place is going out of business."

"Okay, thank you."

Marie parked her car and walked the block toward the bank. As she got closer she could see that the parking lot was full of people. There were three additional police cars parked in front of the bank entrance. Many people were drinking coffee and reading the paper, talking with each other. The crowd was well controlled at least to this point. She knew though, as time went on, the crowds would get bigger and if the bank didn't open on time she didn’t want to be around to see them vent their anger.

After looking through the crowd for a familiar face, Marie worked her way up closer to the bank. Perhaps they’re inside. She approached an officer and told him her problem.

From the look on the cop’s face he wasn't buying her story. "Look lady, I’ve heard the best of the stories. The bank opens at nine a.m. and no one is getting in any earlier. Sorry, but I have to do my job."

"I know you do, but I’m trying to reach my father who is in charge of this place. Look, here’s my identification. Look, if you don't believe me call someone at the police station and they’ll tell you. My father and I were at the scene yesterday when your police chief got killed. Walter Dobbs was trying to save my life and he got killed doing it."

"You're the girl at the shopping center?" He asked.

"Yes. That's what I have been trying to tell you. I think my father is inside the bank with two other men."

"Hold on. Let me get the division commander."

Marie waited as the police officer disappeared into the crowd. Within a few minutes he was back with what seemed to be his boss.

"Hi, Ma'am, my name is Studer... Jack Studer. I hear you knew our chief?" He wore a dark brown suede sport coat with a white shirt opened at the collar. Four gold chains hung around his neck with one hanging lower than the others with the letters ***S T U D*** spelled in gold looking like a highway billboard sign attached to the bottom of the chain. It wasn't quite six a.m. but he was wearing dark mirrored sunglasses and smelled as if he'd taken a bath in cologne.

Marie shook her head. "Not directly, but my father knew him very well. Look, my father and his friends left home five hours ago. I think they might be in the bank. My father is Vice Chairman of the board."

"We tried the doors and the bell. We don't think anyone is in there. We're trying to get someone down here to open the bank."

"Did you try getting in touch with my uncle, Desmond Cain, here in town?"

"Yeah, but the line is busy and we can't get through."

"He's only a few minutes away. Let's go over there."

Officer Studer showed her to a patrol car. They got in and within two minutes they were in the courtyard of Desmond Cain's mansion. Marie got out and walked to the front door with Studer trailing close behind. She rang the door bell.

Slowly the door opened and there stood Polly, the Jamaican housekeeper. "Good mornin'. May I help you?"

Studer flashed his picture and badge at her and the smile disappeared from her face. "Yes, I'm with the Fortune Beach Police Department. Is Mr. Cain available to talk with us?"

"Why I believe so. Please come in."

They walked into the foyer that was absolutely magnificent with its black and white checkered marble floor. In its center was the same round carpet inlaid into the marble that Marie saw on the video tape at the bank.

"Wait here please, and I'll get Mr. Cain."

As Polly walked away, Studer glanced around the room. "Well, one thing's for sure: he won't be waiting on any line for his money. It looks like he's got it all right here."

Polly returned and ushered them into the study where Des was just getting off the telephone.

He looked up. "Good morning. I know why you're here. My phone has been ringing off the hook all morning about the situation down at the bank. I can't believe the newspapers can get away with printing a story like this. It's not like Margaret Neff. I really don't understand this."

"Des, my dad is missing."

"Stu, missing? What do you mean, Marie?"

"That's why I'm here. I haven't heard from him since around eleven last night. He was on his way to the bank."

"Marie, I heard about your unfortunate incident yesterday. I'm so sorry. I'm glad you weren't hurt. Three people died over there and I knew them all. I feel so bad. I just don't understand how everything has gotten so far out of hand. I never in my wildest dreams envisioned anything like this."

"Mr. Cain, I think it would be best for all of us if you'd come down to the bank and try to work this out. There are a lot of people down there, and I'm afraid it's going to get much worse if someone from bank management doesn't talk to those people." Studer advised.

"What the hell am I going to tell them? Everything is fine? We're only good as long as the money doesn't run out."

"Well, it'll only get worse if no one shows up. Are you going to leave this on the shoulders of your staff? Those people want to hear from you, not some hundred dollars a week clerk," Studer said impatiently.

Des ignored him. "Marie, I heard from your father last night about ten or eleven. I don't know where he was. He asked me about the security at the bank, and I told him we didn't have any and that the alarm system is on for the night. That's the last I heard from him."

"I think he could be in the bank somewhere. I'm sure of it. He would have called me. I just know it."

"Marie, what do you want me to do?"

"Come down to the bank with me. Help me find my father, his friend and the guy I hope to marry."

"All right. Let's go." Des said heading for the door.

As they all walked out the front door, Des turned to Polly. "If I'm not back, don't forget to feed the cat."

As they turned off Atlantic Boulevard they could see that the crowd was bigger than ever. Studer looked at Des. "Is there another way I can take you to get into the building other than the front entrance?"

"Go around the bank to the employee side entrance. I can use my security card to get in but the alarm is going to go off once the motion detectors pick up our movements. I can reset the alarm once I get to the front of the bank."

"I'll radio the station and tell them what's going on."

As Studer radioed the police station, Marie spoke with Des. "My father was reviewing video tapes of the security areas of the bank. There are a lot of things he doesn't understand, especially what those guards were doing each day. We have them on tape. You'll be able to see them later. They went to the bank last night to see what was underneath the carpet in the middle of your lobby. They believed something is there. I need you to tell me what it is because they're going to find out sooner or later."

Des' face turned ashen. "There's a vault beneath that carpet Marie. I doubt very much anyone would have the slightest idea what it takes to open it. Your father didn't have access to that area of the bank."

"All I know is I need your help. I know something is wrong. You and Dad worked together for a lot of years. You owe it to him and Mom to help if he's in some sort of trouble."

As the police car pulled up to the side of the building a few people walked up to the car to see what was going on. One man cupped his hands, looked inside the window and saw Des in the back seat. He looked in again and then yelled back to the crowd, "Hey! It's Cain, the head of the bank! He's here in the car! He's going to open the bank!"

Once the crowd heard the news, they began to emerge around the car. Marie became frightened seeing so many faces looking in the window. The car began to rock gently.

Studer picked up the mike. "I better get some help over here fast before I lose this radio."

Someone outside yelled, "Get us our money and we'll leave. We want the bank to open *now!"*

The crowd began to push against the car with more force. "Come out of there!" were the yells from the crowd. Suddenly a half-dozen police officers emerged on the scene and the crowd began to thin out.

Studer said, "Listen, now is the time to get out of here. We can handle things better if you're out of sight inside the bank."

Des opened the door and got out of the car. Marie and Studer followed. Des slipped his card into the slot and the door opened.

A voice came from the crowd. "You can't hide in there forever, so you'd better deal with us now."

Once inside, Marie headed toward the carpet that caused so much controversy. "Well, Des, what's under here?"

He looked across at Marie for a moment and sighed. "Okay, everybody bend down and grab a piece of the carpet and lift. Ready?"

They lifted together, exposing the stainless steel vault with its multiple combinations.

Studer whistled. "Holy Christ! This looks like something you'd find in the Pentagon. How in the hell do you get in there?"

"We can't. The alarm system has to be shut down before any combinations can be used. It's part of the security system." Des responded.

"Do you have the combinations to get in here?"

"Yes. I'm the one who designed this thing." Des answered.

Below, Stu looked at Ray. "It'll be all right. Once 7:30 rolls around someone will be in the building. We can hit the vault door with a chair leg or something and—"

"Hold it. Did you hear that?" Ray said.

"What?"

"Listen."

They both stood motionless.

"There! Hear it?" Ray whispered.

"Yeah."

"Someone's up there doing something with the vault door," said Ray.

Stu ran up the stairs and tapped on the inner side of the vault.

He waited a few seconds and heard someone tapping back.

He tapped again, and again someone repeated.

Stu grinned. "They know we're here."

"Great! Thank God! We'll be glad to finally get out of this rat hole!"

"I hear them!" Marie cried. "They're down there! I heard them!" She knelt and looked at the vault door. "Dad! We're here!" she yelled.

She listened for a reply.

Nothing.

"I know they're down there. They answered. They're there!"

"I heard it too," Studer said.

"How do we get in here?" said Marie.

Des said, "We have to break the glass to the door over there in order to get to the alarm system. It's the only way. We need something heavy."

Studer picked up a stanchion used to rope off private areas of the bank. He walked over to the glass doors and swung it like a baseball bat. The glass shattered into thousands of pieces.

Des walked over to the Wells Fargo alarm system and punched in his five digit code number 93070. "Okay, we're all set." He knelt and spun the left combination a few times then fixed the number at each setting. The red light above the combination went off and the green light appeared. Des moved over to the other combination. He spun the dial and entered the numbers. Again the red light disappeared and the green light went on.

"Well, what now? It's not moving," Marie said.

"Just be patient, please Marie," said Des. He put his finger on the button below the amber glass and pressed his five digit security code number. A glowing red laser beam appeared from the ceiling and shot through the amber glass.

The stainless steel door began to retract beneath the floor. Within seconds a hand appeared through the crack as it opened wider. Marie knew it was her father by the Zuni ring on his right hand. Her heart began to race and she was filled with joy knowing they were alive.

The safe retracted halfway and Stu managed to climb out. He looked at Marie and smiled. "Honey, I don't know or care how you did it, but thanks. I'm so glad to be the hell out of there."

They held each other for a few seconds, not wanting to let go.

"Anyone want to help an old man out of this hole?" said Ray.

Stu reached down and pulled his friend out.

Marie looked down into the darkness. "Come on, Pete! Hurry up, before this thing closes."

Stu put his arm around Marie and hugged her. "Honey, Pete's not here with us."

"What are you talking about? How could he not be? He came with you, didn't he?"

"Yes. He was with us in the vault. Someone knew we were in the building all along. I don't know how this all happened. We had agents all over the place, inside and out. All we know is we heard the vault starting to shut. We tried to get out, but all of a sudden some sort of gas came through the ventilation system and knocked us out cold before we knew it."

"What happened to him?" cried Marie.

"I don't know, Honey... I don't know. We woke up and he was gone and so was all the money and opals we found. The vault was closed and we were locked in. We don't know where Pete is right now, but I'm sure he's safe." Stu tried to sound reassuring.

"Oh God! You know he's in danger! He's a drug agent! They'll kill him! They have to know who he is by now!"

"Hold on there," said Ray. "You're jumping to conclusions. He probably is with the people who cleaned the vault out, but that doesn't mean he's dead. In fact, I would think they would want him alive because he's the only bargaining chip they have."

Stu hugged her closer. "Marie, be strong. You have to believe we'll find him and he'll be safe."

Stu had all he could do to control himself just seeing Des in the same room. How many times had he looked the other way when Des was about to pull off another deal? *Enough of the past*, he thought. *He's at the end of his rope now, and he'll hang for the all the evil that he created because of his selfish greed.*

Stu looked up at the clock knowing that the bank would be opening soon. From the looks of the crowd outside and the noise and frustration in their voices, he knew Peg Neff had kept her word. Exposing Des had been the right thing to do. He looked at Des. "You told me on the phone earlier that you had nothing to do with all this and the killings. I think it's time for you to tell us what you know before we open these doors and you have to explain it to the group out there. Most of them only want their money, but I'll bet a few would like your hide as well."

"I never thought it would come to this. I wish I could turn back the clock, but I can't. The bastards screwed me too, so I owe them nothing. What do you want to know?"

Chapter Thirty-Seven

Twenty high-backed reddish-brown leather arm chairs were neatly placed along the black walnut board table. The board room was the most important room in the bank other than the vault. This was where all the important decisions were made once a month. This would be the command post of the FDIC once they officially declared the bank insolvent.

This room was where Desmond Cain had orchestrated some of the greatest fiascoes in lending one could ever imagine. Someone knocked on the door, then opened it. It was Dave Campbell, Chief Operations Officer. "Mr. Cain, what do you want us to do about the crowds? The police are letting the employees in, but they're very nervous and afraid there's going to be trouble."

Stu said, "Dave, pardon me, but I'm giving the orders now. I want you to go with Mr. Studer here. He'll make sure that police security will be inside the bank. The biggest mistake for us to make is not to open up the bank. How much money do we have in the vault?"

"I'm told we have about three million total, Sir."

"Okay, here's the plan. Anyone who has less than twenty thousand in their account, give them the balance. Those who have over twenty thousand they only get twenty grand maximum. That's it until this mess is cleared up. Just before we open I'll be down to make a statement, outside, so that everybody understands how the program is going to work until the FDIC gets here. Anyone who gives us a hard time will be asked to leave. Any problems and the police will escort them off the bank property. Is that clear?"

"Clear as a bell, Mr. Stuart."

Studer looked at Stu. "I'll be back in a few minutes, as soon as I get my men informed on what they should be doing. I want to talk to Mr. Cain later too." He and Dave Campbell left the room.

Stu looked over at Des. For once he looked like a beaten man. In fact, even his clothes didn't look good on him. His hair was uncombed and he was in need of a shave. No one has ever seen him in this condition before. But it didn't matter. He looked like he wanted it over himself.

"How about we play I tell, you tell?"

Des shrugged. "Whatever."

"Okay, I'll start. What do you know about Jessica?"

"She's my secretary and there's a good possibility I'm going to marry her, so forget about her as a witness."

"When did you see her last?"

"Earlier this evening. She answered the phone, remember?"

"It's the last time she's going to answer the phone at your house."

"What are you talking about?"

"Des, Jessica is engaged."

"What is this, a joke?"

"It's true. I checked it out."

"Yeah? To who?"

"One of your dear buddies... Johnny Mack. She's been sleeping with you all these months, giving you the time of your life, while all the time she's been telling Johnny everything that was going on at your home and at the office."

"You're full of shit!"

"Am I? Johnny Mack knew your every move. He never trusted you after his first deal. You always kept him on a short leash and he never forgot it. He teamed up with Cranston, and between the two of them they figured out a way to use you without you even knowing it. Your Achilles heel has always been broads. It was the one spot that they could penetrate. They needed someone they could trust... someone close and not an outsider."

Des looked at Stu without expression as he continued.

"Des, you never took the time to know anyone. You never knew Mack or anything about his private life. He and Cranston saw the opportunity and used it to their advantage. The chances of you ever seeing Jessica again are slim to none. I believe they all left for somewhere. By any chance, do you know where?"

"I'm not sure."

"Let me tell you something. The Feds aren't here yet, but when they find out one of their own, Pete Langworth, a Federal Drug Enforcement Agent, is missing, I wouldn't want to be you."

"I don't know where they are!"

"What do you know about Tom and Charlotte? Why did they have to die?" Stu asked.

"Cranston killed him. I know people thought it was me, but I hardly knew the kid. Cranston warmed up to him at the bank when he came in. Took him here and there. Bought him a couple of suits and some dinners and put some spending money in his pocket. He had a family with a couple of kids and needed the money. Before the kid knew it he was making changes to documents that involved partnerships Cranston was involved in. Taking fees that were supposed to be paid with commitments and doctoring up the bank tickets to make it look as if he'd paid them. Diverting money to his account and a lot of other stuff. I think the kid was getting nervous and Cranston wasn't taking any chances, so he got rid of him."

"What about Charlotte?"

Des shrugged. "I'm not sure what happened there. She used to be my secretary and she knew everything. She was always tight lipped. I don't think Cranston killed her. I think he had Johnny Mack do it. For one thing Cranston was at the party the night she was killed. Johnny didn't show up at all that night. She knew about the dealings with Morecom Data and Don Zale and the deals that went on. I wouldn't be surprised if Zale told Cranston to get rid of her. He didn't want anything traced back to him, especially anything that would affect his chairmanship of the House Banking Committee. Conflict-of-interest matters worried him all the time, but he did nothing about it. The rewards were greater outside of politics."

"Zale's ass is grass," Stu said. "We're going to have him removed from the House and put him in the big house for the rest of his life. He's a disgrace not only to the country he lives in, but to everyone and everything he's touched. All his accounts here along with the partnership accounts, including yours, are frozen as of this minute."

Des smiled and shook his head. "You're a little late. Most of the money is gone, out of here, out of the country I assume."

"I can't argue that the money is gone, but it isn't gone as far as you think."

"What?"

Stu smiled. "I intercepted a number of wires and had the entries go through so there was no suspicion, but I diverted the money to another account. It never left the bank, Des. I'm talking millions."

"You're one up on them?"

"Well, I'm one up on you, actually. You're still here, and they left you holding the bag. Tell me, what's your part in the vault down stairs?"

"Which one?"

"Both."

Des hesitated.

"Look Des, it's up to you. There is no obligation for you to tell me anything. You'll be telling the Feds soon anyway. I'm just trying to piece things together and maybe somewhere through all of this you can save some of your ass. I never bargained for any of this crap to begin with. Between you and the FDIC I should have my goddamn head examined."

The door opened and Ray came into the room. He took a seat beside Stu. "Marie is all right now. We have her in the employee lounge with a couple of ladies. Let's hope the note these characters left isn't true."

"What note?" asked Des.

Stu looked at him. "I'll tell you later. Just answer the question. What was your involvement in the vaults?"

"It was simple. I rented out the space. I had nothing to do with any of their operation. Cranston ran the whole program with Johnny and a couple of others. I never touched one dollar bill. My business dealings may not have fit your style, but drug money and I don't go together."

"Wait a minute," Ray said. "I just got in on this. Are you saying you rented out the vaults for them to put the money in and you weren't a part of the operation?"

"That's right," Des said. "It was just like our safety deposit boxes, except larger. I didn't want to know anything about the money."

"What did they pay to use these facilities?" Ray asked.

"Cranston paid me twenty five hundred a day for the basement safe and six thousand a day for the shelter vault."

"You actually believe you can convince the authorities that your only involvement was renting the safes at a quarter million a month?"

"That's all I did. I even have a rental contract signed by Cranston." Des replies.

"Good luck with that," Ray said.

Stu said, "We knew there was something big going on in those vaults, especially the lobby set up. Who put that system in?"

"I did years ago, but when I rented it to Cranston he added a few things. How did you find out about the lobby vault? It never opens during the day."

"I happened to be looking at some video tapes. Whoever went in there each time never replaced the carpet in the same place, and that got me wondering what was going on. I have to admit, it was a pretty slick operation."

"I was never in there after it was remodeled," Des said.

Ray said, "While we were in there last night, someone dumped a canister of something into the ventilation system that knocked us out within seconds. Not only did they clean the place out, but the lobby was crawling with agents while we were down there, so I can only assume the same thing happened to them. We haven't found any of them yet. Do you know what's going to happen to you when the Feds get down here and start on you?"

Des shrugged. "Hey, I said before, this is none of my business. I never asked any questions."

"I can't believe you gave Cranston the security numbers to get into the bank after hours to meet with the guards."

"They were his guards. They were made to look like bank personnel, but they worked for Cranston, not me."

"What do you know about Hank Stone?" Stu asked.

Des looked somewhat puzzled at the question. "He's the mayor. Why?"

"What else do you know about him?"

"Not a hell of a lot. He's retired and has a few bucks so he really doesn't do much. That's about all."

"Here, read this." Stu passed over the note left on the counter. He watched as Des read the note.

"I can't believe what I'm reading. Hank Stone? Are you shitting me?"

"Not only did they clean out the money, which we valued at around a million or more, but they cleaned out millions of dollars worth of precious opals," Stu said.

"Opals? So that's how Hank made his money. He sold opals like his father. He was fascinated by them, but it's hard to believe he was involved with Cranston and company."

"Well, it all seems to add up," Ray said. "He probably teamed up with Cranston because he knew he had big money and the ability to make large purchases of opals. Maybe he wanted to corner the market."

"I'm having a hard time choking down Stone's involvement in all this. But, if he's involved, he's on his way back to Australia where he spent a good part of his early life. With all those gems, he would have to be the richest man in the country down there. Anyone wanting a supply of opals would have to deal with him or Cranston." Des still found it hard to believe all of this was real.

Stu said, "You know, you could be right. They're probably headed for Australia, but they're going to be surprised when they check their bank account in Sydney. I'm going to rewire all the goddamn money back here. I have all the account information and the wire instructions. The money will be out of there before they get there. We're not going to have great relations with the Bank of Sydney, but I can prove where the originating wires came from. And besides, Johnny Mack isn't going to fight over drug money and get his ass burned. Remember he has something better."

"Like what?" said Des.

"Jessica and the opals."

Des stood up. "You bastard!"

Des' face was beet red, just what Stu wanted. *Maybe if he pressed a little harder, he would have a stroke and they could save the taxpayers some money.* Stu thought.

Stu looked at Des. "The downstairs vault has to be jammed packed with money because no one has been down to empty it. When the Feds get here they can open it. Maybe they can even catch the guys outside making the drop. Tell me—"

Studer came in. "Hey, Stu, I need to talk to Cain for a moment." He turned to Des. "Cain, you scratch my back and I'll scratch yours. This is just the feather I need in my cap, and you need a friend right now. So tell me, what's their method of cocaine distribution?"

Des knew he was right. Having the right lawyer was one thing, but these cops talk the same language and might be able to add some influence. He was going to need all the help he could muster. He only hoped that at the end of the day Studer would keep his word.

"They move a lot of stuff...thousands of kilos so far, worth about thirty million dollars wholesale, street value around $275 million. That's what I was told. I don't know much more than that."

"Where did it come from?" Stu asked.

"Caracas, Venezuela. It's shipped up from the Colombian cartel and makes its way from Venezuela to Houston, New York, and the Miami airport."

"How in the hell does the stuff get past U.S. Customs?"

"Golf balls."

"What?" said Studer

"Golf balls... by the millions. The largest golf ball manufacturers have set up plants down there. The labor is dirt cheap. So Johnny Mack goes down there and builds a small plant with a print shop. They ship some equipment down there from the States. They hire a foreman to run the place who knows something about the business and packaging and the rest is history. They have it timed so well that they even know how to ship in between the real shipments. They use a balata outer cover because of the skins' softness. They fill the golf balls with cocaine and package them in sets of three just like the real thing. I've seen them and you can't tell the difference. They even fool the damn DEA dogs because of the tight seal around the ball. Once the balls are filled, they're washed in these huge machines with boiling hot water to remove any traces of cocaine dust, and they're packaged in a dust-free safe room."

"You saw them doing it?"

"No. I saw the golf ball and it looked real to me. I was at the club with Cranston one day when he was hitting balls at the practice range. He showed me a golf ball and asked me what I thought about it. I said how the hell should I know, since I don't play golf. He said, 'Here, let me show you.' He put the ball on a tee, looked around to see if anyone was watching, then hit it. Poof! A cloud of white dust was all over me. The ball split right down the middle. That's when he told me how the stuff came into the country."

Studer walked around the room as if in deep thought. He finally took the chair next to Des, pulling it right up next to his. It was as if Des was in a trance as Studer's cold brown eyes met his. "Listen, Bud, I'm only going to tell you this one time. You can save your skin from an extra long vacation. At the worst, you'll do time in a federal prison where life for your kind isn't much different than it is here. But if you aren't straight with me you're history, and your life will be more difficult than you could ever imagine. There are some folks at some of these other places that would just love to get their hands on you. So what's it going to be?"

"What do you want to know? I can only tell you what I know."

"All I want is some straight answers," said Studer. "You bullshit me, it's over. Understand?"

Des nodded.

"Does Cranston own a plane?" asked Studer.

"Yeah, he has a Lear jet. I've been in it a couple of times. He has a hanger at the airport."

"Which one?"

"Miami."

"I'll be right back," said Studer. He scurried out the door, but stopped short and turned and came back. "Where do they keep those golf balls?"

"They have a warehouse right off the Hialeah exit on the West Dade Expressway."

"What's it look like?" Studer asks.

"It's a Butler building... dark blue with a white roof... The sign on the side of the building says Sports Scene Corporation."

Stu walked to the phone on the other side of the room and called Louise. He asked her to get Jerry Pote from Chase Manhattan on the phone so he could begin unraveling the wires back from Sydney and get the money back where it belongs. He also asked her to get Lionel DuPree from the FDIC in Atlanta. "I'll talk to whoever answers first."

"You have a big day on your hands here," Ray said. "I'll do my best to keep Studer company. I don't think I'll be much use to you here."

Des was escorted to his office by two police officers.

The phone rang, and Stu answered it. "Hi, Lionel. Well, I guess today is your day."

"Yes, it is. We heard the news. Our Washington office has been flooded with phone calls for hours. I'm on my way there as soon as I can get packed and get some men."

"Well, I guess it's over here. The place is surrounded by bank customers and police. I hope I'm alive when you get here. I'm sorry to see the bank go under. I know we're super thin on capital, but this community is strong and wealthy. Desmond Cain is finished here. By the time you guys get to him it will be years of lawyers and legal briefs, but at least he's out of here for good."

"I think I'm going to have some good news for you. I've only known you for a short time, but I have seen you in your surroundings. You're honest and capable of running the bank, and most of all you want to see it survive. The one problem is you have a bunch of crooks around you. So with our help and my ass out on a limb in Washington, we might be able to save the bank. There's a lot of heat on the administration not to close too many more banks. The country has to heal and move forward, so with a little luck your bank just might make it."

Stu couldn't believe what he was saying. It was the best news he'd gotten since he'd come back to Fortune Beach.

Lionel continued. "The FDIC is going to infuse about seventy five million in new capital into the bank. For that, everyone is going to pay a price. The old board gets the axe, with the possibility of jail for a few. We'll appoint a new board with two of our people there as well. The present stock you have is worthless so all your current shareholders are going to have to put the stock away for a number of years. If the bank gets rid of its problem loans and makes some money down the road and pays our initial investment back, you'll get your bank back and the stockholders will get their stock back. It's better than us giving hundreds of millions in discounts on those problem loans. The taxpayers are the only ones who get screwed in a deal like that. You guys are going to have to earn your way out of your problems. It will take a lot of hard work and tough decisions, but it can be done, and it's cheaper for us than to close the place. Fair enough?"

"It's a deal. When are you coming?"

"I have to tie up some loose ends on what I just told you, but I should be there tomorrow."

"What can I tell these people outside?"

"Tell 'em you're in business and you're the new chairman. If they want their money give it to them. They'll all be back within the month."

The bank was going to survive. As Stu hung up, there was a knock on the door and Louise entered. "Sir, it's nine o'clock what should we do?"

"I'm coming down, and we're opening the bank." Stu grinned. *"We're in business!"*

Epilogue

Stu couldn't remember the last time it had snowed on Christmas Eve, and it was welcomed on such a joyous time of the year. He looked out through the frost crystals that had accumulated on the living room window. He could see the towering hemlock's standing tall and strong like wooden toy soldiers carrying the weight of the pure white snow. The scene looked as if it was carved out of a Currier & Ives Christmas calendar.

Five years had passed since the ordeal at the Fortune Beach Bank. Life was good for him back home in New Jersey except for the passing of his father, who had died two years earlier on Thanksgiving Day at his office in his bank. His mother, Janice came to live with him and Becca. They settled in the town of Ridgepoint because of its beautiful, rustic landscapes overlooking some of the most breathtaking mountain ranges in New Jersey. It was a nice, quiet town that afforded the lifestyle they wanted. They purchased Bradbury Farm with its seventy eight acres of mountainous terrain overlooking the tiny village. The old farmhouse, which sat to the far right of the property, was built in the early eighteen hundreds by Jason Bradbury, the founder of the Bradbury Brewery, which continues to produce the most popular beer in the northeast. Stu and Becca restored the old house and breathed new life into its wooden frame. Janice moved into the old house, only a short walk from the main house, to give herself some independence.

Stu and Becca lived in the magnificent white-shingled mansion built by the third generation of Braburys. It sat far back from the main road and overlooked a gracious pond that was fed by a meandering stream coming off the mountain behind them.

Stu's father, in concert with the Board of Directors of Morris National Bank, made Stu President and Chief Executive Officer. Harrison Stuart stayed on as the bank's chairman until he died, and Stu was then appointed the bank's new chairman. He had represented the interest of the stockholders to the best of his ability. He sold the bank! Stu, realizing four million dollars from its sale of bank stock while his father's estate, received twenty seven million dollars.

Stu smiled as he thought back to the day he'd walked through the front doors of the Fortune Beach Bank to talk to the hundreds of angry, hostile depositors who wanted their fortunes back. Only a few actually took their money that day.

Good as his word, Lionel Dupree bailed Stu and the bank out of a major problem. It took tremendous vigilance as the bank's new chairman to make the bank profitable again and pay the FDIC back every penny through a private capital offering. Shortly thereafter Stu merged the bank with a local savings bank on the island and walked away, his head held high as he passed through the double glass lobby doors for the last time.

As expected, Des pled not guilty to the charges that he deceived federal regulators and cheated the bank out of millions. A thirty page grand jury indictment in Tallahassee charged him with conspiracy, bank fraud, drug distribution, money laundering, and illegal loan schemes with Alex Cranston and Congressman Donald Zale on the sale and purchase of government owned properties. The trial was the talk of Fortune Beach for months until Des was found guilty on all charges. He was sentenced to thirty years in prison and a five million dollar fine. He was never charged with any of the murders, but life has a way of balancing out to some degree. Des got into a squabble with another prisoner over a dish of bread pudding and a fight ensued. Des was without the bread pudding, with a pencil stuck in his eye and remained in a coma for two years in the prison hospital. He remains paralyzed from the neck down.

It was difficult for Becca for a few years after Des was sentenced. Her brother's actions were always to push the envelope as far as it could be pushed. She blamed herself for not being a better sister than a wife for Stu. Des had genes that she managed to shed early on in her life, and found that greed, selfishness, and honor to oneself all intertwined within family values, and being able to choose right from wrong. Always fearful of ending his life like his father, was Des' life struggle. Becca was never able to convince him that there was more to life than chasing a fictitious fortune.

Studer, Ray and a few FBI agents managed to find their way to Hialeah and the blue Butler building. Not only did they find hundreds of thousands of cocaine-filled golf balls left unattended, but four embarrassed, DEA agents tied and gagged to a metal support beam.

The Lear jet had vanished from the tarmac, but was later recovered at the Ft. Meyers International Airport. The plane was used as a diversion, which threw everyone off guard. When the doors to the jet were finally opened, there in rear passenger seat sat Pete Langworth, blindfolded and left for dead with his hands tied behind his back. He was thankful to be alive. He found out later that Johnny Mack, Jessica, Hank Stone, Zale and Cranston had boarded a United Airlines 747 for Sydney, no doubt with some cash and the opals.

Alice graduated Villanova and was on her way to the Malay Peninsula and the Singapore Bank after the holidays to start her new job.

Pete and Marie married. He got transferred to the Morristown division of the DEA with a little help from friends. Becca and Stu are the proud grandparents of a little granddaughter, Samantha.

Darkness was now approaching, and shortly Ray and Suzanne would arrive for Christmas Eve dinner. This was a special evening for Stu and Ray. Both now retired they formed their new business venture together to be announced at dinner. Collins and Stuart Investigations.

Stu watched Becca's reflection in the window as she drifted into the next room leaving him to his thoughts for the next few minutes. He thought of Australia and *Lightning Ridge* with its sunburned red earth and 120 degree temperatures. One thing for sure that he did not share with Becca was the lure of *Lightning Ridge* and the fascination of those fiery peerless *Oueen of Gems.*

Stu and Ray knew their business was not complete regarding the five felons that disappeared Down Under. Perhaps one day soon they just might surprise them all with a …

"Goo'dye mite!"

The End

LaVergne, TN USA
13 September 2010
196659LV00003B/1/P